INTO
THE
THICKENING
FOG

ALSO BY ANDREI GELASIMOV

Thirst
The Lying Year
Gods of the Steppe
Rachel

INTO THE THICKENING FOG

A novel in three acts with intermissions

ANDREI GELASIMOV

Translated by
Marian Schwartz

Previously published as *Холод* by Eksmo in Russia in 2015. Translated from Russian by Marian Schwartz. First published in English by AmazonCrossing in 2016.

Published by AmazonCrossing, Seattle

www.apub.com

Amazon, the Amazon logo, and AmazonCrossing are trademarks of Amazon.com, Inc., or its affiliates.

ISBN-13: 9781503940819
ISBN-10: 1503940810

Cover design by David Drummond

Printed in the United States of America

Whoever thought that hell'd be so cold?

—Tom Waits, "Lucinda"

ACT ONE

DEEP FREEZES

The best place to pass out is in the tail-end lavatory of a Boeing 757.

Sure, there's nothing wrong with collapsing on some beach like a sad sack, or on a pile of soft couch cushions, but if there's no sand or couch handy at the time, then you're not going to do better than the tail end of a Boeing.

The compartment's so cramped no one's risking anything. At moments like this, we listen to the usual bells that go off in our head and marvel at them the way we always do, whereupon we gently fold up and slide down the narrow wall. If we're standing facing the toilet, our knees rest up against it, so it's more hygienic to turn sideways to the crapper. Then our feet brace us, pressed into the lavatory panel, and we curl to the floor like an embryo.

The airliner speeds us over the clouds, a line forms in the aisle for the lavatory, it's time for the flight attendants to wheel out the meal carts, and we're blissfully absent. We're not in the cabin, or our own body, or dreamland. We're nowhere, and our suddenly orphaned sheath is flying backward at nearly nine hundred kilometers an hour toward that strange frozen city where half of our, or its, life was spent.

The boarding pass in the pocket of our badly crumpled jacket has a name written on it—Eduard Filimonov—though even that barely connects us to this emptied, scrunched-up body. The haggard spinster at the check-in counter got the last name wrong, and the person who knew how to get it right didn't tell her. He hadn't been sure he was going to fly at all. And it hurt to talk. His lips barely functioned.

"Hey! Are you okay in there? Director! Wake up, please."

Someone was shaking Filippov's shoulder hard.

"Can you hear me? It's eight o'clock! Wake up! You're late for your plane."

Filippov pushed away the vile alien hand and tried to hide under the blanket. But he didn't have a blanket. The next second he realized he'd surfaced out of oblivion into the nastiest, most inhuman hangover. Filippov moaned at the insult.

"Don't put on an act," said the vile voice attached to the vile hand. "Nothing on you hurts. This morning you were galloping all over the apartment. And don't go kicking at me, please. You were the one who asked me to wake you. I've already called a taxi. Domodedovo, right?"

Filippov wanted to lift his head, but he didn't have a head. Or rather, he did, but it was someone else's. Someone had left their head on him—disgusting, sticky, and recalcitrant. The alien head wouldn't lift. All his other organs and body parts immediately joined this parade of sovereignties. His stomach demanded to be taken where it could be sick; his forehead begged him to stop pouring molten lead into it; his tongue and throat dreamed of icebergs; and his hands' modest wish was to shake and be covered in perspiration. Filippov felt like the Soviet Union in 1991. He was falling apart. It was as if he'd died, only a lot worse.

As for death, Filippov was approaching middle age, and he'd realized that leaving life would make him just equal to himself when he'd arrived, so he stopped overthinking it. He pushed hard until forty and then let go. After all, up until a certain point in time, there'd been no remarkable, talented, and unique Filippov, up until a couple of squiggles on the calendar. Exactly as there wouldn't be after some other number. He'd just factor himself out and the equation would be solved.

Solving an equation means finding its roots. In that sense he compared himself to the clever old Chinese man who gallops through the mountains in search of magical roots. When he finds the root, the equation is solved. And with it, immortality. Because after death, Filippov planned merely to be equal to the being who wasn't here forty-two years ago, who was hanging out some inexplicable somewhere before the moment of birth, a somewhere where he probably didn't give a fuck about death. He planned just to put an equal sign between himself and that awesome being who didn't give a fuck.

The whole difference between what had gone before and what there'd be afterward consisted now of about a dozen photographs he'd leave behind, which were undoubtedly a mischief, because, after all, it would never occur to anyone to weep over you or put them in funereal frames before your birth—on the basis of there being no you yet in this wide world and everyone around you waiting and waiting but you just not having shown up yet. It was later that they took to doing that. They got used to you being in the access zone and the equal sign never crossed their mind. So Filippov almost wasn't afraid of death as such. A hangover was much worse.

"Are you going to get up or not? What should I tell the taxi driver?"

Having pondered his own demise, Filippov reconciled himself to the necessity of living and tried to marshal all his mutinous organs. Even the shakiest consolation requires the presence of a strong leader.

"Where am I?" he managed to say, overcoming an onset of nausea any other individual would find intolerable.

"The front hall," the vile voice replied gloatingly.

ANDREI GELASIMOV

Filippov unstuck what he had left instead of an eye and ran it over what he had managed to sidestep. Very little fell into his field of vision: a section of wall plastered with old photographs; a blond lock that evidently went with the vile voice; the back of the leather couch where he'd woken up. Or rather, come to. The couch really was in an enormous front hall, as Filippov managed to understand on the second attempt. Directly opposite was a dark, massive front door.

"Think you can quit squinting?" said the vile voice. "Am I supposed to pay the taxi driver or something?"

Filippov called upon the citizens of his internal fatherland to be brave and grabbed on to the back of the couch. After a few rocking movements, which nearly resulted in his stomach declaring its wish to secede from the federation, Filippov was able to find a point of consensus. He froze in a more or less vertical position, swallowed dry saliva, surveyed his hopelessly wrinkled suit, and tried to focus on the vile voice.

"Who are you?" he said.

"Gee, thanks."

"Couldn't you have taken off my jacket? It's a Burberry, by the way."

"You wouldn't let me. You said you'd be cold."

"You could have . . . brought me an afghan . . . But where is everybody?"

"Who's everybody?"

"Well, the people. The people who live here."

He recalled the night's people like a blurry, faceless blotch. Filippov hadn't known any of them before. Even how he'd ended up at this party escaped him; it was a faint glimmer in his swollen, inflamed, and desperately swimming memory. Snatches of some incredibly nasty MTV tune flickered in his head, snatches he really wished he could get rid of, but the song wouldn't let him go. The human blotches had circled amiably to this nauseatingly cheerful music, and his own nausea had imperceptibly fallen in with the general rhythm.

4

"Where's the bathroom?" he managed to ask.

"Down the hall, second door on the left."

———

Smell was the last to return, after hearing and sight—a little late, but it quickly caught up. Not anticipating any new tricks, Filippov was listlessly splashing water from the tap on his plastic, totally numb face when he was suddenly overcome by the suffocating smell of singed wool—and he rushed back to the toilet. After awful convulsions, coughing, and tears, he was able to eject a pitiful drop of bile into the shiny porcelain.

You should have eaten something this morning, his inner voice told him.

"Go to hell," Filippov told the voice, and his reply sounded weighty and booming, amplified by the toilet bowl.

At that moment, he felt like little Alice looking down the rabbit hole, listening to the sounds of her own voice and wondering at the endlessness of the space down that black hole. The lonely drop of bile had slid lackadaisically to the bottomless depths of the sewer lines, but Filippov still couldn't get up off his knees, as if he'd slid down there after it. Indeed, instead of the Mad Hatter or the Cheshire Cat or the hookah-smoking Caterpillar, he was presented with the Demon of the Void, who guffawed at him, demanded more parties, more people, more single-malt whiskey, more expensive food, and more nonstop MTV tunes.

"You're boozing half your life away," the demon jeered at Filippov. "Who's going to give you back that time? You think you're going to get it back at customs like the VAT? Show up at the airport for your flight, present your receipts, show the clothes you bought, and sign a receipt? No, dude, that won't fly. You're sleeping through the second half of your life."

"Oh, go to hell," Filippov repeated, swiping the unending thread of bitter spit hanging heavily from the corner of his mouth. "I've had it with you."

"I've had it with *you*," the demon snorted, vanishing with a whistle into depths more mysterious than anything Lewis Carroll ever could have imagined.

Suddenly, Filippov was again overcome by the smell of singed wool. He shuddered, incapable of getting even a little more out, and the pain born of this vain effort lit up his brain like a flare. The remotest, darkest nooks became visible, and the smell flung him into the distant past, when he and his parents would visit his grandmother for the hog-slaughtering holiday.

They always took the piglets in pairs and named them Mishka and Zinka, as a result of which, for his whole life ever after, Filippov shied away from people with those names. They fed the pigs up for a whole year and slaughtered them in the fall, on the seventh of November. No historical metaphor here whatsoever, of course—they just had the idea of linking it to the holiday that celebrated the Great October Socialist Revolution. Also, you could only keep pork in that quantity in the cellar during the cold months. Little Filippov would hide in the bathhouse or run out the gates so he wouldn't hear the desperate squeals or think about what they were doing to the little pigs, but the smell of scorched bristles after the slaughtered carcasses were burned with a blowtorch permeated everything. Even his mama's holiday blouse reeked of it when he pressed up to her during the feast and everyone was trading shouts under the mistaken impression that they were singing.

"Hey!" The young woman consumed by the subject of his taxi drummed at the door. "Did you fall asleep in there?"

Filippov frowned, spat in the toilet, and trying not to spill his headache, slowly rose from his knees.

"All's well. I'm coming out."

Stopping at the mirror, he finally discovered the source of the foul smell. The right side of his own beard and mustache were noticeably fused, and the tips of his stubble were covered with an unexpectedly handsome scattering of tiny, possibly glass, beads. That place on his face reminded him now of some sea creature with a mass of short translucent tentacles, or the vault of a deep cave covered with fragile and very tiny stalactites. Whitish burn marks shone on his lips like elongated slugs.

Who had set fire to his beard, and why? Filippov couldn't remember.

—————

"You leaving, too?" he said as he exited the bathroom and raised his sorrow-filled gaze at the young woman.

She was standing in the middle of the front hall, wearing an unbuttoned red jacket and holding Filippov's coat.

"I'm going with you."

"Where?"

Filippov stopped and tried to recall his plans. None came to mind.

"The North."

"What for?"

"To see the aurora borealis. And eat sliced frozen fish. You promised."

"Yeah?" He sighed mournfully and smelled the area around him, now perfumed with eighteen-year-old Balblair that hadn't completely dissolved in him. "Is that all I promised?"

"No, to get married, too."

"I see. And who are you? Remind me, please."

The young woman smiled, and Filippov understood why their relationship had taken this turn last night.

"I'm Nina."

"Don't lie."

"It's the truth."

He ran his damp palm over his face, as if trying to wipe off something.

"Fashion model?"

"Yes. I told you yesterday. I've been working for six months already."

"Good for you. Tell me, I didn't give you a credit card, did I?"

"No."

"What did I give you?"

"A phone."

"Give it here for a minute, please."

She took a black iPhone out of her jacket pocket and handed it to Filippov. Scrolling through the texts, he frowned, not finding what he was looking for, then took out the SIM card and returned the phone to the young woman.

"You're beautiful, Nina."

"Thank you. So you're not taking me to the North?"

"No. I don't even want to go there myself."

"And you're not giving me a part in your show?"

"Are you an actress?"

"No."

"Then I'm not."

"Too bad. I believed you."

Filippov took his coat from her and again sighed so deeply that images of the distant but marvelous Scottish Highlands became palpable in the front hall.

Nina had become very sad.

"I envy you," he said.

———

Filippov had to go to the North for two reasons. First, he was a swine. Second, he was a coward. Actually, that's why he'd gotten drunk in the company of total strangers, so drunk that some Nina woke him up in someone else's front hall. How he'd ended up there he recalled only vaguely.

Once in the taxi, he lit up and then immediately threw the cigarette out the window. The whole pack flew out after it.

"You should have given them to me," the taxi driver said.

"Next time."

Filippov looked down and saw why the driver had asked him for the cigarettes. In the deep plastic pocket on his door were tight rows of Marlboro hard packs, L&Ms, Java Golds, and some other crap. There had to be thirty packs.

"Laying 'em in for the winter?"

"They're empty."

Filippov reached out and opened one of the packs.

"Why then?"

"What do you mean 'why'?" The driver grinned condescendingly. "A passenger gets in and wants to smoke—but where's he going to put his ashes? My ashtray broke a long time ago."

"Logical," Filippov said approvingly, and he made himself more comfortable.

The world of idiots was dear to him not only professionally. Even before his success, long before he started winking at his own mug looking at him from magazine covers on newsstands, Filippov liked to act as though people were angry at him, or even trying to pick a fight. Sitting without a kopek to his name one winter at the dacha of some people he knew who had let him go there on the pretext of guarding the house, he'd made friends with the in-house rat, named it Petka, taught it to get into a Salamander shoe box when he gave a special whistle, and then he'd taken this box to meetings with film producers and art directors at the most famous Moscow theaters. When asked what was in the box, he was always honest and lifted the lid slightly. To his old friends from the theatrical institute, who were becoming fewer and fewer and who were absolutely unsurprised at his failures, Filippov explained that Petka was dear to him not just as a friend. Petka had been able to explain to him who he in fact was.

"Judge for yourself," he told one of the last friends who would still pay for him at a restaurant. "In the morning, I get up at the dacha, rummage through all the cupboards, and all I find is a bag of chips. With jack shit in it. I think, 'You dumbass Pink Floyd. Some joke. It'd be nice to eat something.' And all I've got is two little pieces of bread. Because the rats have practically cleaned me out. I strung up that bread, wrapped in paper, so they couldn't get to it. Like on a clothesline, you know, all the way across the room. Like for drying sheets. So, I walk behind it, and this eagle is creeping across, across the line, straight for the bag. Upside down, like a mountain climber. I think, 'Well, they're totally bonkers.' I pick up my bat, walk toward it, swing—and suddenly I can't hit it."

"Why?"

"Well, you see . . . he's creeping so tenaciously. Like a tank. He's looking at me and going anyway. He knows I'm going to whack him, and he doesn't stop. And right then I think, 'Damn it, that's me.' He's like me, see?"

"No."

"Fine then, whack away. Take another half a thou for me. I don't need food anymore."

Filippov and Petka's friendship didn't last long. Once, seriously drunk, Filippov dropped Petka's box in a half-empty Metro car, and when two slick Chechens started beating him he claimed three times that the animal wasn't his, thus disowning his friend and at the same time making it clear to himself that he was a coward.

"Where are we going?" the taxi driver inquired in a friendly way, interrupting those hazy reminiscences.

Filippov opened his eyes but didn't turn his head.

"Where the sun don't shine."

"Why so crude?"

"If you're going to talk, I'll take a different taxi."

On the plane he flopped down and passed out, basically at will. Sitting at the bar before boarding, Filippov had pictured how truly wonderful it would be if his hungover carcass got its own self to its destination, while he, meanwhile, kept sitting here at this bar, disembodied, staring at this glass of whiskey.

He listened to a sad Tom Waits song and imagined himself the hero, underground, trying to convince his beloved to lie down on his grave and press her cheek to the spot where his heart used to be. Actually, Filippov was even sadder than the Tom Waits character, but without the heart. By way of compensation, Tom huskily promised the sky that even if it crashed to the earth, the birds would fall with it and they could all be caught.

Pointless, Filippov thought in unison with the plaintive blues. *They'd run away anyway. They've got strong legs.*

He tried to reach his cold, rigid arms up from beneath the ground to Tom Waits's luscious beloved, but she was paying him no attention whatsoever. Being a wise and discerning necrophiliac, of the two corpses she preferred the raspy, romantic Tom.

However, Filippov's desire that his hungover body travel separately from him was fulfilled. After two hours of flight, his body got up from its seat and went to the lavatory, where it fainted and collapsed, lay there for about fifteen minutes without an owner, drooling out of the left corner of its mouth, and then stirred, grabbed on to the edge of the sink, struggled to its feet, and turned on the water.

Outside, some impatient someone instantly picked up on his languid signs of life.

"Are you going to be much longer? There's a line here, by the way!"

Back in his seat, Filippov sipped the grappa he'd providentially purchased at the airport and looked around as if confused about where he was. He even rose slightly, surveying the cabin.

"Listen, where are we going?" he addressed his neighbor, who was wearing a pink tracksuit.

She looked like a forty-year-old Britney Spears who'd gone to book-keeping school, put on a chunk of weight, and never been in show business. In any case, the skin on her face said more about the sudden coming of spring—when the sun's rays make the snow spongy and shiny—than about any painstaking care taken by makeup wizards. Her short and flirty "virgin's haircut," as Filippov privately defined it, consisted of hair that wasn't the thickest in the world and was bleached to a liver yellow.

Flattered by his attention, the surrogate pop princess took one earbud out and smiled.

"I'm sorry. What?"

"I'm asking where we're going."

The surrogate in pink looked slightly helpless. This was definitely not the question she'd been expecting to hear after two and a half hours of flight. She might well have been counting on something like "Do you like skiing?" or some other nonsense men usually use to start up a conversation.

"Where are we going?" Filippov looked her in the face very seriously, apparently expecting an answer.

The fortysomething princess's pink brain sensed a trick and tensed. The traces of this tension became marked around her eyebrows. She was thinking.

"What do you mean by 'where'? To the North . . . To your hometown."

Now it was Filippov's turn to tense.

"My hometown? How do you know where I was born?"

"You told me."

Filippov's brow furrowed, too. He cleared his throat, wiped his forehead, and then gave his neighbor a suspicious stare.

"When?"

"At the airport. Before takeoff."

She took the earbud out of her other ear and fingered her phone, turning off the music.

"You mean we know each other?" Filippov asked mistrustfully.

"Well, yeah. I'm Zinaida, but you can call me Zina. You mean you don't remember?"

She looked at him in astonishment, trying to figure out whether he was joking or serious.

"No." He shook his head. "I don't remember anything at all. I just fainted in the lavatory. And I think I hit my head in there. I don't even remember who I am."

Princess Zina stopped breathing. Her pink, peroxide life may have known dramatic events, but Filippov's case was obviously the most awesome ever.

"What do you mean you don't remember?" she said at last. "Not at all?"

"Not at all." Filippov shrugged. "Who am I?"

———————◆———————

By this time the flight attendants had reached their row with the shabby, cumbersome cart, and the old woman actively dozing by the window started to show signs of life. She'd been dozing actively and even for show, because at the very beginning of the flight, when the plane was just taxiing, she'd forced Filippov to switch and take her seat on the aisle. Her anxious old-womanish conscience made her feel she had to play out the part she'd declared in the prologue, which consisted of her being very sick, so she even moaned, and the sole remedy for her doubtless incurable illness would be a window seat. She'd managed to crawl over the already seated pink Zinaida, then quickly took off her shoes and rolled her eyes like a martyr so she wouldn't see this whole unjust and cruel world that was afflicting her. Actually, whenever the attendants started handing out anything, she came back to life through an incredible effort of will and detained them for a long time with her demand to be shown everything they had to offer. When she got what she wanted, she deftly peeled back the wrapping, crunched the cookie, and then put her empty glass on Zinaida's lowered tray, raised her own so she could get more comfortable, and, with a meek moan, drifted off into the hospitable lap of suffering.

Now, evidently, she was truly hungry, and Zinaida had to withstand a minor storm. The old woman fretted, jostled, and kept asking, afraid of missing something, and took a long time deciding between meat and fish, while poor Zinaida, who was impatient to fill Filippov, as if he were a suddenly emptied flash drive, passed unbearably hot Aeroflot food trays endlessly back and forth.

In the intervals between these spasmodic transactions, when the old woman's reflections on the attendants' treachery and the frailty of all existence momentarily subsided, an overwrought Zinaida managed to bring Filippov up to speed.

"You're a famous director. Fashionable. Everyone knows you. You mean you really don't remember?"

"Yeah?" he said. "A theater director? Or film?"

"Both. You just won some prize abroad. In Italy, I think."

"At the Venice festival?"

"No. I think it was Rome."

"Ma'am." The attendant, by now worn out from her second back-to-back transcontinental flight, interrupted their conversation. "Anything for you?"

"Too bad," Filippov went on. "I'd have liked it to be Venice. But where we're flying . . . do they know me there, too?"

"Naturally. There are legends told about you there. And every second person boasts about knowing you. No, listen, is it true you don't remember anything?"

At that moment the old woman finally reached her difficult decision and demanded they bring back the meat tray, which she'd managed to refuse twice just a minute before.

"I've forgotten everything." Filippov shook his head as he put the tray in the old woman's reliable hands. "Do I have a family?"

"No. Or rather, you did, but you're divorced now, and that was your second marriage. The first fell apart almost immediately. You married too young."

"Children?"

"One son. He's living somewhere in Europe with your former— well, meaning your second—wife. She took him there to be with her new husband. There was a lot of talk about that in town."

"Yeah? What did people say?"

Zinaida got flustered and focused on her tray wrapper.

"Well . . . people said you beat her. I mean, used to beat her."

"Here, let me help." Filippov took her tray and in a single practiced move pulled off the transparent film. "There you go."

"No, I mean it's all gossip," she went on. "Don't take it too hard."

"Okay, I won't. To be honest, I couldn't care less. I don't remember anyone. You want my dessert? I'm not going to eat it."

"Thank you."

"Bon appétit."

They set to their meal and for a while silently chewed the overcooked stew and watery vegetables. A boy of about five, who was sitting across the aisle, was picking his nose and then licking his finger.

"What else are people saying?" Filippov asked, lowering his dull plastic fork.

"They're saying you're gay."

"Please call the attendant," the old woman by the window demanded. "She gave me fish. I told them I wanted meat."

"Here, have mine," Filippov offered. "Where should I cut it for you? I have a scrumptious filet."

The old woman looked him in the eye for a second and then started fiddling with her fish. Filippov turned his gaze to Zinaida.

"Do you think the part about me being gay is true?"

"I don't know." She shrugged. "You're every bit a man, of course. But even you know it's all so complicated these days. You can't tell at first glance which guy's gay and which one's straight. You run into some pretty hilarious surprises. When I heard that about you, I didn't believe it. But then they even started hinting in the papers. The tabloids, sure, but there were doubts anyway. There's no smoke without fire."

"That's logical. What else are people saying?"

"That you're a drunk and a drug addict. At one point there was a whole to-do about it, but that's died down now."

They were quiet for a while, then Zinaida suddenly dove under her tray table and pulled out a white plastic bag labeled "Moscow Duty-Free."

"Do you recognize this?" She looked at Filippov triumphantly, showing him a white cup with coffee stains inside. But he just shook his head.

"You gave it to me yourself."

"I did? What for?"

"You stole it for me."

"So-o-o," Filippov drawled. "Now we're stealing, too."

"No, you did it for good reasons. You saw me hide a saucer at the bar, and you sat down with me and offered to steal the cup that went with it. You also told me stories about a café in Amsterdam and marijuana brownies. You mean you don't remember anything at all?" She gave him a look of compassion.

"Why did you hide the saucer?"

"You already asked. There, in the airport."

"I don't remember. Tell me again."

She sighed, embarrassed for some reason, and covered her foolish expression. "You're going to laugh."

"No, I won't. Where's that coming from?"

"You already did."

"Yeah? Well, tell me anyway. I'm curious."

She rolled her eyes, as if she really wanted to be candid but at the same time she was embarrassed by what were for her important feelings.

"I wanted to take the saucer as a souvenir."

"A souvenir?" He grinned. "Of what? The bar?"

"There, you see? That's how you talked before."

"But I don't remember anything. I must be getting senile. What do you want the saucer for?"

"On the bottom it says Domodedovo Airport."

"And you decided to swipe it as a souvenir of the airport?"

"Oh, no, of Moscow. I told you then that I was going home for good and they'd never let me go back to Moscow."

"Who wouldn't?"

"Oh, someone. Basically, it doesn't matter. They won't."

"Seems to me you're a full-grown lady."

She laughed, emitting an odd sound as she did.

"Why are you laughing?"

"No one who knows me calls me a 'lady.'"

Filippov listened to her laughter and once again caught that odd sound in it. "Hey, do that again."

"What?"

"That thing you just did. Snort."

"I didn't snort."

"So you say."

"I didn't snort, I'm telling you."

"Uh-huh, you didn't snort. So what's this?"

He imitated her laughter and gave a distinct snort at the end, pulling air through his nose.

"See? That's how you laugh."

Every once in a while Filippov truly did wish he could lose his memory. His life had been far from rough, but there was precious little of it he cared to recall. The list of what he would keep after a sudden and long-desired amnesia consisted of just a few items. In first place were the songs of Tom Waits, which he wanted to remember always. Then came a madly spinning bottle of vodka, glinting in the sun, launched high in the air by his best friend, who, unlike that bottle, was definitely a candidate for amnesia; and the face of his two-year-old son covered with a rough, almost-green crust from his endless allergies, his tears vanishing instantly in the deep, dry cracks on his cheek, as if they were hillsides, not cheeks, and as if he were a small, sad volcano, not a child, and his slopes were covered with cooled lava. Filippov would also retain his memory of the tubby, carefree woman in enormous black pants and a cheap flowered top who one day jumped out in front of him from the Metro like a puffy Beelzebub, put on earphones, nodded, and started rapping: "Call me your girl, then kiss me, kiss me." She formulated her demands in a strong, confident voice and obviously knew perfectly well what to expect from life. That, then, was all Filippov cared to remember. All the rest he easily could forget.

His dream of being permanently rid of useless and tiresome ballast had more than once put him in a playful mood, and then he simply feigned memory loss. But even while desperately playing the fool in front of army commanders, college professors, or all-powerful producers from the federal television channels, he was always a little sad that he, in fact, remembered everything. These gags never had any particular purpose. Rather, they reflected his melancholy over what might have been. This time, though, Filippov wanted to vulgarly extract advantage from his favorite, virtually original ploy. This wasn't about Zinaida, whom he'd met quite accidentally at Domodedovo, or even the fact that he'd genuinely fainted on the plane. No, this was about *why* he was flying to his hometown.

Filippov was ashamed. Everything connected with this feeling had gone out of his life so long ago, and so thoroughly, that now he had absolutely no idea how to behave, how people who are ashamed do behave, so he worried like a virgin on the eve of a tryst with an experienced woman. Ahead lay something new, something big he could only guess at, and now he was awaiting this new thing with curiosity and uncertainty, as if he actually wanted this encounter. Shame exhilarated him, excited him, and drove out his usual depression and boredom. Filippov was ashamed at what he was getting ready to say to probably the last person who remained close to him—the last person he hadn't managed to turn against him yet. He'd never been ashamed of his antics, but right now he was feeling shame for being the kind of person who had the gall not only to commit unequivocal betrayal but also having done so, to show up at his victim's doorstep with a shameless request for help.

Two days ago, in Paris, he'd signed papers to direct a show dreamed up by his old friend and partner from his hometown, a well-known theatrical designer who had done a lot to see that this oddball director from the provinces, who no one needed, not only gained success in Moscow but was in demand in Europe as well. Without his friend's surprising, often genuinely fantastic ideas, doubtless nothing would have come of Filippov, and they never would have let him through any Moscow stage door. In literally a couple of years, the sudden and fresh duo had vanquished the most important theatrical venues, attracting attention with their invariably full houses and scandalous reviews, and the director's equally scandalous behavior. This time, though, the French only wanted Filippov; they had their own designer.

Naturally, he didn't have to sign the contract, but the offer was so good, and Paris in the fall so alluring, and even his agent hinted that after Paris a Broadway option would probably open up for him, that Filippov, who was too chicken to lose all this, ultimately had to sign the papers. That's what he told himself: *I had to.* As if he had in fact had no choice. Now he was flying to the North, to his hometown, first to be the one to explain to his friend that he'd "had no choice," and, second, to get the sketches he desperately needed for the show, in which his friend, as far as he knew, had already formulated all the basic ideas that would more than likely be decisive for the show's success.

Basically, it would be a lot easier to resort to good old amnesia and play out this game with his friend following the tried-and-true scheme, pretending he'd forgotten everything, and in the process somehow improvising, maneuvering, to get a hold of the sketches. But right then, as if on purpose, Zinaida turned up, and Filippov hadn't held his ground. In track and field, as far as he could remember, this was called a false start. He'd also had the vulgar urge to know what people were saying about him back home. Having left that Northern deep freeze of a city more than ten years before, he'd never once gone back and so didn't know what the attitude toward him there was. Up until this moment, he just hadn't given a damn. On Filippov's list of what to consign to oblivion, this place came in at number one.

———

"In ten minutes our plane will begin its descent. Please return your chairs to their upright position, replace your tray tables, and fasten your seat belts."

Filippov opened his eyes and glanced at Zinaida. She was looking at the back of the old woman, who was glued to the window, evidently wanting to view the limitless fields of clouds not only with her eyes but also with her shoulders and chest.

"Our estimated arrival time is twelve o'clock," the voice on the loudspeaker continued. "Local time now is eleven twenty. Temperature in the city, forty-one degrees below zero."

"How much? How much?" someone behind him drawled.

"I'll be damned," another voice piped up. "In October!"

Filippov didn't remember for sure what the temperature was supposed to be in his hometown in late October, but he definitely knew it wasn't forty below. That was more like December weather. Basically, all these cold snaps surfaced as fairly abstract memories—like childish insults or someone else's dream, and not even the dream itself but how people tell it. Getting mixed up and reliving it, they try to convey what unconsciously disturbed them nearly to tears, but they can't, and everything they say is totally boring—not scary—lifeless and stupid. Words can't convey what comes to us beyond words, what grasps and enslaves us in total silence. That was more or less how Filippov remembered the cold.

Over all those intervening years, his body had lost any memory of freezing weather. His surface no longer sensed the chill physically, the way it used to. His skin didn't remember the cold's pressure; it forgot its weight, resilience, solidity, and resistance. Softened by Moscow, Paris, and Geneva winters, Filippov's surface had a hard time remembering how much effort it took just to move down the street as his body cut through a cold as thick as jelly.

Looking at the back of Zinaida, who was holding out hope looking at the old woman's back, Filippov—totally involuntarily and unexpectedly—plunged into his distant past. Disdainfully sorting through the images and memories crawling out of every airplane crack, he even shook his head slightly, as if to shake them off. Up until this moment, he'd been absolutely certain they'd left him forever, drifted down and withered like last year's nasty leaves champing underfoot in the March mess. But now just the mention of true cold instantly roused that whole tedious scum, which stuck to Filippov, asserting its rights and demanding his tedious love for the past and his attention.

Looking at Zinaida's pink back, he suddenly saw his fifteen-year-old self trailing off to school in the wintry morning darkness and the impenetrable fog that blanketed the town for several months, like fiberglass, as soon as the thermometer dropped below forty below. His cheap leatherette gym bag, stiff from the cold, kept slipping off his shoulder, trying to fall off, and it wasn't easy to right, because fifteen-year-old Filippov was wearing a huge sheepskin army coat, sewn, or rather, constructed, for a sturdy fighter, and puny Filippov could barely move in this construction, kicking its wide hem, as stiff as plywood, out of boredom. In this construction, his own arms felt like prosthetics. Or manipulators in a deep-water bathyscaphe. Not so easy to use.

The coat had been obtained by his father, who had pull at some warehouse, so Filippov couldn't reject the army monster. His father was proud to be a man and a provider, too, like everyone else, and once he'd had a drink after work he told endless stories about what a clever, useful, and irreplaceable guy he was. Filippov was trailing down his miserable little street past a row of two-story barracks, or rather, past a row of bulky shadows that resembled these barracks, because in the darkness and fog you could only guess what you were walking past. His bag finally slipped off, but he wasn't paying attention and dragged it behind himself over the bluish snow, its top layer hard as concrete, listening to his notebooks rattle around inside in their oilcloth covers, which were as hard as cold rocks. He was trailing along forty minutes before classes started because the principal had forced the teachers to hold political information sessions in the upper classes, and today it was Filippov's turn to inform his sullen, underslept classmates about the theses of the latest plenum of the Communist Party's Central Committee, about the growth in the Communist Party's leading and guiding role in the life of Soviet society, about the inseparability of the party's authority and the state, about the unity of mind and will of the party and people, and also about fulfilling their international duty as Soviet fighters in Afghanistan. Why he was leading such an inhuman life, Filippov at age fifteen doesn't know.

"We're like cattle," Elza mumbled from another, neighboring memory.

How she had come to be in the local theater, Filippov didn't remember. Maybe from Moscow, but maybe from Leningrad. In any case, she behaved in such a way that all the other actors automatically hated her. They didn't like being provincial cattle, the offal of the acting profession, demons of the lowest sort. Actually, they even hated themselves and, by inertia, all humanity. The reasons for this hatred were different in each case, but the result was always the same. Hatred was their greatest love.

Swaddled in unimaginable shawls that no one here in the North wore, Elza emerged from the fog and, by some miracle, recognized Filippov in his rimy cocoon, perishing from hatred. She came up to him and they stood there motionless, like two cosmonauts who have left their spaceship for reasons unknown.

"We're like cattle," Elza muttered, leaning her head toward him so he could hear and pulling away from her face the part of her scarf she was breathing into and which had frozen in a damp whitish crust right up to her sad eyes.

In this memory, Filippov was twenty-five. He was already a widower and was buying his own clothes. In the winter, he looked more like a wandering monument. He wore two pairs of trousers, a thick sweater, a short black fur-lined coat, reindeer boots, a muskrat hat, and huge beaver gauntlets. These absolutely unbending, titanic mittens were stuck into his coat pockets permanently, and they poked out of them, like an odd stuffed animal whose ears have slipped—obviously because of the cold—to the region of his waist. In the winter, the entire male population of the city was dressed this way, each one absolutely satisfied that he was as good as anyone else.

The short sheepskin and fur coats started to cede their unshakable position after Gorbachev's perestroika, when missionaries started coming here. The diamond territory lured them more powerfully than the heavenly kingdom, and all these spiritual Swedish-Mormon born-agains had the best time they could in the former Soviet North. They wailed to the electric guitar in the movie house, danced in the furniture store, and sobbed with a microphone in their hands, rocking and calling out: "Your coming, Jesus!" After their lively sermons, no one in town particularly went for the Mormon thing, but this did bring an end to the hegemony of fur-lined cloth coats. The missionaries arrived wearing imported, brightly colored down parkas, which was obviously the missionaries' true mission. The crude local Mormonophobes laughed at them and assured them that, like fleas, they would freeze in their "cute little jackets," but for the young Filippov, these shining brand-name raiments were a genuine and practically religious revelation. At twenty-five he set his sights ecstatically on a red down parka, and now nothing in the world could stop him on this lofty path. Thus came the end, in his life, to the era of universal black cloth. His break with his hometown was now inevitable.

In addition, he no longer could bear to go to his young wife's grave.

———

"Buckle up, please."

Filippov raised his head and looked at the attendant leaning toward him. The tips of her neckerchief poked out from under her blouse like pretty, stubborn horns.

"And please put that away." She shifted her gaze to the bottle of grappa in his hand.

"Will you show me your ears?" Filippov was looking at the shiny dark hair framing the narrow white plane of her face.

"What for?"

"It's important to me what kind of ears are listening to me—pretty or not."

"Put the bottle away."

"I can't. For me, drunkenness is the ultimate form of sincerity. There aren't any others left."

"Drinking alcoholic beverages purchased elsewhere on board is prohibited."

"Can I buy it from you?"

"Not now. We're landing in twenty minutes."

"Too bad. Want a sip?"

The flight attendant stood up straight and continued on, turning her head from side to side, as if she were following a tennis match. Or decisively rejecting what no man had ever summoned the nerve to ask her out loud.

"Stop," Filippov shouted after her. "I have a question."

"I'm listening," she said in a weary voice, returning to his seat.

"You should talk to the pilot. We seem to be flying slowly. And in the totally wrong direction, I think. I don't recognize the route. Look out the window yourself."

At these words, pink Zinaida giggled and the attendant silently turned and continued her unhurried movement through the cabin. Schoolboy jokes from forty-year-old jerks had bored her a long time ago.

Filippov sipped from the bottle, stuck it in the seat pocket, buckled up, and closed his eyes again, trying not to miss a single familiarly scorching moment. The grappa warmed his throat, then his esophagus, and finally shone in his stomach.

"You are so great," Filippov mumbled as he plunged into his ice-armored past. "You're my beauty."

—

His father's sheepskin coat had made him the biggest laughingstock in school. The girls in his class and the classes below loved to make fun of him. When he wandered home after classes wearing that fur coat, they peeked out of the small windows of their two-story barracks, sometimes even clambering onto the sill, hurrying before he passed by, their skinny knees knocking, poking out from under their house robes, shouting at him gaily: "Filya-Filya! The town dump feels ya!"

In that coat he looked like another Filya, the restive statue of Felix Dzerzhinsky, who in the late Soviet period fled his pedestal out of grief and roamed aimlessly through the frozen city in search of the revolution's other warriors, who were equally lost.

Among the teasing girls from the windows was one who later—literally three years later—became Filippov's wife.

"Smell it?" he would say to her, gasping from exhaustion and happiness after their first secret attempts at love. "Smell that? It smells different. It didn't used to be like that."

He sniffed his armpits, then she did it, and both laughed at the unfamiliar smell, at Filya's clumsy new trustingness, and at the fact that they had to hide while her lonely mother was sitting in the kitchen, having gotten up in the middle of the night for some reason.

"Idiot," Nina said, "you left your coat in the hall."

They choked with laughter, while the light from the front hall fell incriminatingly through the frosted glass onto their thick crumpled blanket.

Basically, being together was fun. Getting ready to go to a dance at a different school, she could now boldly put on thick woolen leggings, because Filya devotedly carried them around all evening in his bag while she bounced around to her favorite group, Ottawan, and howled like a banshee with her hands up. In principle, of course, everyone there was screaming, but the other girls, before screaming and bouncing, ran to the ladies' room and spent a long time pinching their thighs, which were red from the cold. In a strange school, there was nowhere to put your ugly long pants, so young girls wearing pants over thin stockings raced there from all over town like Olympic athletes amped up from doping. It was good if the head teacher or PE instructor at that school didn't force them to wait long on the front steps. When it's minus fifty outside and gets dark at three in the afternoon, when people at bus stops rush the bus just to make out the route number, when fur cocoons roam the streets in the dark and fog and in this silence each person is a submarine unto himself, when champagne forgotten an extra half hour on a balcony on New Year's explodes the thick bottle into tiny shards—in short, when ordinary winter comes in the North, Ottawan good times at a different school came at a very high price.

The fun didn't last long. A year after the wedding, Nina died. Filippov forgave no one, quit school, became a cynic, and got a job as fire warden at the local theater. At that point, the country was drunk on glasnost. Everyone was talking about everything, and there were virtually no more secrets, so Filippov had to crawl into the deepest darkest corner he could find. The provincial theater, infested with quiet no-talents and kind scroungers, could not have suited him better.

The massive elderly janitor, a woman, who Filippov had to work nights with, once expressed her unambiguous attitude toward the resident Melpomene. After drinking half the bottle of vodka she'd laid in for her shift, she headed for the toilet. Since tsars don't take the long way around, she decided not to go around the stage, and even that route she cut short. When he made his rounds, Filippov discovered her right on the dimly lit stage. The janitor, like a triumphant actor being given a benefit performance, was squatting in the very center of the turntable and babbling triumphantly in the dark. Filippov didn't know what to think. He himself despised the whole local troupe by then, so he absolutely did not condemn the art-weary lady, but a month later she was found frozen to death on the outskirts of town, and he gave some serious thought to the theater's mystique. At the time, he had yet to consider the cold's unusual qualities.

An intrigued Filippov hastened to the municipal library, where he came across Friedrich Nietzsche's book on the birth of tragedy. Filippov gulped it down, contemplating the theater of antiquity and his own tragic lot, and in the reading room got to know the dark-haired but blue-eyed Inga, who was writing her thesis on Old Slavonic pronouns and bore a striking resemblance to Isabelle Adjani, whom Filippov adored from a black-and-white booklet, *Artists of the French Cinema*. Due to his lack of funds, the booklet had been stolen from the bookstore. In the photographs, Isabelle had barely turned eighteen.

In the booklet's photos, Filippov the young widower morbidly sought out the signs of another life foreign to him, and only these minor details—the glove on the table, the half-smoked cigarette in the ashtray next to the white cup, the scattering of daisies on the mildly distraught Isabelle's dress, the little dog in her arms—only they allowed him to believe in that world, that it was material, and that somewhere right now there was a Paris, where there were allées lined with plane trees and a river that didn't freeze three meters thick and where no one jostled you in a long, mean line as you checked your icy mitten for your vodka coupon, hunched over from the cold in an enormous sheepskin coat. In principle, the flights of Soviet spaceships that the TV show *Time* repeated over and over during the days of his childhood and youth were much more real to him than a dog's leash in the hands of eighteen-year-old Isabelle Adjani, which he suspected involved some kind of trick.

Of the French film star and her unusual resemblance to her, Inga herself knew nothing, and for the most part she couldn't have cared less. Nothing in the world could have made her agree to remain in anyone's shadow. This young she-wolf wielded her otherworldly beauty at her own sole discretion. To Filippov's question of why she'd given herself to him after their first meeting, Inga replied without thinking, "You look French." Where she came up with that and what image she had in her head of a Frenchman remained a puzzle, but this assertion of hers flattered Filippov and also linked him to the black-and-white Isabelle

Adjani not only because of Inga's capricious beauty but also because of the suddenly acquired "French" status she'd bestowed upon him so unexpectedly and generously.

After Nina's death, Filippov hadn't wanted to live, either. At the funeral, he pushed aside his family and classmates standing at the grave, leapt in, and demanded that they scatter earth on him, too. They refused, dragged him out of the cool, shallow pit, and brought him around as best they could. Within a few months, he had ceased to regret this. Apparently, he had a lot to learn about life, and it was too soon to leave without learning it. Inga, the tragic muse sent down to him, did not simply surprise him—she stunned him with her attitude toward love, sex, and the human being's biological nature. Filippov was puzzled and disoriented. Taken aback. Evidently, this is what saved him. Her unbridled might, straight out of antiquity, shook him like a rag doll, and he awoke to life once again.

Because sex was nothing more than sport, Inga changed partners the way a sprinter changes lanes at the stadium. For a couple of weeks, she'd run down one lane and then switch to another, the only difference being that the abandoned running lanes couldn't plague her with their whining and broken hearts and lay peacefully right where someone's hand had drawn them. In this sense, ideal sex for Inga probably would have been a superquickie with a real running track.

One way or another, Filippov spent the two weeks given to him in diligent and delightful labors that distracted him from his sullen hatred for the world. For reasons of her own, which were obscure and therefore all the more alluring, Inga called these labors "riding." She also called them Figure Sex School.

They would "go for a ride" in all kinds of places. For Filippov, the most vivid experience was "riding" in the library's listening room. The municipal library was justly proud of its huge collection of classical music, and a secluded room with soundproofing and a door that locked from the inside had been set aside there for normal people. No one could have imagined how well all this not just suited but seemed created for the obsessed Inga. The "ride" began to Beethoven, reached its culmination with Wagner, and concluded with a Boccherini minuet. Never before could Filippov have imagined anything more powerful and, at the same time, elegant. Apparently, it was there, gasping slightly, that she'd told him, "Yours is as stiff as a cliff. No, a lighthouse."

Meanwhile, for some reason, she had a husband and daughter. When the child met Filippov, this taciturn four-year-old was supposed to call him Papa, which Filippov absolutely did not understand, but Inga lived by her own rules. If his mama was "riding" with someone at a given moment, that meant the rider was her papa. French and Papa—that's how it had to be. Obviously, she was shielding the child from bad thoughts about the fact that Mama might get into this with some strange man.

When she got bored, she suggested a three-way ride. She engaged her ugliest friend for the purpose and, as additional reserve, a friend of Filippov's. Since the other girl barely counted as a person, in Inga's understanding, it was his friend who played number three. He tried to demand a better part, but the blue-eyed brunette had firm rules about her girlfriends. In the end, her three-way consisted of unlucky Max and the other girl occupying the next bed, and Inga making biting jokes under the wheezing Filippov about how his friend obviously wasn't a cliff at all and definitely no lighthouse. Max was a modest clock tower that always told the same time.

"Five thirty," Inga laughed underneath Filippov, but her laugh didn't throw him off. The novelty of her attitude toward life just astonished him.

At the time, he hadn't read Aristophanes or Apuleius yet.

Actually, the contrast between utterly innocent Botticellian beauty and total depravity didn't torment the young Filippov for very long. Exactly two weeks after reading Nietzsche on classical theater, he took Inga home, where he made an unforgivable mistake. All this time she'd never once taken off her bra in front of him, saying the mood was wrong or there wasn't enough time, as if taking off her bra took half an hour. But this time Filippov showed some grit—and barely managed to conceal his disappointment looking at her sad, swinging tits.

"You know," he said, being a young and honest aesthete, "I like your face more than your body."

A few days later, as sad as those tits, Filippov lay in bed with the ugly girlfriend, who glanced at the next bed and whispered to him hotly, "Will you marry me if I get knocked up?"

By that point, the pain from Nina's death was almost a thing of the past.

———

Right before touching down, the plane swayed and pink Zinaida clutched Filippov's shoulder, bringing him back to the dimly lit cabin. Addled by the quickly downed grappa and unexpectedly vivid memories, he didn't even manage to say anything sarcastic after the passengers' friendly applause upon landing, which usually annoyed him. He just rose silently from his seat and stood there meekly in the aisle, waiting for them to bring over the stairs.

A minute later everyone else was standing as well. What power makes people jump to their feet after landing, knowing they won't be let off the plane right away, remained a great mystery for Filippov. As he had long since noticed in his perpetual flights, nationality and citizenship played no role in this whatsoever. Americans, Europeans, Asians—virtually everyone liked to jostle in the aisle. Moreover, pulling on their coats and jackets, they worked their elbows so energetically that if you flew fairly frequently, you could well master the basic moves of martial arts. Even if you couldn't elegantly dodge the next blow, you could at least quietly give as good as you got.

This time, the passengers were clothing themselves in thick down parkas. Filippov could have sworn that at Domodedovo, at check-in, no one had had bulky winter clothing with them, but no sooner had the plane slowed down on the tarmac when literally everyone was holding a down parka, and some, snuffling, had already pulled on tall reindeer boots decorated with colorful beads. No fur-lined cloth coats were to be found, by the way, so the missionaries in the nineties had not come in vain. Filippov managed to be happy for his countrymen, but right then the kids started waking up. Considering the number of warm things they'd naturally forgotten about on the "mainland," which now had to be pulled onto them fairly quickly, a faint wail rose in the cabin. Filippov's grappa had run out, so he could do nothing to muffle the cacophony. Actually, he didn't have to do anything; the kid nearby got a good crack from his own dear mama. Exhausted by the sleepless night, the seven-hour flight, her rug rat's endless whining, her husband's absence, and the drastic change of time zones, she wasn't about to stand on ceremony.

"Just try yelling again," she clarified through clenched teeth, jerking the ties of his muskrat cap a little lower than his instantly silent but still menacingly half-open mouth.

Filippov experienced a tremendous warmth for her. If she'd squeezed through the crowd in the cabin and quickly done the same thing with the other vile squallers, he would have been boundlessly grateful to her, but she'd had enough with her own.

"Just you try kicking," she told him ominously, bringing her straight index finger, as long as a tank barrel, up to his frightened face.

The youngster decided not to tempt fate. Blinking, he maintained a patient silence while she sealed off his crying hole with a huge fluffy scarf. She pulled it around to the back of the kid's head, and, to make quite sure, she stuck a white kerchief under the scarf. Evidently, she wanted to seal his mouth very securely.

Now just try to shout, Filippov thought gleefully. *You can just slobber there.* He seemed to have forgotten why the locals covered their face with a scarf.

Meanwhile, the scarf-winding epidemic spread through the cabin. Scarves, shawls, and kerchiefs twirled in the air, whistling like cowboys' lassos. The people's faces that had suddenly become dear vanished under this woolen arsenal so fast that Filippov, despite his aged misanthropy, couldn't help but feel the sting of loneliness. Wool was eating people up, leaving nothing but shapeless dolls in the aisle.

Filippov himself had nothing but his laces to wind around himself. He felt like an orphan in his stupid Dirk Bikkembergs coat, in the midst of this wool bacchanalia. He didn't have a fur cap, either. The old woman who'd been sitting next to him and who now had mysteriously ended up several meters closer to the exit looked around, winked at him, and twisted her fur hand at her fur temple. She was evidently implying that Filippov had been too nonchalant for his own good with his Dirk Bikkembergs.

The next moment all this swaddled realm heaved a sigh, stirred faintly, and, like a festive but silent Chinese dragon, crept toward the exit. As it went, the dragon shed on the emptied seats its crumpled newspapers, plastic cups, magazines, napkins, and other trash, which at that moment suddenly became sweetly nostalgic to Filippov because it all linked him to Moscow, his life, another world—not to what was whirling in an impenetrable fog outside the gray windows, awaiting him distastefully on the frozen staircase. By an effort of what in normal people passes for will, Filippov suppressed the desire squeaking piteously inside him to stay where he was. The plane would have to return to Moscow without him.

The exhausted, smiling attendants pressed up against the cockpit door. From the open hatch, the cold insolently grabbed them by their pretty knees in their thin stockings, but they stubbornly bundled up in their fur-trimmed parka hoods and nodded at the creeping dragon and smiled, smiled, smiled. The pilots, who had hidden their smiles somewhere in back, were waiting for this all to be over and so were trying not to move a muscle where they were. Filippov pictured them standing quietly on the other side, their palms pressed to the steel-clad door, to make it at least a little warmer for the girls.

"Thank you very much," he said, smiling vulgarly as he approached the flight attendants. "It was perfectly marvelous."

"Good-bye," the one Filippov had asked to show her ears responded on autopilot. "Thank you for flying with us."

Uttering this absolutely impersonally, in the next moment she recognized Filippov and livened up and managed to scowl, but the sight of his thin coat with a joke for a collar and nothing covering his balding pate evoked first surprise in her and after that pity. Filippov noted this sympathy flashing across her pretty face, and he lashed out.

"I'm being met." He winked. "Come with me? I'll give you a diamond."

The expensive coat on Filippov said a lot. It was clear that a jerk flying from Moscow in threads like his wasn't about to kick the bucket at a bus stop; he was probably being met by a big car as hot and steamy as a bathhouse. Any human feelings that might have been in the attendant's eyes were extinguished, and in the voice of a *Matrix* autochthon she said a warm good-bye to the next passenger.

When he'd taken a step out on the stairs, Filippov realized in a fraction of a second just how out of touch with reality he'd become in the last few years. Naturally, he knew he wasn't going to go straight from the plane to the jet bridge in the fashion of standard European flights, but he was still counting on at least some kind of transport. Before, as far as he remembered, the passengers were met right there by a long rundown bus that then spent a long time looping around the concrete, flinging the arrivals from side to side. People leaned awkwardly and held on tight to poles and their suitcases; they swore and scoffed, but they did nonetheless ride. Now, having hopped the awful half-meter gap between the plane and the shaky stairs, Filippov looked mournfully at the file of passengers stretching through the icy fog, trailing across the airfield to the terminal.

As he went down the metal steps, which rang alarmingly from the cold, Filippov covered his mouth with his hand to avoid taking in a full breath of icy air. He still remembered what that could lead to in weather like this. Thousands of diamond needles bit into his bald spot, cheeks, and forehead as he trailed behind the others. Clenched like a crooked little worm, he listened to his own breathing, which in the absolute silence now seemed to belong not to him but to the raspy, unintelligible, and infinitely lonely Darth Vader.

Harsh, Filippov thought disjointedly. *Totally harsh.*

He kept his head down as he walked, but he still made out another three large planes on the airfield. Next to each, passengers were crowding and hopping in place, languishing from cold and impatience, being allowed on the stairs only one at a time. After showing their boarding passes to the swaddled figure at the foot of the stairs, they hastily clambered on board. Filippov, for some reason, kept turning around to look at them, slipping on the iced-over concrete and tripping, unable to rid himself of the sensation that he was seeing this for the last time and that once they all flew away there would be no way out for anyone.

This is how he understood what a terrified soul must feel, more or less, at being delivered to Purgatory in full view of those favorites for whom Saint Peter had already opened wide the pearly gates.

"Tell me, is someone meeting you?" Zinaida had caught up to Filippov and latched on to his arm.

———

From the window of the enormous SUV, which looked newly purchased and in which Zinaida's husband had come to meet her, everything looked exactly as of old. The square in front of the station hadn't changed one bit in the last ten years. Hunched recognizably over the entrance from the port highway were smokestacks wrapped in fiberglass. Naturally, Filippov remembered that the entire city was covered in a metal web of heating mains, but the sight of them was still a shock. There weren't even any wires in the Paris sky, but here, along every street, and here and there over pedestrians' heads, stretched kilometers of very sturdy pipes. From time to time, fiberglass was wound around the heating mains, where it hung in ugly shreds, swaying in the fog and wind. In his youth, this had reminded Filippov of Gothic novels, where there's always something nasty hanging and swaying in dimly lit, gloomy, and damp vaulted dungeons.

The indigenous cars busily cloaked themselves in clouds of exhaust fumes out in front of the airport, which had seen its share of sad northern views. The various Uaziks, like pushy, nimble riffraff, had old quilts stretched across their hoods, wintertime-style. Their side windows sported the squares of modeling clay Filippov had forgotten about a long time ago. Actually, he wasn't sure the drivers used modeling. It may well have been some kind of putty. In the winter, for scientific reasons unknown to Filippov, these squares were the only unfrosted spot on the car windows, and those ensconced inside proudly gazed through them at the pedestrians suffering minus fifty.

In the fog, vague silhouettes of new arrivals and the people meeting them scurried across the open space between the airport terminal and a small barracks-like structure. Filippov vaguely remembered that this barracks served as baggage claim. Why the bags and suitcases couldn't be handed out in the warm terminal remained a mystery. Actually, questions like that didn't occur to the hardy locals. They just scurried through the cold there and back, hauling their luggage, wrapped for extra security in blue plastic wrap. The heavier the luggage, the faster they warmed up.

Looking at these strong and unpretentious people, their Uaziks, their heating mains, and their life, Filippov thought he might throw up. This wasn't just a reaction to his hometown. The grappa had worn off, and his fussy system was demanding additional fuel. In vain hope, Filippov swiveled his head, but there was no alcohol in this stranger's car. Then he cracked the door open, hunched from the cold, and leaned over the dwindling asphalt covered with oil spots and patches of gray ice. His body convulsed, sobbed piteously, and then moaned, but he vomited up exactly zero. The fog instantly thickened into the Demon of the Void.

"I'm coming to get you," the demon jeered. "Fill me up. I'm sick to my stomach."

Filippov took a deep breath and looked up at the gray sky, as if hoping to find the rabbit hole he'd fallen down into this Wonderland.

"You shouldn't have opened the door," said the figure of Zina's husband as it materialized directly in front of him out of the fog carrying an enormous suitcase. "I don't care how stewed or baked you are. This is a Land Cruiser, not a Studebaker."

"Very funny," Filippov said, politely praising his unfunny joke.

Actually, in order to justify himself in his own eyes, he felt like immediately adding something insulting, but he didn't have the strength left for nastiness. He leaned back in his seat and slammed the door. The next moment, Zinaida dove out of the fog next to her husband. She was carrying skis. She'd started to say something quickly and angrily, but her husband wasn't listening. He walked around the car, opened the tailgate, put the suitcase inside, and said to Zinaida, "Let's not do this now." Then he slammed the door and started arranging the skis on the roof. Filippov listened to the racket, his own nausea, and Zinaida's grating voice. Something had upset her. Something had happened while he was sitting in their car admiring his long-abandoned hometown.

"What's her name?" Zinaida asked irritably, getting into the front seat and slamming the door hard.

"Listen"—her husband sighed—"I just traded in the car. Why do you have to do this?"

"Pavlik, spare me about the car," she wailed. "I'm not feeling so good as is. You still haven't answered me, by the way, where you got the money for it. So enough of the smooth talk. What's her name?"

Pavlik turned around to Filippov guiltily and pulled his shaggy cap off his head, revealing an equally shaggy head of hair. In principle, it made no sense, given that state of affairs, why he needed a cap at all. Pavlik's hair stood almost straight up like the brilliant Doc Brown from Zemeckis's movie at the moment the time machine gets fired up. Maybe he was just afraid of his wife. In any case, being nearly bald at his forty-two years, Filippov did envy him a little.

"Let's just talk about this at home," Pavlik said softly. "Why do this in front of a stranger?"

"Oh, don't mind me," Filippov chimed in. "I like this kind of stuff. Only let's stop by somewhere first. I need a drink. Otherwise, I might get sick and soil your floor mats."

Pavlik pulled a nice leather-sided flask out of the inside pocket of his down parka and held it out.

"Rabbit out of the hat?" Filippov asked.

"No, Hennessy."

"Not bad, either."

Filippov screwed off the top, and for a few seconds total silence fell over the car. Zinaida had clicked shut all her inner locks and was looking blankly through the windshield at the tedious fog. Pavlik was lost in his own thoughts, too. Taking small sips, like an old and very calculating vampire, Filippov sucked down some cognac. The smell of Hennessy gradually filled the inside of the Land Cruiser.

"As for 'Studebekker,' by the way," Pavlik said, "I can tell you that's the wrong pronunciation. Actually it's supposed to be 'Studebaker.' Catch the difference? 'Baker,' like in Baker Street. The London street where Sherlock Holmes lived. But here we say 'Studebekker.' That's just how it happened historically. But it's wrong. And by the way, that was the American truck that served as the chassis for lots of our Katyusha

INTO THE THICKENING FOG

rockets during the Great Patriotic War. Not everyone knows that. Have you ever given their cabs a close look? You can tell right away. A Studebaker has these characteristic—"

"Hey, man, want me to recite you a poem about your wife?" Filippov said as he twisted the cap back onto the cognac. "Just keep the flask close at hand."

"Sure. Did you write it yourself?"

"No, it's a folk poem."

Zinaida surfaced from her stupor and turned around in her seat. Her face now looked nothing like that happy, simple-hearted blob making googly eyes at Filippov on the plane. Now she was inwardly collected and apparently ready to give someone hell. She definitely didn't look like someone who cared one bit that she had a glamorous Moscow celebrity riding in her car.

Filippov struck a pose suggested by a couple of swallows of alcohol and, humming a little, started to declaim:

"Rubber Zina, rubber Zina,
I saw her in a magazine,
I met her on a mezzanine,
I dropped her on her little bean,
And now she's muddy, not so clean.
Rubber Zina, rubber Zina,
She didn't bounce, which seems to mean,
She may be made of plasticine."

He fell silent. Pavlik and Zinaida looked at him, obviously at a loss.

"Well?" Filippov asked. "Powerful stuff?"

"Is it erotic?" Pavlik conjectured.

"Why?"

"The rubber part's like a sex shop ad."

"No." Filippov shook his head. "When I learned it, we didn't have sex shops yet. At theater school, I had to recite this all the time for speech class. I had trouble with my *z*'s and *s*'s. A minor defect. The teacher found the poem for me specially. There was more, but I don't remember the rest."

"Your memory's back?" Zinaida asked Filippov.

"Partly." He nodded. "Can we go? At the moment I'm not nauseated."

Before leaving the port settlement for the highway to town, shaggy Pavlik asked Filippov where he should take him. Naturally, he should have gone straight to his friend's, prostrated himself before him, repented, blamed the French producers for everything, and most important, asked for his help. But he chickened out. The illusory joy that grips us at the news that the dentist can't see us today was suggested in his instant reply: "A hotel. A decent one. I do seem to recall there were a couple of so-called hotels."

"No, no." Pavlik laughed affectedly. "They took down those woodpiles a long time ago. A lot's changed here in general. When was the last time you visited?"

"Never. Stop. Which way are you going? Town's not there."

The car jumped out onto the port road and turned not left but right—where there was a crossing to the other shore past the big hangars. Not once in his whole life had Filippov ever used this crossing, but he knew that in the summer a ferry operated there, and in the winter, cars crossed the river, now a road of ice.

"I need to make a stop." Pavlik turned around, and a plea for understanding shone in his eyes, like a dog's. "If I go from town afterward, it'll be way too far."

"Then let me out. I'll take a taxi."

"That won't work," Pavlik said to Filippov as if he were a child. "All the Moscow flights have arrived, and the taxis have gone off. You won't find anyone at the port."

"Then I'll take a bus."

Pavlik actually burst out laughing at those words. This annoyed Zinaida so much that she demonstratively covered her ears with her hands.

"A bus? You really haven't been here in a long time. They aren't heated. We've still got those Soviet-made Liazes going around town."

"The fleapits?"

Pavlik turned around with a smile.

"Ah, you remember what they used to be called."

Filippov snickered. "Certain things you don't forget."

"I'm afraid that with your outfit, you'd get downtown frozen solid—like a halibut in the store, or a cod."

"On the other hand, it's a sure thing I won't rot."

Pavlik readily burst into laughter. Despite his wife's sullen silence, he was obviously thrilled at the unexpected meeting with the hometown boy who was famous in Moscow and who'd turned out to be such a regular and entertaining guy.

Filippov looked at the puny firs flashing by in the fog, at the faceless warehouses and commercial structures pressed up here and there to the frozen earth behind the airport, at the tedious territory, so alienated from ordinary human needs and plans, and at the gray sky, which breathed such limitless and definitive indifference that even Filippov, who rightly considered himself a champion in that discipline, felt a chill somewhere between his shoulder blades that took his breath away, like when he was a kid and such a nonentity that the older kids didn't even bother to drive him out of the yard during their games. He looked at all this and tried not to listen to Pavlik's chatter informing him of temperature records, prices for heaters, and some endless something else—something that lulled him, reconciled him to his arrival, and put him in a traveling mood. It was all good. He was riding in warmth, not wandering around in search of a taxi through the chilled station square. The cognac nearby, instilling confidence in the future, now sloshed unctuously in a flask. And his difficult meeting and conversation had been put off at least until tomorrow. It was all good.

No, it was good I flew in, Filippov told himself. *I was wrong to be tense. Tomorrow we'll resolve everything and I'll go straight home. And then to Paris. Fuck hearth and home.*

Still, something was wrong. He tried to fight off a sense of mounting, totally irrational alarm, but this feeling was lapping somewhere very nearby, washing up against the far-from-firm shore of his cognac happiness, and little by little Filippov began to have his doubts about riding with strangers who had offered to drop him off in town but were now taking him God knows where. His old friend, paranoia, suddenly decided to remind him of the number of dead bodies picked up on the town's streets by police patrols weekly during Filippov's youth.

"Seven or eight," he muttered—and Pavlik immediately cut his chatter short.

"Excuse me, what?"

"Where are we going?"

"It's not far now. Don't worry. We'll get you there safe and sound—better than DHL."

Pavlik laughed gleefully at what he took for his own wit and then started badgering Filippov with stupid questions. He wondered why Filippov's beard was singed, what his creative plans were, what was happening with the weather in Paris right now, and how much a ticket to the Lido cost. To suppress his idiotic fears, Filippov expressed interest, too, inquiring about how much good fish was in town, whether he could have reindeer boots made, and why workers with blowtorches were sitting three meters up on the heating main at the exit from the port. Pavlik shrugged and replied that you could see that all over town, but he didn't know the reason.

"Maybe some kind of precaution."

"All over town? When you've already got a blast of cold like this?"

"Well, yeah, that's just the time for precautions. Have you been to a burial lately?"

"Whose?"

Pavlik glanced over at Zinaida, who'd had time to enlighten her husband as to Filippov's star status but hadn't warned him about his eccentricities, and now, swallowed up by something extremely important to her, she wasn't listening to their conversation at all and obviously had no plans to lend her husband a hand.

"Doesn't matter whose. Have you ever seen a dead man in a coffin?"

"Sure, I have. What does a dead man have to do with this?"

"What he has to do with is you tell him about prevention. So he doesn't get too upset."

"Ah . . . So that's what you're getting at." Pavlik nodded warily, pretending to understand his passenger's metaphor. "That's, sure, yeah . . . You're right about that. Only I was talking about something a little different."

"We're all talking about something a little different, my man. So that's enough avoiding the subject. Hand over the cognac."

As they drove up to the river crossing, Filippov felt good again. The incredible thickness of gray wadding overhead even seemed to have thinned slightly, and a little bit of sun had broken through to them at the bottom, though it didn't make it any brighter. On the river, the fog had obviously gotten blown off, and as soon as the car had bounced over a gigantic pothole and jumped out onto the ice, visibility increased significantly on all sides.

"Hey, wait up," Filippov said. "I thought we were only going as far as the crossing. You mean you think you're going to the other side?"

"Oh, it's very close here," Pavlik said in a rush. "We'll dash across in the blink of an eye. And there it's right on the shore."

"The blink of what eye? Where's the shore? I don't even see it."

"Yeah, well, once we go around the island here you'll see it right away. Or after the second island. There could be fog there again, though."

"What islands? Where are you dragging me?"

"We won't be long at all. I promise."

Filippov recalled flying into his hometown twenty or so years before, returning from Vladivostok, and the huge Il-62's tiny shadow floating for an eternity—or so it had seemed at the time—amid the assemblage of barges, steamers, and launches. If it had taken a long-distance airliner that long to cross this river, then how long was it going to take this silly SUV? Especially if you took into account all the hummocks, detours, and islands.

"Let's go back," Filippov said. "You're getting on my nerves. I have to get to the hotel. I have a meeting."

The part about the meeting was a lie, of course, but even that failed to make the slightest impression on Pavlik.

"I can't," he said, and he stubbornly gripped the wheel. "Anyway, no one forced you to get in the car with us."

Filippov looked over at Zinaida, the very image of a tedious smartphone addict—temporarily and, evidently, very seriously unavailable.

Filippov's father, who served on a submarine in the early 1960s, would beleaguer him with stories about autonomous excursions and about how the sailors, who went out of their minds during their long transits, would turn around the films they'd long since learned by heart and run them backward. This obviously entertained the submariners, but Filippov, who was now experiencing very similar feelings, was in no mood for laughter. His own film was winding in reverse, and he looked mournfully on landscapes that had come back into his life, and his memory, readily and with mocking love, wiped away the ice of the present.

Around him now, the water splashed and the summer breeze was noisy; the mosquitoes droned about their millennial hunger, the seagulls screamed like mad, and the sun should just have been about to peek over the water's edge. Everything here was practically like at sea: the sun rose not from behind the forest or a hill, but from behind this border of water that would have sufficed for an average-size European sea. This river only pretended to be a river, as it disdainfully put up with being called. In fact, it was a sea, of course. A sea. It simply moved sideways, palpably and heavily displacing itself to the right, opening up to the eye a flat space, boundless in every direction, where islands, ships, and motorboats were drawn like blotches. But it lacked what in a normal person's perception makes a river a river—it had no opposite bank, and you got the feeling that it wasn't even necessary, that a river could go on living calmly with a single bank, that that was enough for it, that having two banks was for garden-variety rivers as long as this one was wide. This one was so majestic, so divinely wide, that it was a great honor for even one bank, and had it had just a little more unearthly arrogance, then it might have gotten along without any banks at all, not a single one—just water and sky.

Filippov huddled, shifting his distraught glance from the horizon to the snow-scattered island slowly slipping out of his field of vision. Stretching toward him from the smoothed channel was a path drowning in deep snowdrifts. Why it was here and who had trampled it through, Filippov couldn't imagine. For a second he considered what kind of life might go on here in the winter under these conditions, and that horrified him. If a mightiness so unlimited was not only halted but simply immobilized, shackled in many meters of icy armor for virtually half the year—which meant half one's whole life—then the reason for this silent immobility had to be absolutely omnipotent. The river exercised complete sway here over space, but the cold unequivocally held sway over the river.

"Here it is, the other bank." Pavlik joyfully poked at the windshield. "You can see it over there. Look, look. I told you we'd get there fast. You shouldn't have worried."

Filippov leaned forward and saw a dark strip of forest.

"That's another half hour away."

"What do you mean another half hour? The road's about to get better. The winter road's packed down harder from this end."

With a quick jump onto a small hillock, after which the channel stretched along the Lena's native bank, the car dove back into thick fog. Firs on both sides of the road kept floating out of the fog like the masts of sunken ships. The blurry images out the window were powerfully reminiscent of a child's magic lantern show, like the one at the very beginning of Bergman's *Fanny and Alexander*. Pavlik cheered up noticeably and started back in on his rigmarole. Now he was informing Filippov about the weather and the qualities of the local fog, and somehow, imperceptibly, he inched into foggy phenomena in general, including in culture. Filippov missed the moment when he made the leap to theater.

"So you do agree?" Pavlik said heatedly, demanding that Filippov confirm what he, entranced by the matte scenes out the window, hadn't even heard.

"What? Agree with what?"

"That Shakespeare couldn't have written all those brilliant plays."

"Why?"

"What do you mean 'why'? He was a half-educated actor and couldn't even write properly. You do know that he didn't leave a single clearly signed document, right? He signed them with a dot! Can you imagine? He put a dot below, or some scribbling."

"And what of it?"

"What do you mean 'what of it'? We've been misled."

"You don't like his plays?"

"No, I do. But he wasn't the one who wrote them!"

Filippov shrugged. "What's the difference?"

Pavlik actually gasped from indignation and turned his head helplessly, as if he wanted to look Filippov in the eye and understand why he was mocking him like that. "Are you serious?"

"You're like a fledgling in a nest now." Filippov started to laugh. "You know, they're always showing them on the Discovery Channel. All naked and repulsive. Their mama flies in with worms for them, and they turn their little heads just like that. Come on, open your beak."

The rest of the way, Pavlik maintained an injured silence.

———

Getting out of the car at some tall gates, he didn't even answer Filippov about how long he'd be gone and, naturally, didn't leave him the flask.

When situations like this arose—and they had rather frequently in his life—Filippov couldn't help but remember his production based on Chekhov's *Seagull*, in which all the parts had been played by disabled people: A paralyzed Arkadina was wheeled around in a chair, and Nina Zarechnaya had no arms. Filippov had dreamed of finding a Trigorin without a head at all, and that remained just a dream. But Treplev was played by a seventeen-year-old boy with a dyskinetic form of cerebral palsy. The illness had turned the youth into a mumbling and muttering being incapable of coordinating his own movements, but had left him such a handsome and clear mind that Filippov, interrupting the rehearsal, could wait indefinitely for a vivid, paradoxical, and always fresh image to be fashioned from his mumbling.

When this boy once told him that the criterion for determining disability was above all social inadequacy, Filippov immediately was overjoyed, diagnosing himself for all to hear with what he immediately termed *communicative disability*. He declared that he was no longer accepting any accusations of boorishness and greediness, because he, too, had a disability, moreover a tier-one disability, naturally, and you weren't supposed to insult the disabled.

Punished now for something he didn't believe he was guilty of in the slightest, Filippov mourned the flask and didn't repent his behavior one little bit. In fact, he couldn't have cared less about the problem of

Shakespeare's authorship, or debates about whether Anne Hathaway was his wife, or about the fact that the present-day Anne Hathaway had recently gone to a fashionable Hollywood party without underpants, or about the liberal opposition, which, although it did sit on Moscow's boulevards fully clothed, on the other hand defiled it like a true gypsy camp. He was deeply indifferent to everything discussed with such heat and splutter on television and the Internet. Moreover, he was sincerely amazed at others' lack of indifference. For him, in fact, it was a puzzle why, say, a woman's pubis, perfectly nice, no doubt—that much he allowed—could produce such a sensation. After all, everyone upset by the young actress's discomfiture—even if we take it on faith that this discomfiture wasn't intentional—had no doubt had something to do with or at least seen this remarkable detail at least once in their life. Filippov didn't get where the novelty in this was, and he was prepared to agree a thousand times with Macbeth—no matter who dreamed him up, by the way—that life "is a tale told by an idiot, full of sound and fury, signifying nothing."

Sometimes it even seemed to him that this "idiot's tale" had captivated the ordinary person to a significantly greater degree than the circumstances of his or her actual life. Practically everyone Filippov knew liked to talk about what in no way affected them personally. It was as if they'd erected a fortress wall around themselves—a Great Wall of China of inexhaustible nonsense. They'd barricaded themselves in the inner courtyard of their paltry and, as it doubtless seemed to them, insignificant lives. While leaving this clumsy but inevitable self-humiliation on their conscience, Filippov nonetheless pitied those ordinary people.

He absolutely didn't care whether Shakespeare did or didn't write his plays. But the fact that he himself was now sitting in a car in the middle of the forest, gazing out at this fog and this cold—for some reason, that was important. Filippov still didn't understand that reason, but in the fog he was already picking up on if not its outlines then at least its scale.

When Pavlik's figure materialized out of nothing, directly in front of the car, Filippov shuddered. Unaccustomed to the local tricks with distance, he wasn't prepared for objects popping up out of the fog at no more than a few meters away. None of the usual methods for orienting yourself in space worked here in winter. Sounds, too, drowned helplessly in this gray cotton wool. It was much easier to determine who was around you—or who was getting close to you—by using your imagination than by trying to actually see anything.

"Come with me." Pavlik exhaled a furious cloud of steam as he opened the back door. "I can't manage myself."

"Where are we going? Have you lost your mind or something?"

Filippov clutched his coat collar to protect himself at least a little from the wave of burning cold that struck him.

"You're the one in a hurry. Let's go. I'll give you my cap." Pavlik pulled off the shaggy construction with one hand while pulling on his hood with the other. "Be quick about it. You're the one holding us up."

All the nasty presentiments that had gripped Filippov as they drove away from the airport rushed back like a nest of riled snakes. Pavlik's shaggy cap didn't help one bit.

Jumping out of the car, he tromped hurriedly over the thin but firm crust of his sneaker soles, which stiffened instantly in the cold, but he couldn't catch up to Pavlik, who was waiting for him beside a big house whose unfinished porch gaped like the wide-open abdominal incision of an unfortunate patient on an operating table.

"Follow me." Pavlik waved to him. "This way, this way."

He disappeared around the corner of the building, and Filippov beat a path after him feeling doomed. His hands, which he'd hidden from the cold in his pathetic pockets, were being pressed down by a cast-iron vise, his feet slid apart, and his breath seized up so harshly it didn't remind him of air at all. Filippov got the definite sensation that he was breathing sparkly diamond needles that were poking into his warm, soft, defenseless lungs. Squeaking like a trapped hare at these strange attempts at breathing, and tripping a few times over construction materials frozen into the path, he wended his way to a huge metal container filled nearly to the top with construction detritus. Pavlik was pulling the container by the edge hard, trying to move it for some reason. "Help me!"

Before Filippov could even contemplate what this was fraught with, he latched his frost-twisted claws onto the metal edge. In the next split second he was pierced by a blow that those condemned to the electric chair never have time to tell anyone about. Like Buddha under the Bodhi tree, he saw the truth and at last gained a full picture of the essence of human suffering.

"Why don't you have gloves?" Pavlik shouted in his ear. "Try the other side! Push from there. Push with your shoulder!"

Filippov got unstuck from the container and hobbled over to where he'd been ordered. Leaning into the metal surface, he obediently began pushing the gigantic garbage bin, but his sneakers kept slipping ridiculously, and he slid to the concrete-hard snow. Since his hands were back in his pockets, he fell awkwardly, hitting his head with a booming thump. The shaggy cap came in pretty handy for the blow.

"Come on," Pavlik shouted from somewhere behind the steely sky. "On my count. One! One!"

Filippov's shoulder felt the container shuddering from Pavlik's vain efforts and barely refrained from maniacal laughter. Sprawled out on the frozen earth beside the metal giant and having absolutely no idea what it needed to be pushed anywhere for, he pictured the scene as a bystander would, and realized he'd never seen anything funnier in his life. Without removing his hands from his pockets, he tried to get back on his feet, but he fell again, banging himself this time, too, and started laughing now in full voice.

"What's with you?" Pavlik said, appearing from behind the container and squatting beside him. "Why are you lying there?"

"I . . . I . . ." Filippov was choking with laughter. "I'm tired. I stretched out for a nap."

"You shouldn't lie down. Get up right now."

"Shouldn't you go fuck yourself? Why'd you drag me here, anyway?"

"Get up, I'm telling you!" Pavlik pulled on Filippov's coat as hard as he could, and Filippov finally got back on his feet.

"I have to get into the building," Pavlik went on. "See the little balcony on the third floor? I have to move the container under it, and I'll crawl up there."

Filippov leaned his head back and looked at the unfinished, railing-less balcony.

"Not through the door?"

"It's locked."

"That means no one's home. We've dragged ourselves here for nothing."

"I have to make sure. They wouldn't have left. I brought them the money."

"You'll come again."

"I have to make sure no one's here. They'll ask me."

Filippov turned his head and noticed some big boxes heaped up by the fence.

"Maybe those over there will work." He jerked his head. "We can put one on top of another, and you can climb up."

A couple of minutes later, Pavlik had disappeared behind the balcony door and Filippov had wandered around the building toward the porch. He went up the steps and kicked the door. The lock clicked, and the door opened.

"Come on in," Pavlik said, letting him in. "It's a lot warmer here. I'll look on the third floor, too. I haven't checked all the rooms there."

"You think they're hiding from you?"

"No, but they may just be sleeping it off. Construction workers. You know how that goes."

When they got back to the car, Filippov demanded the flask from Pavlik and didn't take it from his burning lips until "beads of happiness" welled up in his eyes. That's what he called the tears that came on after strong drink, when alcohol was drunk not by the shot, in one go, but poured into the system in a nice steady stream—like fuel going into the tank at a gas station.

"I don't understand," Pavlik muttered, fussing with his phone. "No one's home. Now there's no one else I can call. What is this? Danilov told me for sure he'd be waiting."

"Listen, let's go." Filippov finally tore himself away from the flask. "Or else I'll drink and drink—and I'm not eating anything. That's bad for you. I need some kind of chow, otherwise it's trouble."

As they drove back out onto the ice, a distraught Pavlik lost control of the steering and the car nearly hit a huge block of snow pressed like concrete.

"Hey," Filippov shouted, grabbing the handle over the door. "Let's be a little more careful, my man. You might accidentally kill me."

Looking at the vast white field, he once again felt as if he were on a plane cutting through and hovering motionlessly above a solid shroud of clouds. He didn't think he was claustrophobic, but occasionally in those moments he got a heavy feeling not unlike what he'd felt at the first funeral he'd attended. It happened exactly a year before his Nina died. Standing by the coffin of his classmate, who had drowned in this same river, Filippov couldn't find the strength to look through the window in the lid at face level. The body had spent nearly a week under the water, so it was buried in a soldered metal box, the kind they were bringing home dead boys in from Afghanistan. His classmate's name was Slavka, and he himself had only just returned from the army, having steadfastly withstood adversities he didn't even want to tell anyone about. Slavka died trying to save children caught in a strong current.

The huge metal coffin had been brought for him from the enlistment office, where Slavka's father was the top official. Filippov had loved Slavka for his directness, for his powerful and utterly invincible naïveté, for his belief in the good, and that was why, even though in those days Filippov was already sure of the meaninglessness of life, he still couldn't look through the window's thick glass.

"Look, over there, next to the island—it's a car." Zinaida pointed vaguely forward.

Filippov leaned over and saw a cherry-red Zhiguli with tinted windows. For some reason the car was stopped not on the smooth channel but slightly to the side of the winter road, as if the driver had been on his way to the island but got stuck in impassable snow.

"I wonder what took him that way?" Filippov said.

"Maybe something happened?" Zinaida suggested.

"Vodka happened," Pavlik muttered. "They booze up and race around in their jalopies. Here's where they ran off the road."

He pointed to the side of the road where a fairly tall snow parapet had been smashed through by the Zhiguli flying off.

"By the way, are you aware that among the native population their system lacks the enzyme responsible for digesting alcohol?" Pavlik went on while Filippov kept his head turned, not taking his eyes off the orphaned car floating by out the window. "That's why they get drunk so fast, you see. The Cossacks who came here in the seventeenth century quickly realized all this, and an epidemic began of getting the locals drunk."

"Stop," Filippov yelled, pulling on Pavlik's hood so hard that for a second he even let go of the wheel. "Brake!"

Someone was running out from the snowbound Zhiguli, toward them, lifting his knees high. He was holding a tire iron. Waving the iron, he was shouting something, but they couldn't make out what he was saying.

Surprised, Pavlik, who had managed to stop the car, immediately put it in gear and leaned on the gas.

"Stop! Where are you going?" Filippov dug his fingers into Pavlik's jacket, but this time Pavlik deftly freed himself by jerking forward, bent over. "Have you lost your mind? What if they need help?"

"What if it's not help they want? What if they drove that way so we'd go out onto the ice? I can't stop. I've got a lot of money on me, and anything can happen around here. It's better you not know."

"Have you been watching too many Westerns or something?"

"People drive this way all the time. They'll help him."

Filippov turned around and for a long time looked at the man, who had finally climbed out onto the road, hurled his iron after them, and was shouting and shouting something and just wouldn't stop.

———

Twenty minutes later they drove back past the airport and hopped onto the road to town. By way of compensation for the long detour and less than delightful experiences, Filippov demanded Pavlik's flask, which sent his mood on the upswing. Actually, after the fifth or even sixth foray at the other man's Hennessy, he unexpectedly soured on it. Leaning back in his seat while deftly maintaining the look of an animated being, he rode totally prostrate past the port's five-story apartment buildings, past the port school, and past the port's House of Culture. It was here, shortly before her death, that his young—like him, barely more than school-age—wife liked to shake a leg. Filippov, who was then in his third year at the teachers college, made several attempts to horn in on her convoy, but he never did gain admission. Nina went to this House of Culture for folk dancing by herself. Red slippers, pinned blond braids, and sarafans whirled around there, but not for him.

Who they did whirl for Filippov didn't learn right away.

The guys who lived by the port had historically been considered much cooler than everyone else. Their precious Montanas and Wranglers fit as if they'd been poured into them, because they'd been bought not in public restrooms and underground passages during fitful forays to Moscow but in actual brand-name stores in the Baltics and Warsaw Pact countries, where their otherworldly fathers had flown as crew commanders, copilots, navigators, and flight engineers. In the early 1980s, Toto Cutugno started singing for these ineffably otherworldly fellows way before the townies. After high school they didn't go to the local literacy project, which for some unknown reason was called the "teachers college," but flew off in big handsome planes to the Riga Institute for Civil Aviation Engineers, from which very, very few returned to the North, and those who did basked in the rays of feminine adoration, dropping words they'd picked up in Latvia, like "paldies," "Jūrmala," "Dzintari," "beating the crap out of Balts," and so on down the list. Compared to the insipid local boys, they looked like Humphrey Bogart in *Casablanca*, even if you took into account the fact that not a single local girl had ever heard of that film.

Apart from the obvious Aeroflot eroticism, which rested not least of all on the elegant flight uniform—raglan leather jackets, gold chevrons, stripes, wings, and the other attributes of these modern and traditionally mischievous cupids—the flyboys occupied a special status in town strictly by virtue of geography. The only way to get from here to the mainland hassle-free was by air. Due to the permafrost, which was constantly afloat in summer, the railroad remained science fiction. Highway transportation was made extremely difficult by the abominable roads and the total distance between places. Naturally, heavy barges came and went when navigation opened, delivering to the city vital cargo, but who wants to feed the mosquitoes on a great Siberian river for weeks the way they did in the nineteenth century? In the cold, you could leave town by car over the winter road that any body of water turned into as early as autumn, but the epic distances and colossal risks easily killed any desire for follies like that. Even children knew that when it's fifty degrees below in the taiga and the engine dies, you first have to set the spare and then the other tires on fire. While all this business is burning, someone might drive by. The warmth lasts about an hour and a half. If no one's come by then, that means you're SOL. Especially since you don't have wheels anymore.

So people loved their flyboys here. An awful lot really did depend on them. They garnered salaries inferior only perhaps to heating engineers. The people who worked at the heating plants had no competition.

Considering all these circumstances, you had to admit that young, nervous Filippov, eaten up like cheese into one big hole by endless self-doubt, had zero chance against flight engineer Venechka. Where that guy had popped out of remained a mystery for a while, but soon after, well-wishers whispered that dance-rich Nina had met him at the Falcon, the cult—not that people said that then—Young Pioneer camp. This early erotic educational institution, which lived for the intense but brief Northern summer, accepted boys from port families and girls wishing to part with their innocence. The more innocent pubescents stamped dejectedly around the Pioneer campfire as "Signalers," "Beacons," and "Geologists," while the proud scions of Aeroflot's falcons got themselves such a hullabaloo going at camp that come fall the teachers' councils in the city's schools weren't just counting their chickens. Moreover, for afternoon snack at Falcon they were given enormous bunches of grapes. The main fruit in the North in those days was the potato, but for their pampered children the flyboys could simply arrange a vitamin flight from Fergana.

Nina got into Falcon without any pull whatsoever. Having among her relatives not even one worthless aviator, she suggested to the camp director creating a colorful and original—as people put it at the time—dance collective, and the director made it happen. So that summer Nina had herself some fun, big-time. She had only a year until her graduation exams, and she had to prepare properly for that unbearably boring period of her life. After that, she knew, there would be no time for trifles like sex. Studying is a schoolkid's main job.

But Venechka the falcon circled over the young'uns every summer. Or rather, preyed, as some of Filippov's friends later described their attendance at receptions in European embassies. The main objective during these receptions was to grab as much as you could. Not so much to eat as to taste, sample, stick your finger in everything. And so it was that Venechka, instead of a summer vacation, when all the other aviators and their entire families climbed on board and winged their way south somewhere, cut his circles around the weakened little fools, easily getting everything he wanted from them. De jure, he was listed as a phys ed instructor at the camp; de facto, he worked like a tomcat for his cream. By light of day, he handed out shabby ping-pong paddles to the unnecessary and uninteresting lads; by night, he prowled under the windows of the camp counselors and purred about something eternal in his cozy phys ed cubby.

In this sense, men fall into two main camps—canine and tomcat. The behavior of sexually mature cats with an eye to life differs strikingly from the rules of the chase in the dog world. While mutts band together to politely follow the lady of their heart and patiently await signs of sympathy on her part, tomcats couldn't care less about their beloved's feelings. They wear down the herd, chase a very frightened young female up a tree or into some dark corner, and after that, do their damnedest to get in her good graces. Flight engineer Venechka undoubtedly fell into the feline camp.

It was way too late when Filippov—or rather, at the time, just plain Filya—learned about his young wife's past exploits. Naturally, Nina hadn't planned on continuing these summer "visits," but after graduating and getting married, she suddenly felt like a grown-up, and the behavior she had previously justified by her lack of experience, virginal languor, and general eagerness to live now found justification in her eyes as an indispensable attribute of a married lady's life. Anyway, that's how they talked about it in the French films Filya—whose aestheticism and arrogance could be so tedious—was always watching. With the French, women were constantly cheating on their husbands, and they didn't suffer from it one bit; in the end they could just take a gun and knock off a tiresome lover, or husband. Whichever. Those kinds of twists and turns intrigued Nina, but even under the influence of all those films she wouldn't have sought out Venechka herself. Venechka fell on her like snow on her head in the wings of the municipal Pioneer Palace, where for old times' sake Nina was still performing with the children at the New Year's parties. He squeezed her damp hand and immediately suggested they put on a dance together at the port House of Culture. It soon became clear he was no more interested in choreography than he had been in phys ed.

And they were off.

Very soon after, Filya started being pestered by strange phone calls. If he picked up, no one said anything. Whoever was at the other end of the line was silent in anticipation of him getting sick of repeating his stupid and helpless "hello." After a minute or two, Nina would always call a girlfriend, or her mother, or someone else, and agree to meet, but Filya wasn't in the least suspicious. He was so wrapped up in himself, his future, and his assured destiny that he thought these calls were a coincidence that for some reason were getting more frequent but were no less silly.

One time an unknown male voice set up a meeting with him, promising him significantly to impart something important, but Filya didn't attach any great importance to it. Or rather, he did, but in a completely different sense. In those early and fairly awkward years, he was deeply convinced that everything that happened to him was related only to his future greatness, and if someone mysterious wanted to talk to him, then that very mysteriousness was directly related to nothing other than his, Filya's, chosenness. The voice warned him to show up alone; Filya would recognize him because he'd be holding an English-language *Rolling Stone*.

Enchanted by this run-up, Filya hurried to the meeting like a quivering deer, but after loitering around the North Cinema for nearly an hour and a half, he'd only frozen his cheeks and nose. He never did see the magazine with the seductive title or the possessor of the telephone voice.

The next day, the white spots on his face had turned into crimson bruises, his nose was outrageously swollen, and dear Nina laughed for a long time, looking into the mirror over his shoulder while he attempted to shave.

He learned the truth about her monkey business from her best friend. The good girl gave him not only the addresses, password, and secret signals but was delighted to initiate him into everything that used to go on at Falcon. Wounded, Filippov thirsted for details and naturally wasted no time obtaining them. Preparing to tear Venechka to pieces, he seared himself for an entire week with images of other people's love. Flaring his nostrils, sniffing the smell of his own singed flesh, he dreamed up pictures more and more horrible, dreamed of dying, dreamed of killing, and tore himself up because he didn't understand his own situation.

As obvious as it was, his wife's betrayal seemed unreal. He himself felt unreal, and he tortured himself like a character forgotten by his own remiss author. Up until that moment, the text of his life had been written out more or less distinctly, and he'd been moving through his role, acting out the mise-en-scènes, emotions, curtain calls, bows, and exits expected of him. But now, after what dear Nina had done to him, the play had come to a screeching halt and he'd frozen downstage in the blinding footlights. What was expected of him now, Filya didn't understand. Any movement—this he felt—would be inauthentic.

Actually, something was already starting to glimmer before him. The broken threads by which an unknown puppeteer had led him for so long across the stage still dangled helplessly from his unscrewed arms and legs, and listening feverishly to Tom Waits, clutching at his songs like a strap in a shaking bus, he was already beginning little by little to dream of something strange, something unusual, something his own and fresh. Many years later, when for some reason he suddenly remembered that distressing ordeal, what came to mind immediately was Tom's song "Make It Rain," a heartrending complaint about his perfidious girlfriend saying he'd lost any pride he'd ever had and demanding someone send down immediate and cleansing rain. It was the raspy cuckold Tom's idea that a downpour would put out the fire of inhuman pain in his raspy chest torn up by his cuckold status. Tom Waits insisted that he was Cain now, not Abel, demanding that the skies open up and rain come crashing down immediately. So, too, Filya now dreamed of a downpour that would wash away into some dirty sewer his sweet, unfaithful Nina, and his memory of her, and, most of all, his own incomprehensible shame for something that was in no way his fault.

"Hi," Filya had said to flight engineer Venechka when he opened the door of his port apartment. "I'll be quick. You and I are going to have a duel. Prepare yourself."

In recognition of the moment's solemnity, they bought six bottles of vodka at the supermarket. It was impossible for two people to drink up that much, although the situation did demand extreme gestures. They decided not to get any snacks—the single combat had to be held in its pure form.

After the second bottle, when no victor was declared, they decided to test themselves on a dare. They went outside and wandered as far as the police department, where they lay down in front of the door on the shoveled asphalt—directly on the stinky gasoline spots from the police cars. Filya lay down first. Venechka was behind him by just a second, because he was thinking he was inevitably going to get fired from flying.

"Well, embarrassed?" Filya asked him from below.

"Who? Me? Watch your mouth."

A minute later both were sitting in lockup. That's what they'd been counting on, actually, because given the February weather, lying on the ground any longer would have been problematic. Although the vodka was warming, naturally.

"I was still first," Filya insisted. "And you lost, you punk."

"You'll answer for that 'punk.'"

To the captain on duty, Filya reported in his convoluted way that this was an act of grief.

"Yeah? And just what are we grieving?"

"A loss . . . A difficult, irrev . . . irretrievable loss."

"What did you lose?"

"Our peace of mind."

"Well, I can guarantee you a couple of weeks of peace of mind."

"That's no use, c'mrade captain. We're grieving for our dead brothers."

"I don't understand."

"A few days ago, in a terrrrrrible disaster, seven Amerig . . . American astronauts perished. They were like brothers to us, c'mrade captain . . . This is a terrible loss. It's breaking our hearts. Think about it. For whom the bell tolls . . . It tolls for you . . . I mean, not you . . . I mean, me . . . I'm a little mixed up . . ."

After drinking some tea and talking something over with his colleagues, the captain ultimately let them go. Especially since he knew Venechka's father. Basically, in the port, everybody knew everybody else.

Back at the dissolute flight engineer's place, they opened the third bottle. The walk through the cold, their loss and retrieval of freedom, and their conversation about the *Challenger*'s recent explosion, as well as the alarm that arose as a result for the fate of humanity, aroused in them new strength, so it was decided to continue their battle. Their idyll was nearly spoiled by Venechka's mother, who came home that night from work and categorically refused to see either her son or his young friend drunk. They agreed they'd take a basin from the bathroom into

Venechka's room, lock themselves in, and not bother his mama, in case they felt like peeing or throwing up.

Which they did, fairly soon after. Both at once. Venechka started feeling very sick, and down on all fours, he sadly hung his turbulent head over his mama's basin. At exactly that moment, Filya felt an urge to relieve himself. Standing directly opposite the modestly vomiting flight engineer, he let loose a merry and ringing stream into the basin. Filya was absolutely sure of himself, therefore he had counted on easily hitting the huge, slightly rocking enameled circle, but he didn't take Venechka's condition into account or his head's lateral range of motion. When the stream struck the bottom of the basin hard, Venechka, who hadn't expected this turn of events, was startled by the other's splashes and shrank to the side. Everything might have worked out, but, unfortunately, he was a flight engineer, not a navigator, and after two and a half bottles of vodka in two hungry faces, he'd chosen the wrong direction for the outflow. Landing right under Filya's powerful, life-filled stream, for some reason he froze humbly, the curly hair at the back of his neck shining as handsomely as under that real summer rain Tom Waits wanted so much in his song. Filya, enchanted by this picture, couldn't make himself stop but kept going. On and on and on.

———

Twenty-two years later, finding himself by the will of his drunken fate in virtually the same spot, Filippov woke up in the backseat of a stranger's car. His implacably impending sobriety had given him a terrible headache. His throat was so dry it felt as if they'd put an emery board down it and generously sprinkled it with what shakes out of old fiberglass. His hangover hadn't gone anywhere. It was lying low, pretending to have been frightened by the cognac out of the stranger's flask but making it blatantly obvious that the fright was feigned. On the other hand, Filippov now knew where childhood goes.

"Up yours," he muttered, and he gripped the flask, which was slippery from his sudden sweat, and rested his now-intelligent gaze on the back of Zinaida's nervous neck.

At that moment, Pavlik's Land Cruiser gave such a powerful jolt that Filippov took a hop in his seat and Zinaida grabbed the overhead handle.

"Could we notch this down?" she said.

After shouting at her husband, she turned to Filippov. "What did you say?"

"Good cognac. It brings back . . . pleasant memories. Have some?"

He offered her the flask, but she pushed it away abruptly.

"No, thanks."

"Don't be afraid. I'm not contagious. I just look it."

"Did you know, by the way," Pavlik interjected, "that Richard Hennessy, who founded the cognac house in France, served in the Irish battalion of King Louis XV and wasn't even French?"

"Maybe that's enough of your Wikipedia," Zinaida said, cutting him off before finally saying what had obviously been eating at her the whole way and what she had until now had the strength to keep quiet. "You have to tell me. Has she moved for good? Did she take a lot of stuff with her?"

Talking about the history of French cognac was obviously more fun for Pavlik, but his familial duty in the form of his tired and angry wife demanded a discussion of more vital matters.

"You know . . . You should talk to Tyoma yourself. He's all grown up. At least he makes his decisions for himself. Naturally, I realize it's not easy for him right now. Ending up here at his age . . . After Moscow . . . Basically, he doesn't talk to me."

"Who does he talk to?"

"His girlfriend. Theoretically, she's very sweet. Only I almost never see them. They stay in his room all the time. They practically never come out."

"How is that okay?" Zinaida threw up her hands in impotent hatred. "A strange girl has moved into my apartment, and you call her 'theoretically, very sweet'!"

"Zina . . ." With his insinuating tone of voice, Pavlik was obviously apologizing to Filippov. "Tyoma did ask us to leave him in Moscow. His behavior here is a young man's protest."

"I should say so! And if he'd asked you for poison, would you have come running, too? 'Here, son, the very best cyanide.' Listen, I'm sick of being used! I wasn't the one who forced us all to move here, by the way. And without me, he'd have nowhere to live. Not here, not in Moscow, not in the middle of nowhere. I said I'm sick of it. If we have to come back to the North, then the whole family comes."

"Hallelujah," Filippov said.

Pavlik glanced at his flask, which Filippov was still holding.

"Are you going to drink some more or should I take back the cognac?"

Filippov took a big gulp to stock up and twisted the cap back on.

"What's her name?" Zinaida said, spacing her words, having a hard time restraining herself.

"Listen." Her husband chose his words cautiously, putting the flask back in the pocket of his down parka. "Let's talk about all this at home. All kinds of things could have changed now with us gone."

Filippov, who was grateful for the Hennessy, decided to help him out. "Pavlik, tell me, please . . . On the runway at the port, I saw three big planes at once. And all three were being loaded simultaneously. What's that about? Has the schedule here changed that much? It used to be there was just one flight to the mainland, I thought."

"Well, here's the thing." Pavlik livened up noticeably. "The cold forced fog to drop down. They probably postponed the flights, so they backed up. And now, as soon as a window opened, for good measure, they . . . You were really lucky you skipped through. For the past couple of days all the flights from Moscow have been diverted to Magadan."

"Yeah? And what's there?"

"Nothing. It's just bad fog here."

Filippov nodded and fell silent, staring out at the gray half-gloom. His hometown, which he still hadn't had a good look at, was behaving like his hungover body—aloof and doing everything in its power to emphasize that it was a separate entity and didn't bear the slightest relation to him. He hadn't been able to establish trusting relations with his body or his hometown. The Hennessy had just created a more or less comfortable illusion of contact for a very brief time.

Like the befuddled Alice in her whimsical Wonderland, Filippov took a close and wary look at what should have been comprehensible and close to him but the place aroused nothing in him other than confusion, alienation, and total incomprehension. On top of that, it felt odd that Lewis Carroll's frail and scarcely hard-drinking heroine had experienced feelings identical to his. You'd think at her age a fantastic country would have been the dearest thing. Games, little animals, swimming in a pool of tears. Certainly no worse than a hyperfrozen Arctic homeland for a fashionable director coming off a serious bender. At the same time, Filippov couldn't help but admit a definite similarity to Alice. He, too, from time to time, was confronted with bottles on which even the unaided eye could read "Drink Me."

Neither the hills on the horizon nor the enormous, plaintive emptiness through which the highway ran toward the city could be seen, due to fog. His memory quickly filled in all of that, and Filippov frowned squeamishly. Stunted bushes pretending to be trees grew only in the city, while here, along the airport road, there was no vegetation whatsoever. In the summer the oppressive heat made for only dusty, pale grass.

"On the other hand, they aren't blowing up anything here," Filippov said, continuing his reflections out loud.

"What aren't they blowing up?" Pavlik readily aimed toward him his well-disposed ear, hidden somewhere in his head of hair.

"The Metro. In Moscow, nearly every year. Once they hit two stations at once. Forty people blown to pieces."

"Oh, that. Yeah, yeah, horrible. No, as far as that goes, it's more peaceful here, of course."

"More peaceful?" Filippov asked, and he thought for a moment. "But what if the local power station—or whatever you call it, that makes the heat—what if it suddenly shut down? What do you think—would the town die fast in that kind of cold?"

These words actually made Pavlik shudder.

"Bite your tongue. Where'd you come up with an idea like that?"

"No, just theoretically."

"I don't want to talk about things like that, even theoretically."

"You could at least guess how many hours before the radiators in people's buildings started bursting, couldn't you? How would people behave? And what would happen after? Would panic break out right away or only later?"

Pavlik started turning his head anxiously.

"Why do you want to know? Why bring it up at all?"

"I need it for my work."

"Your work?"

Pavlik furrowed his thick brows warily. Filippov leaned forward and gave him a friendly slap on the shoulder.

"Yeah, for a show. I want to get a sense of the image of a dying city."

"And what show is this, if it's not a secret?"

"Albert Camus's *Plague*."

"*The Plague*? But I thought all that takes place in Algiers, doesn't it?" Once again Pavlik couldn't let slip an opportunity for his erudition to shine. "In Africa, if memory serves, radiators don't burst from the cold. Even in the North."

"Who cares? It's important for me to understand how the city would react. After all, it senses its own demise. It sees certain symptoms.

The rats crawl out of the cellars. And the inhabitants think it's just a bad omen. There's going to be a famine, or something like that."

"Our buildings don't have cellars."

"I know."

"They're on piles."

"Yeah, I know. What a thing to harp on! I have to have a sense of the mechanism of disaster. How it starts ticking. Understand? 'Tick tock, tick tock, the end to all is near.'"

"Creepy."

"Correct. From the very first moments, the viewer should be shitting his pants."

Zinaida, who'd been listening to their conversation with interest, frowned at Filippov's choice of words. But Pavlik played along. He was flattered to have someone off a magazine cover coming to him for professional advice.

"Well, in weather like that, the radiators in apartment houses would burst the next day. You could probably burn furniture for another twenty-four hours."

"And after that?

"After that, I don't know. After that—kaput."

"Forget about the end. I'm not interested in the end right now. What's important is how it starts. Plus the scale of the tragedy. How many people live here now?"

"About two hundred thousand."

"Pretty decent. You can't evacuate a horde like that on planes. And by the time spring comes, the city would have frozen solid. How would they survive here?"

"They wouldn't."

"Fuckin'—"

"Pavlik!" Zinaida shouted piercingly.

Directly in front of them, a Land Cruiser almost exactly like theirs flew out of the fog like a fast-moving black lump. The other SUV was heading straight toward them at top speed in the oncoming lane. A silver BMW was on its tail. At the last moment, Pavlik managed to avoid a crash by throwing the car to the right, and both oncoming cars flew past, missing them by just centimeters. Filippov was hurled roughly into the door, Zinaida kept shouting something, and the car thrashed down the shoulder's washboard of frozen ruts and potholes. When the Land Cruiser finally came to a stop, Filippov let go of the door handle and touched his banged-up head, leaving blood on his fingers.

"Great drivers you've got here," he muttered. "World art nearly suffered a grave, irrevocable loss. Fuckin' A."

———

Next to the hotel Zinaida had brought him to, several guest workers were spread out, squatting. Despite the serious cold, they were doing some kind of work by the heating main. Cigarette smoke and an undertone of a foreign language coiled over them like steam over an ice-free reservoir. The filthy quilted jackets over the worksuits, the black work caps with the white strings at the crown, the dark faces, the very pose of a small, wary beast pressing close to the ground—all of this instantly brought to Filippov's mind an image of the hundreds and thousands of other people hunkering down all over the country, people wearing more or less the same clothing and with more or less the same faces who inexplicably chose exactly this pose when they needed to rest.

Maybe, Filippov reasoned foggily, *in a past life they were all short creatures: sheep, dogs, hedgehogs—something along those lines—so now they feel awkward at human height. Maybe they get dizzy?*

"The best hotel in town," Zinaida said, parking on the square next to the covey of hunkering repairmen. "Although you probably remember everything by now. Do you recognize your hometown?"

Filippov nodded cautiously. "When I was here, people called this square the Five Kopek."

"They still do. Let's go—I'll help you get settled."

"Do I need help?"

The reception desk was located on the third floor, for some reason. The girl at the desk was a local. No longer accustomed to Yakut faces, Filippov stared straight at her with interest, like a total boor. Long ago, back in the Soviet friendship-among-peoples days, when here, in the Far North, outsiders who had flown in for the financial perks predominated numerically, locals didn't work in hotels. You didn't see them as sales-clerks, construction workers, utility workers, or policemen—as if the usual city professions didn't suit them. Retaining their natural purity, they hunted, raised deer, carved ivory, toured with dance troupes, per-formed as throat singers, and did scholarly research to prove they were mankind's ancestors. They held high positions in the party and the very highest in the Young Communists, played the Jew's harp, and smoked Belomor cigarettes. Filippov recalled from his early childhood the typi-cal very old and tiny Yakut granny with the inevitable cigarette in her mouth. There was no large family, as they got ready to go out of town in the summer to celebrate Ysyakh, their pagan New Year, who failed to bring along a granny like that, and she would sit in the place of honor in the family circle, squint her narrow, knowing eyes at the bucket of kumys, smoke her Belomors, and smile enigmatically.

"What, are you mocking us?" Zinaida was pressuring the girl at the desk. "What does that mean, someone has taken the deluxe room? Get him out! Do you understand who has come to pay our city a visit? You mean you have world-class stars staying with you every day?"

The young woman shifted her infinitely indifferent gaze to the "world-class star," and Filippov got the feeling that for exactly a sec-ond the entire millennial tundra, with its deer, nomad camps, lichen, midges, lost geologists, and hard frosts, was looking at him through her narrow eyes. Judging by her reaction, Filippov had not conquered the tundra. His singed beard, busted forehead, and eyes watery from prolonged drinking were obviously insufficient argument. They'd seen "stars" like him in this hotel before.

Bored, Filippov turned away from the reception desk, which was covered in cheap plastic. The opposite wall sported washed-out, slightly askew photo wallpaper. The birch grove with the withered tree in the corner personified Northerners' vain aspirations for a real forest and the kind of "Euro renovation" fashionable fifteen years ago.

"Where are they pouring here?" he asked tundra girl, interrupting Zinaida's passionate monologue. "Does the hotel have a bar?"

"A baar? Yes." The young woman nodded and pointed to the stairs. "Over there, rownstairs."

Hearing the half-forgotten but unexpectedly dear-to-his-heart assonances, Filippov immediately remembered that around here "baar" meant "there is," and consonants were always approximated in the direction of the local phonetics.

"Taank kyou," he politely said, and with unsteady step headed for the stairs leading to the second floor.

At the teachers college, which he never did finish due to his wife's death, a few of the instructors liked to revamp Russian pronunciation in their own fashion, too. Or rather, not so much liked to as couldn't pronounce any other way. For them, "phys ed" was "piss ed," the "files" in the dean's office became mildly entertaining "piles," the variable x was the rather perplexing "ekhas," and in the most natural way, "folio" became a disease. Certain misunderstandings did arise, but given a degree of ingenuity, they were all resolved by harmless student guffaws.

"Hey there, *tabaris*," Filippov greeted the slender, narrow-eyed young man behind the register as he entered the room tundra girl on the third floor had called a bar.

A few flimsy light-colored tables, obviously from some school cafeteria gone bust, plus heavy, pompous chairs, with twisting, polished backs and red velvet seats that didn't match at all, constituted the room's bizarre furnishings. To match the chairs, hanging on the windows were unwieldy theatrical curtains snatched at the waist by wide, dusty sashes with enormous buttons. There was no one at the tables. However, each did sport a salt cellar filled to the brim.

Just the way we like it, Filippov thought.

The young man at the register, huddled with the chill, tore himself away from his accounts, hiding his slender dark fingers in his armpits, and shifted his indifferent gaze to his one and only customer, who repeated "Hey, *tabaris,*" as he approached the bar.

"Hello," the bartender answered in perfect Russian. "Only you're pronouncing it wrong. And *tovarishch* went out of fashion a long time ago."

"Are you a linguist or something?"

The slender young man nodded.

"I'm in my second year."

"At the teachers?"

"No. A while ago they opened a branch of Tomsk University here."

"Cool. So tell me, as one linguist to another, what've you got to get me off?"

The boy swiveled his head, turning to the row of poison-colored bottles behind him, as if he didn't know what he had there. The sight of this battery of bottles evoked in Filippov an advance but quite real onset of nausea.

"Only don't offer me any of that. No offense, but I don't drink anything colored."

"Maybe a little something white then?"

"Vodka?" Filippov fired back.

He was always touched and slightly amused by Frenchmen who spent scads of time in restaurants first seating people at the table, then ordering salads, and when the time came to choose the cheeses became so thoughtful and deep that Filippov's sense of irony got the better of him. He was constantly kidding his Paris friends and assuring them that the idea for Auguste Rodin's monumental *Thinker* must have come to him in a restaurant. A Frenchman contemplating a menu simply demanded being captured in bronze.

Like a Russian pondering whether it's time for him to tie one on again.

Actually, there was another reason for Filya's pensiveness, too. He was trying to guess how this was going to go. Experience suggested that his plan was fraught with immediate consequences and he might just as well vomit right now, but his elegant and essentially mathematical calculation led him to a net positive.

"Standard, Parliament, or Bulus?"

"What's Bulus?"

"The local vodka made with glacial water. The glacier's more than a thousand years old. It's very close to here. In Kachikatsy."

"Let's have the Kachikatsy," Filippov said. "The Scots can stuff it. What generation of what plaid clan uses water that's a thousand years old in their whiskey?"

As soon as the philosophical question was decided, it was time for boring prose.

"What do you want with it?"

Suddenly sad, Filippov stared at the sandwich corpses wrapped in plastic and displayed—obviously for the parting ceremony—right on the bar.

"Fish, maybe?" the linguist suggested, pointing to the wrinkled pink flesh under cellophane.

"Did you catch it last century?"

"No. They brought it yesterday. It's cold outside—what could happen to it?"

"Yeah." Filippov sighed. "It's not just cold *outside* here, by the way." He rounded his lips and breathed out a little of his very own, almost immanently reeking breath—which obediently condensed into a little white cloud. "See that? What's that supposed to mean? Skimping on the heat?"

"I don't know." The linguist shrugged subtly. "Basically, the cold came early. And as usual, the utility workers weren't ready in the fall. Temporary heat outages. We've had a team of repairmen working there, by the front door, for two days."

"I saw how busy they were." Filippov snickered. "With workers like that, we'll freeze to death like bedbugs tonight."

"The rooms are getting full heat. It's only chilly on the second floor."

"You call this chilly? It's okay that I'm sitting here in my coat?"

"Feel free. I don't care. Maybe a sausage sandwich then, if you don't want fish?"

Filippov didn't answer right away, rubbing his now-cold bald spot.

"Do you have rat-tail sausage?"

"Why rat-tail?"

"Have you ever been in a sausage factory?"

"No."

"If you had, you wouldn't ask. They switch off the meat grinder for the night."

He raised his eyebrows significantly, but the bartender wasn't catching on. Filippov had to raise his eyebrows again. The bartender still didn't get it.

"So?"

"Don't be dense. Imagine a giant meat grinder. As big as a train car . . . or this bar of yours. Although this isn't a bar, of course. Call it whatever, just not a bar. A waiting room in a village bus station. I'll tell you what real bars are like afterward. Once on the Ramblas in Barcelona, I got seriously hammered in one establishment . . . Fine, that doesn't matter right now. So, you've got your meat grinder. Grind away, grind away. Cows and hogs . . . Meat and bloodiness all day long. Twisted guts. Just like it's supposed to be. You mix it all up now, pulverize the bones, brains all over the walls—basically, totally awesome. More ground meat than you can shake a stick at. At night you have to go home. Your workday's over. What do you do?" Parodying a scene from *Desperado*, Filippov leaned across the bar toward the bartender with a Tarantino-esque false dramatic pause, which had to be followed by an invariable platitude. "That's right, sonny. You push the button."

The young man behind the bar stopped shivering, observing with interest as Filippov acted out with his hands, voice, and even his face an industrial meat grinder after being turned off.

"And silence," he said softly, ending his noisemaking. "The rest is silence."

For a few seconds neither said anything, neither even moved, and then Filippov made a striking gesture he'd picked up from a certain actor at the Tambov Dramatic Theater performing in a children's show, *The Singing Piggy*.

"And at that moment," he began solemnly, hypnotizing the bartender with the killer combination of the Tambov gesture and Edvard Radzinsky's sepulchral intonations. "At that moment, the rats appear. Have you read *The Inspector General*?"

"Yes."

"Well, these are nothing like the rats in Gorodnichy's dream. Remember? They came, they sniffed, and they went away. No, my dear man, there aren't just two. And they don't go away. They've come for the night, a hungry horde, to eat, not sniff. Can you imagine all the stuff left in that turned-off meat grinder? You think they clean it? Or you think the rats miss even one night? The hell they do! They go to work like a train keeping its schedule! Eat all night. Stuff their nasty, ratty faces. Now just imagine what happens come morning. When those . . . well, what do you call them . . . sausagers . . . come back and one of them switches the meat grinder back on. You think the rats finished eating, said thank you, and quietly went away? Or maybe they have this boss rat from the Rat Emergencies Ministry who sits on the clock and at exactly six thirty in the morning tells them, 'Guys, fuck off. It's time to scram. Those mean men will be here any minute, and they'll wipe that smile off your face.' You think so? I have my doubts. Something tells me they don't have a good, sympathetic, attentive rat like that. Which means that when the sausagers switch their barrel organ on in the morning, the insides there are full of rats. God's creatures, stuffed and trusting. And all of them, squealing wildly, are quickly turned into sausage meat. Now, tell me honestly, are you sure that every morning someone separates that 'first-run' sausage meat from the main batch? Some specially trained, experienced sanitary person? No? Me neither. So, give me my vodka. I'm ready now."

Impressed by this ferocious improvisation, the bartender looked askance at his sandwiches wrapped in wrinkled cellophane. His confusion was understandable. First of all, never before had he given such deep thought to sausage, and second of all, he'd never encountered anyone this unusual before.

"What do you want with it then?"

"How about nothing, for the sake of purity. I should give this thousand years of yours a proper tasting."

He didn't pick up on any millennium in the local vodka, however. Not even half a millennium. His nausea rose the same as from ordinary vodka. Filippov instinctively pressed his right fist to his mouth and held his breath. Somewhere inside his restless body, a volcano had been awakened. Nevertheless, experience and many years of practice had tempered him to such an extent that ultimately he emerged the victor in this unequal battle.

Thus the ancient Greeks, knowingly inferior in numbers to the Persian host, nonetheless did not lose their dignity in the battle at Marathon.

"You put one over on me." Filya sighed and looked at the now-quiet bartender. "Ilya Lagutenko was right when he said vodka's hard water. I've only had it worse with the vodka of my childhood. On the other hand, it only cost six rubles."

"Six rubles and twenty kopeks."

"How the hell do you know that?"

"I remember."

"Genetic memory?"

"No, I drank that vodka myself."

"Come off it. In a previous life?"

"Why? This one. Under Andropov, I think."

"What year were you born?" Filippov went on his guard, realizing now that he wasn't being played but still not believing his own eyes.

"Sixty-eight."

"You've got to be kidding. You're forty?"

"Nearly." The bartender smiled. "You mean you can't tell?"

"Wait up, but you said you were in your second year."

"Yes. By correspondence. I do have to pay, of course, because it's my second degree, but it's interesting. My first degree is as a mining engineer."

"Hot stuff," Filippov said with emphasis. "You're well-preserved. I thought you were about twenty."

"No, thirty-nine."

"And I'm forty-two. Listen . . . What about—?" All of a sudden he started to laugh. "What's going on? That's fucked up. You mean you've spent all these years in these freezing conditions, these everlasting freezing conditions of yours? What's it called? Anabiosis? Cryo-something? Really, how could you? No, this doesn't happen."

"Why not, though?" the bartender said. "That's how things worked out."

"Yeah?"

They both fell silent, each with his own thoughts.

After about ten minutes of this silence, Zinaida walked into the bar. Her cheeks were burning. Her greasy bangs were hopping belligerently.

"Get your deluxe?" Filippov inquired languidly.

"I'm doing this for you, by the way." She looked at his glass. "You're drinking again?"

"I am," Filya admitted. "What else am I supposed to do? Want some of the local vodka? Produced from the purest glacial water. Or-fucking-ganic vodka. But unbelievable filth."

Filippov found nothing outstanding in his drunkenness. Five years ago, when, after a tedious string of life failures, artistic disasters, and total obscurity, genuine success came crashing down on him, he hadn't considered it drunkenness at all. At the time, at thirty-seven, he suddenly had access to kinds of alcoholic beverages he'd simply never known existed. Or he had, but he hadn't believed it, the way people don't believe in other people's obscure gods. From that moment, the cheap vodka, bathtub beer, and other swill that formerly had made up his *carte des vins*—which if you didn't want to risk your life you just didn't drink a lot of—was whisked out of his life like a bad dream, and approaching with a heavy tread to take its place, in elegant—a couple of times even crystal—bottles, was alcohol with European labels like "XO," "Single Malt," "Reserva," and "VSOP." You could drink as much of it as would go down; your system absorbed it easily. Those abbreviations made Filippov happy, but it took more than a year for this happiness to share not only his suddenly fat wallet but also his tongue and soft palate. And a full understanding of the taste triumphs of alcoholically progressive humanity dawned on him much later, followed by a need to justify his enthusiasm. For him, success had already lost the unique charm of novelty and could not serve as significant grounds for getting drunk. He had to turn to morality.

"We're like children, you see," Filippov would say the morning after a fabulous binge as he examined his reflection in the mirror and lightly slapped himself on the cheeks. "We didn't mean anything bad."

The absence of any evil intention as a motive for drinking worked effectively for a couple more years. Filippov enjoyed the new aspects of his life and at the same time, unlike other lushes, felt neither ashamed nor guilty. During this time, his curiosity led to the world of dry wines, which, seemingly, had been barred to him for good in his tender Soviet adolescence by the bitter Hungarian Riesling and the macabre Bulgarian Bear's Blood. Nor did strong drinks disappoint. Orujo, chacha, tequila, pisco, various kinds of schnapps, and Moroccan boukha distilled from figs lured him with their aromas, which he missed in Russian vodka, although at the same time vodka itself always found a distinguished and perfectly honorable place among his personal guideposts.

He was also stimulated by the fact that in the mornings, he felt like he was in another dimension. A hangover frequently brought with it a new and totally surprising view of ordinary things, and sometimes a scene that just wasn't working for his actors at an evening rehearsal would suddenly reveal to him, come morning, a surprising, vivid facet, and by the next rehearsal the actors would be shrugging in amazement, giving each other the thumbs-up, and from time to time even applauding their own brilliant lord and master. All this couldn't help but facilitate new experiments. The only thing Filippov didn't touch was liqueurs. He could splash a drop of cassis into a goblet of white wine, but all the rest he disdained.

Actually, even this cloudless period in his romance with alcohol ended pretty quickly. Basically, everything connected with spirits passed quickly in his life. Filippov could open bottles faster than anyone, poured fast and precisely, got drunk fast, and got sober exactly as fast— by changing the proof. This was his trade secret. He knew that after a few glasses of wine, which would always knock him for a loop, a decent swallow of Scotch or bourbon would immediately restore him to his former quick reactions. However, soon even the hangover itself became so familiar that the morning's illuminations abandoned him, doubtless preferring other, more exalted drunks. New and strange thoughts on directing stopped coming to Filippov.

This silence from the higher spheres worried him, and he seriously began thinking about living sober, but right then an amazingly fresh, and in a certain sense even poetic, doctrine of alcoholism came to his rescue, as pure and beautiful as a child arising from sleep, and Filippov readily fell at its feet, folding up the unfurled banners of common sense and social responsibility. To his own surprise, he suddenly told her that drunkenness was simply another form of sincerity. And who more than anyone else, one might ask, should be sincere if not an artist?

"I don't know, I don't know." Zinaida shrugged. "I think more than anything else an artist should be alive. At this rate you'll be digging your own grave very soon."

"As to being alive—that's not a fact," Filippov objected, pointing out his empty glass to the bartender. "Are you up on how well the dead sell? If Michael Jackson were to die now all of a sudden, you know how much he'd rake in? But alive, no one's cared about him for a long time."

"Michael Jackson I get. He's got records and songs. But what have you got to sell after you die? The scenographies for your shows?"

"Ooh, the words we know. Scenography." Filippov nodded to the slow-moving bartender. "Come on, come on—pour. Don't be shy."

"You can make all the fun of me you want," Zinaida said, "only the problem's right in front of you. You passed out in the car. And before that—you were the one who told me you'd passed out on the plane. Two blackouts in one day."

"In the car? I did?"

"Who else? Me?"

Filippov tore his gaze away from the newly filled glass and gave Zinaida a wary look.

"Don't lie."

"Now it's 'Don't lie.' You were stretched out on the backseat for twenty minutes totally passed out, and now you're trying to deny it."

"When was it I was stretched out?"

"Almost the whole way after the crossing."

"Don't lie."

"Enough already. I'm tired of it."

"Zina, don't be rude to me. Who raised you?"

"Who raised you?"

"Wait one little second."

Filippov turned toward the bartender.

"Have you heard of Mannerheim?"

"Yeah, it's some Finnish vodka."

"It's not about being Finnish; it's about how you drink it. Marshal Mannerheim demanded the glasses be filled to the very brim. Can you pour a full one? So it's got a bit of a hump? True, the Finns freeze the glass and the vodka especially for this. That makes the surface tension stronger. Almost like oil."

"Why freeze it?" the bartender said. "It's plenty cold here as is." He shrugged and carefully topped off the glass.

Filippov leaned over it, assessed it, and then nodded. "Not bad. You have to make sure the vodka comes a little over the edges. A mound like this. Now watch, Auntie Zina."

He neatly picked up the glass off the counter and smoothly bore it to his already open mouth. At one point the vodka swayed ominously over the edges of the glass. Filippov froze, waiting out this disturbance. Then he decisively brought his chin to the glass and swallowed its contents in one go.

"See? And you're making me out to be feeble. I didn't spill a single drop. By the way, that's how Marshal Mannerheim chose his officers. Sure you don't want any? You're chilled through. Have a go. Look, you've got goose bumps on your neck already."

He reached out to touch her before Zinaida could pull back. That is, she did pull back, but with a delay. An awkward moment.

"No," she said. "I'm going. They're expecting me at home."

"Who? Your son's girlfriend?"

These words made Zinaida freeze like a hamster in a cage when you tap the top of the bars unexpectedly.

"You're looking at me as if I were the one who killed Kenny."

"Who?"

"If you don't know, there's no point trying to explain. I was trying to make a joke. By the way, if you knew that, it would be easier for you to find a common language with your son."

"What business is that of yours?"

"Me?" Filippov shrugged, carved out a wolf's grin from a kiddie show, and shook his head. "None. It was just by the way. You really don't know who Kenny is?"

"I already said so."

"All right, don't be angry. By the way, you insulted me, too, with your lies about me passing out. I was just playing possum. Iron self-restraint. Long years of training."

"I wasn't lying to you."

"Listen, don't start. It's gotten boring. I remember the whole way from the airport to the hotel."

"You do? Good. Then tell me what happened on the road."

"And will you snort for me?"

Zinaida once again was taken aback.

"In what sense?"

"The literal. The way you snorted when you laughed. I just loved it. Please snort. I have to remember it. I'll show my actress later. She can laugh like that, too. In one show, she has a laugh at the beginning of the second act, and it's not working. But if she snorted like you, it would. I kept telling her at rehearsals, 'Imagine I'm sitting on a streetlamp bare-assed.' She did laugh well for a couple of performances, and then she stopped. My bare ass didn't strike her as funny anymore. Please snort. Come on—is it so hard? I have an important scene hanging on this."

Zinaida looked at Filippov for a second, then doughtily wrinkled her nose and snorted.

"No, that's not fair," he drawled disappointedly. "You've lost the whole organic nature of it. Any fool can do that. On the plane you did it very differently. It was enchanting. Such a good little cartoon piggy."

"You want *me* to snort?" the bartender offered.

"No, thanks. I need the female sound."

"I can do it like a female."

"That's something I definitely don't need. Anyway, it's not interesting anymore."

Filippov was truly bored and once again pointed out his empty glass to the bartender.

"A Mannerheim?"

"No need. Pour the usual."

"I'm waiting," Zinaida said. "I held up my end of the bargain."

"Do we have a business going here or something?" Filippov cast a sidelong look at her.

"You have to keep your word."

"Fine, then." He sighed. "Just let me have a drink."

He downed his third glass, frowned, sniffed his fist, and blinked to clear away the oncoming tears.

"Basically, listen," he said. "After the crossing on the port road, some moron drove straight at us. We were run off the road. I hit my head. Then that asshole jumped out of his car. No, wait. He didn't. There was another car there. And a few people sitting in it. They dragged that asshole out of his jeep and started . . . Yeah . . . And your Pavlik tried to stop them." Filippov paused. "Because it was a young woman."

"Well?" Zinaida said after waiting a few seconds. "What happened after that?"

"After that . . . For some reason I don't remember . . . By the way, where's Pavlik gone to? Why did you bring me to the hotel alone?"

"There, you see? You don't even remember anything about Pavlik. And you passed out much later."

"Lay off this passing out thing. Who was the girl? And why were they chasing her? No, hang on—I'll remember. I just have to re-create the staging. Come here."

He jumped off his barstool and dragged Zinaida over to one of the tables. "Sit."

Filippov sat her down on a pretentious chair with a polished back. Then he himself, scraping another chair's heavy legs over the tile, sat behind her.

"So, we were sitting like this. Pavlik was here on the left. Let me put a chair here for him, too. Another car flew past us and stopped over there. Then the second car . . . No, wait a sec."

He jumped up from his chair and ran toward the big table in the opposite corner of the room. "This'll be their car. These three goons are walking over from there." He hunched over and displayed a might and threat nonexistent in nature.

"And they're running toward this SUV. In slow motion." For some reason, Filippov started demonstrating the three men running in slow motion, heading toward the other table, which he evidently had playing the part of the third vehicle.

"They run up . . . drag the driver out . . . and at that moment . . ." He rushed toward Zinaida, plopped down on the chair next to her, and then abruptly opened the nonexistent door. "At that moment, your Pavlik scrambles out and runs toward them." Filippov demonstrated the same slow-motion run for Pavlik as for the attackers, looking around as he does and opening his mouth without making a sound.

"He shouted something, but we couldn't hear it. The door had already slammed shut. And I was right here." Filippov rushed back to his chair and collapsed on it, throwing his head way back and pressing his palm to it.

"But I saw it all. Those three dragged the driver out. The driver resisted. Your Pavlik ran toward them." Filippov fell silent. "It gets fuzzy after that. There's a fog."

"That's it?" Zinaida snickered as she turned toward him. "And you said you'd remember."

"Know what? I'm sick of you. I told you what happened on the road. What more do you want? I even remember what she was wearing. Black jeans, high reindeer boots. Tall, narrow boots. A dark sweater—dark blue, I think. A gray scarf, long, wound around a few times. A dark mink cap with earflaps. Like a man's. That's why I took her for a boy at first. Get it?" Filippov gave Zinaida a triumphant look. "Little Miss Know-It-All."

"Fine." She nodded. "Then what became of Pavlik after? And why was that girl running away? Who is she?"

Filippov was silent.

"We did discuss all that," Zinaida said.

"Who with?"

"You."

"When?"

"An hour ago. Right there, in the car. Only after that, you passed out, and now you don't remember anything."

Filippov became sad and hung his head.

"Do you have something to play a CD on?" he asked the bartender a minute later.

The bartender dove under the bar and hoisted onto it a paunchy boom box.

"Put this in," Filippov said, walking up to him and taking a Tom Waits CD out of his coat pocket, a CD he carried around and importuned bartenders with all over the world. "Track three."

The CD clicked into place, something responded in the speakers over the bar, and Filippov nodded and listened to the dear raspy voice:

You'll be lost and never found
You can never turn around
Don't go down to Fannin Street

Feeling fucked over, Tom droned on through the speakers about how easy it is to lose yourself, all it takes is one wrong turn, and Zinaida shook her head, looking at Filippov.

"You really don't remember anything. Nothing at all."

Curtain.

ENTR'ACTE

THE DEMON OF THE VOID

He started popping up in Filippov's life gradually. He'd flit by at one party or another, at important premieres, and for quite a while, even when he recognized him, Filippov wouldn't try to talk to him. The array of personalities at these events was always more or less the same, so you never picked out anyone in particular. Everyone recognized everyone else, and no one gave a fuck about anyone else. Filippov assumed he was someone's friend, a common acquaintance he didn't have to talk to.

Later they started to nod upon meeting, exchanged snide comments once, and Filippov decided he liked the stranger. He had an appealing knack for fresh and fast remarks, with a light cynicism, without ceremony, and at the same time with a charming simplicity. But they really saw eye to eye when it came to slander. Finding themselves side by side on a crowded sofa at the embassy of a certain small but very rich European country, they dissected everyone at the reception so sweetly that Filippov, who had been about to die from boredom, roared back to life and recognized kindred blood in the stranger.

By their next meeting at some presentation or the awarding of some prize at the President Hotel, he asked around, but none of his acquaintances knew the fellow personally. Everyone assured him he was someone's friend, but a minute later that someone would deny knowing him and send Filippov off to the next candidate. Actually, this stopped bothering him almost immediately. He decided his witty interlocutor was the typical freeloader who insinuates himself into fashionable parties, and this largely coincided with his own views on life.

Catching sight of his new friend, Filippov delightedly took him by the arm, dragged him to the nearest secluded corner, twirled the button on his expensive jacket, and whispered hilarious vulgarities about everyone who passed or stopped for a sociable clinking of glasses. He was blissfully happy not to know his companion well. Filippov would definitely have been wary about telling someone from his own circle all these things about his colleagues, partners, friends, and former lovers.

The stranger was invariably ecstatic and, as a reciprocal move, told him piquant details about those same people, details even Filippov didn't know and that livened him up no less than a thin white line on a dark mirror. It was from this character no one knew that he learned the interesting way one of his former actresses had set her sights on a well-known "factory, newspaper, and shipping magnate" who had rashly set eyes on her. Attempting to deprive the poor sod of any choice and tie him securely to her, the inventive priestess of Melpomene had used cocaine vaginally every time before sex, which brought not only her trusting fiancé but the beautiful aspirant herself to bewitching orgasms.

"Look how easy it is to be perfection," his remarkable new friend said, smiling at Filippov. "And you keep going on about talent, talent, talent."

Once he told a marvelous tale about original sin.

"The kind god who created the world had the idea of populating it with sensible mortal creatures and, for starters, sculpted life-size models of them. The god placed these statues in a large stone house and posted a guard outside and ordered him not to let the evil spirit into the building. The evil spirit was known for his dirty tricks and, naturally, would never pass up a chance to participate in the production of the first men. As usual, the evil spirit didn't wait long and bribed the guard, promising him a warm fur coat, because the action took place in our native lands, and the guard was on his last legs, literally freezing at his post. The evil spirit penetrated the building, defecated everywhere, and out of mischief or, perhaps, disrespect for the sculptor's talent, defiled the unfortunate giants from head to foot with his filth. After all this outrage, the good god turned the luckless guard into a dog and turned the sculptures inside out, so you couldn't see the shit. Ever since, people have been filled with you-know-what."

Filippov was sincerely glad to learn the stranger was from the same part of the world as he was. That brought them even closer together. A couple of times they ended up in the same car returning to Moscow after fancy parties outside of town, and he managed to initiate Filippov into his secret concept of "the void."

"Understand me, my friend," he said quietly. "There's nothing neater, tidier, or handsomer than this doctrine. I've been working on it for years. You have to agree that each person is trying his hardest for mastery. Everyone wants to master something, to fill himself and his life with something pleasant, important, and precious. But that's a mistake. It's one of the saddest errors in the world. No matter how much a person acquires, it still isn't enough. He's always tormented by the thirst for something more. Or at least the suspicion that there's something more. Only the void is capable of ideally filling the human soul. It alone doesn't leave a single unoccupied spot in the soul. Pure physics, brother. You can't argue with that."

Enchanted by this logic, Filippov got chummier and chummier with the stranger until the moment, one day, he woke up and found him in his apartment. At first, he decided they'd gotten smashed the night before and the stranger had simply spent the night, but by the next day his new friend hadn't gone anywhere. Soon after, the stranger revealed to Filippov his true identity.

ACT TWO

·······

FREEZING POINT

Filya was awakened in the most utter darkness by an unpleasant clicking, as if people were playing wooden spoons in the next room. At the same time, the perky spoon players were also whining ever so slightly. He tried to distract himself from this hotel amateur hour, trying to fall asleep using a trick he'd come up with for occasions such as these, but it didn't work. Filya mentally drew the reason for the sound; however, instead of the usual lulling scenes, he got glimpses of tin rabbits devoting themselves to enthusiastic, bone-rattling love. He was ready to leap out of bed and tear the entire hotel to shreds, but catching his trembling lower jaw with his wet hand, he instantly stopped the detested clicking and whining.

Actually, while groping for his watch on the nightstand, he detected even stranger sounds. The blanket covering him didn't rustle when he reached for his watch but suddenly squelched and then made a sloshing sound. Filya tried to lower his right foot off the bed to stand up and turn on the light, but his knee bumped into something hard, and the squelching and sloshing were repeated. Totally befuddled, he froze, trying to wake up, and then cautiously felt around, came across some plastic bottles, and realized he was sitting in a full bathtub. The water was icy.

Filya spewed some ugly and booming curses when he remembered he really had filled the tub before he'd intended to collapse on the bed. He'd long been a devotee of this procedure, naively supposing he was battling dehydration. Spirits dried his flesh until it was like flammable peat, and drinking on high-altitude flights, he had recently learned, dehydrated his talented carcass twice as fast.

The only thing he didn't understand was why the light had gone out.

Filya wiped his face with his wet hands, hoping to make out something in the pitch dark, but he had locked the door to the bathroom, because that's what he always did in hotels, out of some vague fear, and the light in the bedroom was off. So there wasn't any strip of light under the door whatsoever. He couldn't even tell where the door was. Filya was racked by a far-from-faint trembling.

At least I didn't drown. The idea stirred in his mind, not that this thought was any consolation.

Attempting to remember which side of the tub had the tile wall, he pushed himself up on his trembling arms, swayed to the right, and smashed his head so hard he collapsed back into the icy water. Moaning from pain, cold, and despair, he got furious, leapt to his feet, slipped immediately, and sat back down in fright to regain his balance. For some reason, with one hand he covered his male equipment, shriveled to child size. Then he reached to the left with the other and, not bumping into any obstacle, cautiously stepped over the side of the tub. The bottle left there last night tinkled underfoot. The cheap whiskey had hit him hard.

Filippov froze, trying to figure out whether he'd broken the bottle or not, and then took a timid step. He tried to step on the tips of his toes, so as not to cut himself if the bottle had broken, but his legs were shaking so badly and the icy tile was so slippery that for stability he had to drop to his full foot. Otherwise, he risked crashing to the floor and banging himself on the toilet, for instance, or the sink, whose locations he really didn't remember.

First off, he had to find the switch, so he pressed his shoulder to the wall and moved along it, fumbling over the tile somewhere around head level. The wall turned out to be incredibly long, like the hole that curious Alice fell down in pursuit of the rabbit. Filippov slid along the wall for an eternity until he ran into a corner. No switch there. Or there was, but at a different height. Trying not to consider that possibility, he moved on.

His feet were solid ice. The shoulder touching the wall was burning from some scrape. His head was crowded with thoughts about a nasty contagion covering the hotel tile, and the switch just wouldn't come to hand. Suddenly, he remembered the towel rack and stopped, crossing his legs under himself apprehensively. The construction consisted of three impressive nickel-plated rods arbitrarily pointing in different directions and, consequently, his face could now run into one of those rods. Picturing himself with skewered eyes, Filya squatted slightly and then slowly moved on in a half squat. The switch turned out to be at stomach height. The reason for the placement was anyone's guess.

Filippov flipped the switch a few times, and the neon tube over his head hummed and blinked a warning and then lit up his gray, crooked little body in the cloudy mirror on the next wall. Filya was surprised at just how small the bathroom in fact was, and he himself, too, and he frowned disdainfully at the sight of the naked wretch in the mirror and shifted his gaze to the upset square bottle in which he saw the last smidgen of alcohol that hadn't spilled.

"Damn it, I'd already reached the point of Red Label," he moaned.

The window in the bedroom was closed. Tugging on it, Filippov confirmed that the terrific cold that was turning his breath to visible steam had not come in due to his drunken desire to air the room before going to bed. The radiators were barely warm to the touch. His whole body quaking and now back to whining from the cold, he tried to find his underwear but quickly gave up on that plan. After a brief battle he was able to pull the pants and boots he'd abandoned at the threshold over his still-wet legs and feet. He wanted to run out into the hall as quickly as possible, because, according to his feverish calculations, the hall should have retained at least some warmth. At least, as far as he remembered, it didn't have a single window onto the street. Not bothering with his tiny shirt buttons, he threw the hotel blanket—covered in large and what looked like dirty checks—over his shoulders and dashed for the door. Skipping past the open door to the bathroom, he braked. The disgusting blended swill left in the resting bottle might come in very, very handy. Filya went back for the whiskey and, now holding the bottle, finally exited the room.

The half-dark hall receding into the distance, with two rows of doors as alike as the numbers in a theater checkroom, was empty. Either the hotel was now defunct and the guests' stiffened corpses had frozen to the hospitable mattresses, or else cold like this was a completely ordinary thing here and everyone was used to it and each person had at the ready a fine bearskin in their room that they could calmly wrap up in and not rush through the hall in wet pants and a crude checked blanket. Filippov twitched first to the left, but after trotting twenty meters or so and not finding the front desk around the corner, he went back and, like a proud trotter, ran to the right. What specifically he was hoping for from the hotel staff, Filya still didn't know, but running down the red carpet—even on wooden legs—did warm him up a little, and at the opposite end of the deserted hall he stopped for a second to take a swig. The sight of the red carpet receding into the half-dark infinity cheered him up, but he quickly drove out the images close to his heart.

"Velkum houm," Filippov muttered in English after taking a big and greedy swallow from the bottle.

At that moment, the blended swill—there'd been absolutely nothing else to buy in the local stores—seemed a perfectly tolerable beverage. His throat, covered with goose bumps from the cold, even inside, gratefully accepted the amber moisture. Glassy tears came readily to his puffy eyes, and Filya froze, like an exhibit at Madame Tussauds, riveted by what was happening to himself, to the cold, to his lips stung and burning from the spirits, to the low-grade whiskey slipping into him with difficulty, to his stomach, which it hadn't yet reached, and to the taciturn hotel, which didn't give a flying fuck about the cold. Why should it? The whiskey surprised his stomach more than it did Filya himself, who had drunk worse things.

He straightened up and stood stock-still for another second, shaping his lips into a ring and checking whether his breath was turning to steam. His burning lips cracked at this effort, and Filya felt a stinging in the corners of his mouth again.

"Damn it," he growled, unable to keep himself from licking his wound.

———

The young woman at the reception desk was sound asleep, her head resting on her arms. Her long ponytail shone in the light of the neon lamp as if someone had coated it with grease. Filippov had never encountered in anyone else hair as black and thick as Yakut girls had. It wasn't just thick; it was fat. Each of the hairs had its own separate thickness, and together they were not just a hairdo but an independent, powerfully vibrant organism. In ages long past, these women's menfolk could have simply spun this hair into string for their bows, seines for catching fish, harnesses for reindeer, or ropes to save the brave hunter so consumed by the hunt that he'd fallen into a bear pit. Filippov had to curb himself from touching this thick treasure, glossy as tar.

The big clock on the wall said half past five. Due to the long flight, continuous drinking, and tremendous jet lag, Filippov had lost all track of time. Whether it was morning now or evening, he just couldn't tell. More than likely, of course, the young woman was sound asleep after pulling the night shift, although she could have all kinds of reasons for taking a nap in the evening, too. Filippov knew a couple of famous actors who shared dressing rooms with restless youths on purpose so that they wouldn't sleep through the evening rehearsal. There were rumors that once, at contract time, one of them had demanded they add a clause about the right to a paid postprandial nap.

Unlike Filippov, Sleeping Beauty was dressed appropriately for the conditions. The one-size-fits-all Chinese down parka in khaki with an enormous hood, like a space-suit helmet, a scarf wound around her neck several times, and beaded mittens, which her head was lying on, ensured her fresh body a healthy sleep, whereas hungover Filya, in his little blanket over his damp shirt, was quaking like a stray mutt on a nasty winter's night. Looking at the young woman breathing evenly in her fairy-tale sleep, he even thought he could feel her emit warmth herself. Reaching out to make sure, Filippov realized with amazement that he'd not been mistaken. Waves of warmth were coming from the black-haired receptionist.

Filya stood over her for a few minutes, reaching out with one and then the other hand, still unable to lower the blanket he was clutching at his throat. He couldn't care less about the nature of this miracle. The main thing was that it had happened. He warmed himself in this woman's rays as if at a stove, trying not to wake her, with no concern whatsoever for the mechanics of local miracles. Not even a shadow of amazement stirred in his mind. What was important was to warm up a little. Actually, when he'd stopped shaking like a jackhammer, he remembered various shamanistic things, but when he leaned a little lower over the young woman he saw something plugged into a large surge protector next to her chair: a heater.

Electrolux. Filya read the handsome gray letters on the snowy white panel with just his lips, as if afraid of startling her.

Green numbers glowed softly on the small display.

"Twenty-five degrees," he whispered quite involuntarily, like a man bewitched.

Walking around the counter from the other side, Filippov squatted beside the heater, gave it a second or two's thought, and then carefully pulled the plug. The heater seemed hot to the touch, so Filya took off his blanket and wrapped it around the Swedish miracle. He had to leave quickly but quietly. Filippov rose onto tiptoe, took one step, and another, and then, like the careless Albrecht trying to flee Giselle's dead and angry friends, hurried away from this cemetery of iced-over hopes. He ran to the turn like a fleet-footed deer, stopped, and leaned against the wall. His heart was pounding madly right next to the heater. Filya was jubilant as he entered his own corridor.

The empty bottle of Red Label was right where he'd left it a few minutes before.

"Freeze here, you beast," Filippov whispered maliciously, casting a glance at the empty vessel and pressing to his belly the warm, blanket-wrapped heater. "No one needs you anymore. I hope you die!"

Disdainfully skirting the bottle, he headed toward his own room, but the farther he went down the hall, the less confident his step became. The endless row of doors on the left-hand side discouraged him more and more. Finally, he stopped. When he'd left his room, he hadn't given a thought to how he would find it upon his return. At his moment of flight, it simply hadn't occurred to him to remember the number on the gray door. Moreover, now he even doubted his room was on the left side.

"It could just as easily be on the right," Filippov muttered, turning around toward the deserted, orphaned bottle and trying to figure out how he'd been moving in relation to its present position when he was looking for the reception desk. "I stopped right here and took a drink."

He went back to the bottle and set the heater on the floor. His ditched girlfriend was close to the right-hand wall, which meant that Filya was probably keeping to that side while he was moving. That meant his room was probably on the right, too. He would hardly have crossed the hall when he'd exited his room.

"But what if I was on autopilot?" Suddenly, he had his doubts. "Keeping to the right is a habit . . . No, it's not a hundred percent. Damn it."

He turned his head, listening to his intuition, but his intuition was totally silent. It liked both sides of the hall. Deciding his heart would tell him when he was facing the door to his room, Filippov moved slowly down the carpet. The cold had already made its claim on him again, but Filya didn't take the blanket off the heater. He was busy counting steps. He didn't think there should be more than fifteen of them from the bottle to his door. At the sixteenth step he stopped and looked at the door to his left. Not a peep from his heart. Then he shifted his gaze to the right. Total silence.

"Damn it. I did run in the other direction," he said, recalling the dash from his room toward the cluttered stairwell.

Considering that run, it made no sense to calculate the distance from the bottle. His reference points were thoroughly confused. Filya returned to the heater, and experiencing wrenching twinges of conscience, he picked up the bottle off the floor in hopes there was at least something left for him. The vengeful creature wouldn't give up a drop.

"To hell with you," Filippov growled. "Terrific."

Once again, the cold was seeping into his bones. The heater had cooled off completely, so Filya pulled off the blanket. But there weren't any electrical outlets in the hall. The only thing left to do was return the stolen treasure to its place, plug it in, and sit quietly by its side until morning, like an old Indian in a blanket, whom everyone had abandoned. Without a drop of liquor.

However, recalling the young woman sleeping at her desk, Filippov paused for a second. Then he ran at an inaudible trot back to the front desk. The blanket stayed there like that, lying on the floor.

Before he could run the few meters to the desk, he stopped to calm his breathing. Waking Sleeping Beauty would be a total disaster. He tiptoed toward her, leaned over her giant hood, and fell silent, trying to shiver with the least possible amplitude. On the desk, under her crossed arms, on which rested her disproportionately large, black-haired head, lay the room list with the guests' names. Filya had remembered that page a minute before. Creeping out from under her left beaded mitten were the poorly printed letters *lippov* and then the number 237.

"How could I forget a number like that?" he muttered, hastily collecting his stuff in the corridor.

This time the empty bottle was among them.

He was holding the heater, bottle, and blanket when he walked up to his room door, pushed it with his foot, and realized he didn't have the key.

Filya exhaled a small cloudlet of steam, and for five or six seconds it hung there like a frozen computer. There was no one to reboot him here in the hall. Quickly, though, his gaze was once again intelligent, since he remembered that he'd had the key under his arm as he ran out of the room. His hands had been busy with the bottle and blanket. And his pants pockets were too narrow to hold the plastic key chain, which was the size of a kiddie shovel.

"So what became of it?"

In the hall, as far as the eye could see, the key wasn't lying either on or next to the carpet. That left just one place.

Filya ran to the reception desk for a third time.

As he approached Sleeping Beauty, he noticed that her head was turned the other way, and the pacific expression on her face had been replaced by a censorious one. Perhaps she had sensed that the heater had gone missing, her sleep had ceased to be untroubled, and she was just on the verge of asking herself whose fault it was.

Filya dropped to all fours, so that in the event of alarm, her eyes wouldn't fall on him right away. He started to investigate the space around the desk, but the key was nowhere to be found. When he'd crawled practically under the sleeping receptionist, she started squirming in her chair, evidently trying to surface from a disturbing, swiftly cooling dream. Filippov froze with hand and knee raised, but the young woman didn't wake up. The key wasn't under her desk, either. Actually, as Filya admitted to himself, it couldn't have been. But where won't you look when you've lost something important?

His losses did not end at this, however. Far from it. Upon his return to his room, his teeth chattering again from the cold, he discovered on the threshold the blanket and whiskey bottle he'd left but not the stolen heater. Someone had stolen it again.

"What kind of people are they," Filya moaned, dropping to the floor next to his door. "They have no shame, damn it, no conscience."

At that moment, he had the sense that someone was standing on the other side of the door. He didn't catch anything specific, but it was as if someone had sighed. Or was trying to hold back laughter. Or a large bird had spread its wings.

Filya stopped his teeth from chattering and his droning due to the cold to listen to the hotel's nocturnal silence. The bird in his room fell still as well. Convulsively grabbing the doorknob, Filippov rose to his feet, straightened up, and stared into the peephole. He now had the definite feeling he was being looked right back at. The only reason chills didn't run down his spine was that they'd already been there for quite some time.

The next moment, whoever was looking at him from his room moved away from the door, and Filippov distinctly saw light fall across the peephole.

"Open up!" He banged on the door. "Do you hear me? Open up and fast!"

The light disappeared in the peephole again, and a moment later he heard an unfamiliar voice.

"Who's there?"

"Knock, knock," Filippov muttered. "Open the fuck up."

———

In life—no matter how clear, pigeonholed, and boring it is—there are these times when we understand with absolute clarity that at this very moment anything is possible, and we understand this coldly, disinterestedly, and, at the same time, furiously. Suddenly, we understand that the plane might crash, our spouse might not come home, the person standing next to us in the Metro might be carrying a deadly virus. Moreover, a friend who died long ago might call out to us in an underground passageway, the midnight sky might shine from end to end, a fish might talk, and a black cat might consider us a bad omen. There are moments when anything seems possible, anything our imaginations can conceive.

In such instances, death might well seem to await us in our provincial hotel room. Not that bald freak in the hooded cloak from Bergman's *Seventh Seal*, and not that shrimp with the braid from the joke about the canary, but our own proper, ordinary-size death, which for some reason has let us be for a whole forty-two years. And then we turn around and start running away, even though we've told ourselves a hundred thousand times that we're not afraid of death, that dying is just going home, or to the harbor, as fearless Tom Waits sings. But the red carpet is already conspiring with our inflamed fantasy, has already become an uncrossable mire, and our feet are sinking into it, getting stuck, and our flight is starting to look more and more like distressed bellowing. Here we are bellowing with all our might down this carpet until a door opens behind us and a human being finally peeks out of the room into the corridor, a living creature. But we're still not prepared to recognize him, or rather, her, because we're busy running, our dash for the world of the living filmed on very slow stock.

"Stop! Where are you going?" the creature in the flesh says melodically, and we turn around mistrustfully, slow the swift viscosity of this waking dream, catch our breath, and once again bring the surrounding world into focus.

"Who are you?" Filippov said. "Why? Why are you in my room?"

"I found the key on the floor. Over there." She pointed to the end of the hall, as far as Filya had managed to run during his recent flailings. "I'm Rita. Do you remember me? Today on the port road."

"Rita?" Filippov pressed his entire body to the wall and slid to the floor. "Rita? It's really you? You shouldn't do that to people. You nearly killed me."

———

He came to smack-dab in the middle of his life. Or rather, in the middle of what at that moment he took for his life. Rita was dragging him by the hand down the hall. With her free hand she was holding a bottle of red wine that had turned up out of nowhere and was even open already. The coat buttoned up over his collar was tightly wound with someone's scarf, which gave off the intolerable smell of perfume.

"Where are we going?" he said.

Rita didn't answer him, and Filya came to the conclusion that he'd only thought, not said it. Taking swigs from the bottle as they went, he managed to be vaguely surprised that his fastidious body might in his absence not only have sprawled out unclaimed in the lavatory of the Boeing's tail, it had already dressed itself, had found and opened a bottle of wine, and now was trailing somewhere after a beautiful young woman.

"Capable beast," he thought out loud about his physical shell.

"What?" Rita turned to him.

"Where are you taking me?"

"I explained it to you."

From the room they were walking past at that moment and into the corridor jumped a guy in a black down parka and a huge fox hat. Holding a television. He bumped into Filya and set off nearly at a run, and a moment later had disappeared around the corner. Something was happening in the other rooms, too. Glass was breaking; things were being dropped. The sounds of a nasty racket were flying at them from everywhere.

"Let's go." Rita pulled Filya by the sleeve. "Don't stop. We have to keep moving."

Filippov distinctly saw a cloud of steam detach from her lips at these words.

"I don't understand," he said.

She had barely managed to drag him out of the hotel when the light behind them went out, and all six floors, including the glass door lobby, plunged into total darkness.

"Finita la commedia," Filya said, leaning his head back and gazing at the darkened hulk behind him. "Everyone is free to go."

He turned around and froze in place with an open mouth, and thick steam poured out like from a dormant geyser. There was an endless stream of people walking past the hotel.

They were moving down the street, down the sidewalk, through the parking lot, even down the hotel steps. The rare streetlamps, straining a yellowish semblance of light into the fog, had already picked this swaying black mass out of the darkness, but someone was already turning them off, one by one, and absolute darkness was rolling toward them from the central square. The windows in the building opposite blinked and went out, too. The crowd floating down the avenue was now lit only by the headlights of stranded cars. Helpless, like life rafts in the ocean around a sinking liner, they emitted a muddy light, picking out of the darkness the endless backs and coiling breath of the thousands upon thousands in this throng of humanity.

Bewitched by this scene, Filippov was awakened by a powerful pain in his left earlobe, which was a sure, although long-forgotten, sign of frostbite. Rita was now dragging him around the corner from the hotel, and he was rubbing his ear while automatically taking sips of the instantly iced wine. He couldn't shake the feeling that this was all a dream, that above all this was a layer of water—kilometers, megatons of the Arctic Ocean—and all these inhabitants of the underwater kingdom had contrived their own wordless exodus in search of dry land, the promised land, or—just the opposite—an even deeper spot for themselves.

In the car, where the warmth pierced him even more sharply than the cold had before, and where he was immediately struck by a faint trembling, Filya tried to concentrate on what Rita had started talking about so loudly after she jumped into the passenger seat, but then he realized she'd been talking for rather a long time and he simply only now heard her, as if outside was outer space and the sounds in it didn't reach him.

"He's got this vile mug—like a mollusk's. That miserable Cthulhu."

"What?" Filya said, gazing at the solid, faceless mass he guessed was outside the car. "Whose mug?"

"The investigator, that Tolik. Imagine, he goes, 'Call me Tolik if we ever meet outside the station.' And I go, 'Why should we ever meet anywhere else?' On his own turf, he's not Tolik. There he's this whole Anatoly Sergeyevich. Anatoly Sergeyevich Cthulhu. He hides his tentacles under his desk."

"What tentacles?" Filya couldn't tear himself away from the window. "Where are they all going?"

Rita switched on the overhead light and turned toward Filippov.

"I was telling you in the hotel. There are heat outages in town. Something happened at the power station, or the heating station—I don't know what they call it. The radio said they'd get it fixed soon. But they let everyone leave work. People are going home."

"You mean it's evening?"

"Yes."

"I see . . . But why are there so many of them?"

"I'm telling you. Everyone was told to go. The whole town's on the move. There are plenty of students here, too. There was a comedy slam at the university."

"But why on foot? Have the buses stopped?"

"I don't know." Rita shrugged but didn't lean back. She kept looking tensely into Filya's face, as if expecting something from him, expecting him to come out with some decision.

"But where are we going?" he asked after a pause, during which he'd tried in vain to stop the shuddering that was hammering at him.

"Nowhere." The driver turned to him. "We're just parked. I'm not driving through this crowd."

Filippov thought his face was vaguely familiar.

"Who are you?" he said, taking a big swallow from the bottle and splashing wine on his chest.

"This is Tyoma," Rita said. "I was telling you about him that whole time."

"Tyoma?" Filippov rubbed the dark splashes on his coat lapel. "Your mama wouldn't be Zina, would she?"

The youth smiled, and Filya immediately recognized the pink princess's smile.

"Yes, she flew with you from Moscow today."

"Aha, and this here is the young woman who nearly killed us afterward."

"I explained already," Rita said heatedly. "I was supposed to meet you all earlier, but Danilov took me out of town. That's why I drove off in his car and his guards chased me."

Filippov belched, shook his head, and motioned for Rita to stop.

"Listen, let's not do this all at once, and let's not do it now. This Danilov, this chase—this has nothing to do with me. How did you know I was flying in? Who are you, anyway? Why did you come to meet me?"

"Your friend said you were flying in. The artist. You called him the day before yesterday from Paris."

"And you know him or something?"

"No, my mama sees him socially."

Filya snickered and looked at himself in the mirror, rubbing his burning left ear. "Yeah, I came incognito, so to speak," he said. "But with this face . . ."

"Same thing happened to me," Tyoma said when he caught Filya's look. "Didn't shave for a few weeks, and then at a party in a club I decided to drink flaming absinthe on a bet. My friends said, 'Let's light it up.' Well, they did. They were all clean-shaven. But my beard caught fire—and the bartender barely managed to toss me a towel. Good times. My burns were more or less like those."

He pointed to Filippov's face in the mirror and laughed quietly.

"Did it hurt for long?" Filya asked.

"I don't remember. Five or six days. What happened to you?"

"Something like that. Probably."

All of a sudden, without saying a word, Rita opened her door wide and hopped out of the car. Tyoma was leaning toward the windshield, trying to make out what he could in the dark and haze, while Filya, who had already subdued his shivering, took his first decent swallow. The wine was god-awful, but Filya was glad that it poured down his throat rather than his chest. He'd had enough shivering in his life, even without these crazy swings in temperature.

"What are you doing?" Tyoma asked Rita after she dove back out of the dark and into the car.

"I thought . . ."

"You thought what?"

"There was a kid there. Let's go. The crowd's thinned out."

"So you've started seeing things?" Tyoma said.

"Hey, why are we shaking like this?" Filya interrupted. "I thought we were on the central avenue. Or are the streets here completely screwed?"

"The wheels froze a little," Tyoma replied. "The car's heavy, and it stood in one place for at least forty minutes. They get square when it's freezing if you're not driving."

"Is it going to be like this long?"

"A couple of minutes."

"That much I can stand." Filya sighed, leaned back in his seat, and carefully pressed the now-shaking bottle to his belly.

He never did get an answer to his question of where they were going, but after the warmth that had poured inside him and out, that didn't bother him anymore. The car quickly stopped shaking, and Filippov could without fear apply himself to the glass friend that had come from he had no idea where. They were both being taken somewhere without being told where, but the main thing was that they were together—Filya and his good, reliable friend, so full of life and promise, who would have to betray him, though not soon, when it turned into an empty and indifferent creature.

"You were asking why everyone was on foot." Tyoma's voice penetrated Filippov's blissful anabiosis. "Look what's happening at the bus stop."

His cloudy headlights were aimed at an antediluvian bus swarmed by inhabitants of the local underwater kingdom. Once again, Filya felt like he was under several kilometers of water, although now he was no longer Filya but Jacques Cousteau, or Steve Zissou, Bill Murray in a submariner's red cap, an inquiring scientist leaning against the porthole of his deep-water bathyscaphe.

"What are they doing?" he asked.

"Trying to board the bus."

People wearing clumsy clothes that maximally impeded all their movements were crowding around a bus, looking like a giant colony of sea crabs besieging a sleeping fish. Their voices could barely be heard in the car, which made the entire scene even more unearthly and frightening—and, to Filya's eye, gorgeous.

"Wait up." He tapped Tyoma's shoulder. "Can you stop for a second?"

"Sure, I can."

"Add some light. Shine it over there."

He pointed toward where the whirlpool of human bodies was swirling and seething like a genuine maelstrom.

"No. I'd have to drive onto the sidewalk."

"Well, go ahead. I can't see anything from here."

"Have you completely lost it?" Rita said. "There are people there."

"You worry too much," said Tyoma, infected by Filya's investigative daring. "I'll be careful."

The car listed while driving over the curb and stopped at an unpleasant angle, which made Filippov lean to the right. The cloudy fog lights were now shining straight at the gaping opening of the bus's back doors, which was too narrow for the besieging crowd. Heads, arms, and shoulders flashed in the opening, but everyone's desperate efforts to board were leading to the exact opposite result. By trying to get inside, each person wasted their strength and produced more than enough energy to block everyone else's strength and energy, so they swayed helplessly in a thick human muddle.

"I never cease to be amazed at the local customs," Tyoma said. "In Moscow, people would form a line and board calmly."

"That won't cut it here," Filya spoke up. "The Northern temperament. The last in line are still going to think there won't be enough room for them. And they'll be right. There won't."

"Tyoma, let's go, please," Rita said nervously. "Mama's expecting us."

"Then call her," Filippov said.

"I can't. There's no signal."

"That's nuts," he said in disbelief. "Come on, give me your cell."

Rita handed him her phone, and Filippov quickly pulled out the SIM card and inserted his own. There really was no signal.

"F-f-fuck," Filippov exhaled. "I'm waiting for a very important message. Does this happen often here?"

"Of course not," Rita said. "I don't remember this ever happening."

"Damn! Fine, let's get to your place quick. I'll check from your home phone."

"How are you going to do that?"

"I'll call my voice mail. Let's go!" Filippov poked Tyoma in the shoulder. "It's not interesting here anymore."

The car rocked like a boat again and drove down into the roadway, smearing its dirty light over the crowd one last time. Filya didn't give a rat's ass now about these flickering arms, heads, and faces—or rather, not even faces, but hoary masks that left only a narrow slit for the eyes, while all the rest was covered with a solid crust from the breath that escaped and immediately froze on these people's scarves, kerchiefs, and eyelashes. At any other time, Filippov wouldn't have passed up the chance to compose a life for these people, put a few vivid individuals into this sticky biomass, and be aghast at their loneliness in the faceless crowd and the impossibility of tearing away from it or even just freeing up their arms. He would have invented families for these unfortunates: dear ones not knowing anything and going out of their minds in their apartment, which was getting colder by the minute, and friends who kept dialing their number. He would probably have invented all sorts of things, but right now he was seriously worried about the phone signal being lost all over town. Therefore, he didn't see the bus, which had been waiting patiently at the stop up until now, finally shudder and get going, floating away into the fog like an awakened whale, while the crowd at the back doors sighed with one big shared chest, and the sturdy, the strong, and the decisive, who had begun to push, immediately cut through, and those who were weaker fell underfoot. But no one was looking down there, at them, anymore. The bus sailed farther and farther into the fog, and people were hanging out the unclosed door, like dark fungus growing on a tree, little by little falling off, disappearing, gradually restoring the bus to its proper bus look.

———

When the car stopped, Filippov started feeling sick. His face had become oddly cold from the inside while at the same time being covered with sweat. He thought the Demon of the Void might be just about to show up with his idiotic jokes, but he didn't. Apparently, he had no use for other witnesses. He preferred an audience of one: Filya.

In vain anticipation of his old friend, Filippov sat in the stopped car, his eyes bugged-out and his mouth wide-open. He was being tortured by an air bubble rising from somewhere in his stomach, which just couldn't escape. Rita and Tyoma turned around and looked at Filya sitting there silently, but they didn't say a word. Filya thought their looks seemed sinister.

"I'm not going anywhere," he said when he'd finally burped up the air that had paralyzed him. "There's someone standing in the dark there. Take me back to the hotel."

"Stop it," Rita said. "There's no one there. And the hotel isn't all that safe. What if they don't have electricity until morning? Come on. Don't make trouble."

She opened the door and hopped out of the car. Filippov knew there wasn't anyone outside, but he was already beleaguered by vague fears concerning Rita and her companion, who had yet to explain to him where they were taking him or why. Continuing to fight a sudden panic attack, he applied himself to the bottle, though it came up empty.

"Beast," Filya muttered, letting the worthless glass corpse thud to the floor. "You picked quite the moment."

Rita and Tyoma, both wearing tall felt-soled deerskin boots, easily climbed onto the high, iced-over porch, while Filippov lagged behind, flapping his arms helplessly. When he slipped over the icy crust in his stupid Kris Van Assche sneakers, he expelled a small waterfall with a dull moan. Judging from the taste of what Filya threw up, he hadn't digested the wine at all, it had just been poured from the bottle into the wineskin that was his stomach and then onto the icy crusts built up in front of the porch. Having served more than once in this sense as alcohol's beast of burden, Filippov wasn't the least chagrined. He waved his companions on and leaned against the railing in anticipation of a second wave.

"Very bad wine," he told Rita and Tyoma when he followed them into the pitch-dark entryway. "Real rotgut. Like 'Vera Mikhailovna' in her distant childhood."

"What Vera Mikhailovna?" Rita asked, shining her cell-phone display on Filippov's deadly white face.

"What was popularly known as vermouth. Except it wasn't."

"Let's get going." Tyoma pulled him by the sleeve. "My battery's running low. Anyway, it's probably warmer in the apartment."

It was really cold in the entryway. Not like outside, certainly, but the steam was pouring from Filya's mouth. He inhaled noisily, sniffed, rubbed his newly strange face with his stiff hands, glanced at Rita walking behind him and lighting the way for him with her phone, made a joke of tapping his frozen-hard sneakers like hooves, and from time to time bumped into enormous crates, which were crowding the entryway. At the same time, his directing reflexes automatically coerced his brain. Imagining—against his will—this pathetic procession as an onlooker, he saw either an anthill in cross-section in whose cramped passage three insects were now crawling with their little lamps, or a twisting dead-end burrow where rabbits were rustling, or the obstruction of a bottomless mine shaft where miners bereft of all hope were trying to break through to the exit, and these images made him feel more and more dreary, desperate, and angry.

"Are you telling me people still store their potatoes like this?" he muttered through his teeth after ramming into an ammo case with a hell of a giant lock and now intentionally kicking it.

"Of course," Rita replied, passing in front of him. "Where are they supposed to store them?"

"Right," Filya growled. "Don't go to the store. Listen, is this going to take much longer? Or are you waiting for me to break my leg?"

"Two more floors," Tyoma replied as he kept going up.

Rita followed him, but Filippov didn't budge. Waiting for the phones' pale glow to stop trembling past the railing of the next flight of stairs, he dropped to the floor and fell quiet between two potato crates. The smell of rotted damp earth calmed him. His fear retreated, and Filya pressed his cheek luxuriously to the rough side of the left-hand crate. The boards were unplaned, and he had this crazy urge to rub his face against them and grate his dark, incomprehensible fear to mush. *I'm not going anywhere,* he thought sweetly, then immediately hissed in pain. In addition to the abrasions, he clearly felt two or three splinters stuck in his cheek.

Above, Rita's felt soles slapped softly and quickly. Filya leapt to his feet and stood close to the crate, making indecent doggy movements.

"What are you doing?" Rita asked in amazement when she aimed her phone at him.

"Dominating." He turned toward her. "I'm the dominant male. These freaks have to know their place."

"What freaks?" The astonishment in her voice had reached its upper limit.

"The crates. If you knew what they've done to me. I've hated them since I was a kid."

"Cool, cool." Tyoma started to laugh, leaning over the railing above and shining his phone on Filippov, too. "Rehearsing a new show?"

"No. I'm searching for the meaning of life."

"Let's go. There's got to be more of it up top."

Ten seconds later they stopped by a flickering, leatherette-covered door, and Tyoma rang the bell.

"Shine a light on the lock," Rita said.

Putting away her phone, she jangled her keys, and for a few seconds in the stairwell there was almost total silence, which Filya alone broke. Whether it was because he felt like he was suffocating, or out of fear, Filippov was taking in cold air and exhaling it intently, with great noise and effort, the way you do at a doctor's appointment when the icy stethoscope is pressed to your chest and you're asked to take a deep breath. Filya was wheezing like an excited French bulldog. Rita was fiddling with the door and getting more and more irritated. Tyoma held his phone over her shoulder until the display went out and their whole silent threesome was plunged into the total darkness of the grave.

"Damn it," Tyoma said softly.

"What's going on?" Rita burst out, banging on the door with her hand. "Mom! Open the door, Mama!"

In the darkness, something clanged, there was a gust of long-awaited warmth, and in the opening before them yet another human figure appeared. Like Rita and Tyoma before this, the figure was holding a flickering phone instead of a flashlight.

"What took you so long?" Rita said, walking past the figure into the apartment. "I must have been fiddling with that lock for half an hour."

"How am I supposed to know who's doing the fiddling?" the figure said. "You were all so quiet."

She shone her phone on Filippov and Tyoma, still not suggesting that they come in.

"The lights went out about forty minutes ago," she said. "I'm afraid alone."

"The power's out all over town," Rita said, somewhere way back in the apartment. "Do you plan on standing there long?"

———

Rita's beauty could get Filya pretty worked up. If in the hotel—with full light still, but in interiors of somnolence—he'd thought he'd been abducted by some totally unearthly beauty, then here, he had enough trembling light from a pair of candles to scope out how matters in fact stood. Rita's beauty was more assumed than it existed physically. It shone from her; it was intended but didn't declare itself directly. It seemed her beauty didn't want to foist itself on anyone, as happens with proud but shy people who can't make up their mind or who find it beneath themselves to take part in the general merriment but also don't leave altogether, staying close by, haughty and reserved, as if telling everyone around them, "I'm here, and I'm someone to be reckoned with."

No, it wasn't about her outward appearance. In photographs where the authentic inner person is absent and only its shell is registered, or, even worse, the photographer's fantasy, she probably looked quite ordinary. Just a face, just a smile, her hair like hundreds and hundreds of others have. But when all this was set in motion, in steady, vital pulsation, in change, in constant development, in sliding, in the continuous, unbroken tango she led her life in, her features filled with the vivid meaning of the being who lived inside her and had simply not reconciled itself to this just a face, just a smile, and hair like hundreds and hundreds of others have.

Apparently in the hotel, Filya had instantly and unerringly caught the breadth of precisely this inner being and not the sum of her ordinary nose, ordinary eyebrows, in no way remarkable mouth, and heavyish chin.

You can't fool us, he thought proudly, delighting in his unfailing professional instinct. *We see everything.*

Actually, he couldn't rule out the idea that he simply had to explain to himself why he'd agreed to leave the hotel at the first summons of a young woman of such ordinary appearance. No matter what, his self-image must never suffer.

Something as nontrivial as his near stupor, however, didn't threaten this self-image in the least. Filya couldn't care less that upon entering a stranger's apartment he once again nearly passed out. If it hadn't been for Tyoma's quick reaction, he would have gladly stretched out in the big, cold entry and let strangers worry about his carefree drunk body.

Tyoma, who was standing on the apartment threshold behind him, grabbed Filya by the shoulders, put his arms around him the way a parachute instructor does with a first-time jumper, and dragged him through the endless entry into Hades. In the kitchen, they put Filippov on the small sofa in the corner, like linen ready for the laundry—with care, but a little distractedly—and went on with their lives, which Filya began to observe with interest, trying not to give away his viable status. Actually, deep down, he guessed he wouldn't be able to give it away even if he wanted.

In the kitchen, unlike the entry and, evidently, all the other rooms, it was warm. All four burners on the gas stove shone with a pale fire. The humming oven was open, and heat streamed out of it and through the kitchen in magical waves. From time to time, Tyoma would move close to a burner, lean over it, and warm his hands next to the oven, as if he hadn't come here in a warm and comfortable SUV but in that solidly frozen bus that the desperate crowd had taken by storm at the stop. Obviously, something else was eating him up. Rita was repeatedly touching the cooled and inexplicably ringing and clicking radiator, checking to see whether it was giving off heat, as if it might have started during those thirty seconds when she wasn't touching it.

Besides the gas in the kitchen, there were also a couple of candles burning, which allowed an attentive but at that moment not very lively Filippov to delve further into the secret of Rita's beauty. That was truly what he had on his mind, this beauty. It's what Rita herself, Tyoma, their friends probably, and in general, any observer who held his gaze on this young woman would have had in mind, except, by all accounts, her mother.

"Beauty, Filya, is like a nuclear weapon," Inga, with her amazing resemblance to the French film star, had once told him. "The whole time you've got this urge to drink, right? Hard to believe, but the temptation is probably just like what those guys have with an atom bomb. There's this crazy urge to throw it at somebody. All the time."

Filippov had recognized her the moment they carried him into the kitchen. Recognized her but decided to act as if he didn't for now. He became a crouching tiger and a hidden dragon.

———

Inga had changed, naturally. Even a turtleneck sweater and a thick top with a flirty hood inappropriate for her age couldn't hide what there had been no trace of before. Where twenty or so years ago a pair of listless nipples had swayed sadly, a real unreal chest now rose up. All the rest had been subjected to time's natural editing. Actually, plastic surgery had made its corrections in areas other than her bust. The captivating features of Isabelle Adjani still peeked through the Botoxing and face-lifts, reminding him of the eternally beautiful and what never was. But ultimately, after all these years, there was only a glimpse of those features now in Isabelle herself.

As Filya recalled the last film of hers he'd seen, he came to the conclusion that Inga had been lucky. In the role of a stupefied teacher, Isabelle had mostly reminded him of the fluffy owl from the Russian cartoon about Winnie-the-Pooh, whereas Inga could still very simply pass for an attractive Piglet—a little older and with a big chest, but nonetheless the same Piglet who'd hit Winnie precisely in his fluffy backside instead of the balloon. For what purpose this cartoon piglet had lured Filya into her kitchen was unclear. But it soon became clear that Inga had taken no part in his abduction.

"Mama, I'll tell him everything myself," he heard Rita's voice say. "Why drag this out? Let him answer for his actions."

"Rita, I've told you a hundred times already, he's not your father. Why did you drag him here at all?"

Now I'm in for it, Filippov thought. *A daughter out of thin air.*

"What makes you think he's not my father?" The girl's voice kept ringing.

"Rita, have you lost your marbles? Tyoma, take him back to the hotel."

"Inga Vladimirovna," he said, "you can't even imagine what's going on outside. It's bedlam."

"So? Because of some panic, this lush is supposed to lounge around my kitchen?"

I'm not lounging. I'm lying here politely and neatly, Filippov thought, not in the least offended by "lush."

Inga walked over to him and sniffed disdainfully, as if his sins would give off a physical stink.

"I read on the Internet that last year he tried to marry a dog in Las Vegas. He even dragged it to a priest."

Filya summoned all his strength to keep from melting into a happy smile.

"For PR, probably," Tyoma said. "Maybe that was when he put on the show about the dog. *Chestnut* or something. Anyway, it's an awesome idea."

"Why PR necessarily?" Rita interjected, also walking over to Filippov and leaning over him. "A person can just love animals a lot."

"Yeah?" Inga said. "And marry them?"

Easily, Filya thought.

———

Back then, in Vegas, he'd wanted to fix his karma. About six weeks before that, he'd accidentally strangled a dog during one of his shows, and after that everything had gone down the tubes. A promising project fell apart, an utterly reliable investor skipped out on him, rehearsals stopped gelling, and, most of all, out of nowhere, his member started bending. During an erection, this caused him genuine pain, and Filya started avoiding his muse of the day. The young woman decided they were getting rid of her, and in revenge she slept with his erstwhile and, naturally, triumphant investor, making a video of their sex and putting a clip on the Internet. That was when Filippov rushed to Vegas, to clear his head, if he could, and patch up his downtrodden status as predator. To make things worse, it started hurting down there not only during an erection.

The accidentally hanged mutt, who died because Filippov had made a mistake and given the order to raise a lowered grating with the animal tied to it, he would scarcely have remembered if not for the Indian fakir sitting on the sidewalk at the casino entrance. Bewitched by his fantastic turban, Filya squatted in front of him, complained about his life, and then offered him some bourbon from a paper bag. After that, they crawled from one hotel bar to another until morning, winding up somewhere on the outskirts of town among faceless little houses that looked like shoe boxes.

Closer to the desert, overhung by a sun as hungover as they were, it turned out that the fakir was not so much from India as he was Moldova, but at the same time was still quite adept at tweaking out karmic subtleties. Switching to Russian altogether, he explained that somewhere Filya'd done some badass shit and he had to perform a rite of cleansing immediately. Filippov tensed and remembered the show about the Marquis de Sade and the mutt that had died because of what he'd done. In the capacity of a humorous and, in one critic's opinion, witty counterpoint, the unfortunate mutt had portrayed a Hachiko waiting patiently for his master, "personifying an array of banal and predictable qualities the mere mention of which in our review would be a clumsy attempt to create an unforgivably crass trend."

The dog had been tied to an ornate grating so it wouldn't run away during the show, and it sat for two hours straight in the middle of the stage, yawning loudly from time to time at the actresses' bared bodies, which endlessly amused the big-city audience, tempted and slightly bored by sadism's cunning ways. When the grating went up and the dog, yelping, started to strangle, the viewers livened up and Filya, sensing success, wouldn't allow the assistant director to lower the mechanism until the very end, so the mutt hung four meters up for nearly half an hour. Had this been a poodle or a relatively small terrier, all would have ended well for the dog, too, but it was as big as a large German shepherd, and under that weight the noose around its neck pulled quite tight. For the first ten minutes the dog was still twisting, desperately beating the stale air above the stage with its paws, and in this time Filippov managed to drive out from behind the scenes two assistants who were in tears and begging him to spare the dog. But then the dog quieted down, and in the now tensely attentive hall there reigned a solemn—later Filya would call it "Wagnerian"—silence broken only by the stormy ovation. After the show, journalists said that the mutt was all right, that it had been taught that trick especially, but it was a one-off, a performance never to be repeated.

Restoring the karmic chain of events in the process of his purifying binge in Vegas, Filya decided not to put off the problem of his spoiled karma for later. There, on the outskirts of town, he picked up a pretty mangy stray, dragged it to a wedding chapel where you could register a marriage even sitting in your car at a special drive-through window, like at a McDonald's, and told the priest he wanted to marry the dog. According to the intention he'd shared with the Moldovan fakir, this should have concluded the dog theme in his life by restoring the ruptured balance and calming the karmic turbulence. Invited as the sole guest to the wedding ceremony was his journalist friend, who'd woken up by then and who Filya, who hated to travel alone, had paid, out of friendship, for his ticket from Moscow and his stay in a five-star hotel. As a sign of gratitude, the journalist was prepared to be sincerely enthusiastic about his escapades and to post to his Twitter feed about their adventures together in golden Las Vegas. Ultimately, the priest turned out to be hardheaded and heartless, but the tweets and photos of Filippov hugging the balding mutt in front of the chapel made their way onto the Internet, and the fakir reassured Filya, saying that even intentions were enough for karma, just so they came from a pure heart.

Recalling this story now, Filippov unconsciously touched his member and sighed, much relieved. This fellow had been quite all right for more than a year. Without taking his hand out of his coat pocket, he gave it another little harder poke with his finger, just to be sure—and it was as if his old sensations of pain had never been. Filya tried to perform his pocket manipulations in such a way that no one would notice his rousing state, but judging from his abductors' tense voices, he was the farthest thing from their minds. At that moment the stub of one candle snuffed out, and on the ceiling, directly above Filya, like in the first scene of *Macbeth*, three gigantic, monstrous shadows swayed. Filya's old love, who had surfaced from the past, her unattractive attractive daughter, and the completely irrelevant boy Tyoma clustered oddly around their last remaining candle, forgetting about their sloshed trophy from the big city.

———

The kitchen was getting chilly. Filya quietly formed a ring with his lips and exhaled to check whether steam would come from his mouth. Things hadn't gone that far yet, but not moving at all was starting to get uncomfortable. The wine was virtually drained, and the droning oven couldn't hold the warmth in that large kitchen, which was built for central heating. With the temperature outside a good forty below, and considering the aged window, which was closed far from as tightly as one would have wished, and the streams of icy air that made Filippov feel not only with his skin but also, as it seemed to him now, the entire surface of his stupid coat—given these difficult circumstances and, most of all, given his stillness, he was probably going to freeze solid and very soon. It was starting to sting a little. The trembling rose inside him first in tentative, timid waves, in spurts, sort of, leaving behind the blissful silence that arises in pauses between attacks of the hiccups, but gradually these pauses became briefer, the trembling more and more noticeable, and Filya more and more sober and unhappy. He realized it was time to get moving, come back to life, and prove himself, but some deep inner languor was compelling him to be patient.

Filippov was absolutely unfazed by the sudden appearance of a grown daughter. This news didn't bother him for a second. Truth be told, he didn't care whether the girl was lying or telling the truth, but his desire not to take part in a discussion on this topic was of catastrophic proportion. In his capacity as a lifeless body, all claims to paternity were received for now merely like general delivery, and whether the addressee ever looked at his mail or not—that was unclear.

"What will we do if they don't ever turn on the heat?" the bustier shadow was saying meanwhile.

"Mom, are you totally insane?" the rather less elegant shadow said in a nervous whisper. "We'd all freeze right here."

A demanding knock at the door reached them from the vestibule.

The shadows on the ceiling froze, hoping, evidently, that the knocking would stop, but the pounding started up again.

"Who is it?" Inga said.

"How should I know?" Rita said. "Go ask."

Filippov felt a wave of cold when the kitchen door opened for a couple of moments, and a few seconds later he heard nervous voices in the entry.

"Mama, I think," Tyoma said softly.

"Damn," Rita said. "What are we going to do?"

"It's all fine. Just keep quiet."

The nervous voices were getting closer. From the intonations, Filippov recognized Zinaida, and after her Pavlik as well. Inga was barely answering them.

"Where is he?" Zinaida repeated. "Tyoma! Do you hear me? Where are you?"

Entering the kitchen, they stopped next to the little sofa where Filya was playing possum. Crazy cold wafted off their backs.

"Zina, I told you, he's fine," Pavlik said.

"Get your things." Zinaida rapped out her words, paying no attention to what her husband had said.

"Maybe we should all sit down and have a talk," Inga said.

"Tyoma, did you hear me?"

"Listen, Zina—"

"Don't touch me! Get your hands off me! Now!"

Inga, who had barely touched Zinaida's elbow, immediately staggered back as if struck.

"Zina," Rita shouted, reeling from the sudden insult, "have you completely lost your mind?"

"No one's talking to you," Zinaida said. "Sit down and be quiet. If I see you next to my son one more time, you'll regret it!"

"Zina." Pavlik tried to pacify his wife. "The girl has nothing to do with this."

"But her dear sweet mama does! You came here instead of a hotel when you were running around on those little 'business trips' of yours? To this apartment?"

Filippov realized that he was probably never going to have a better moment to flee. Rising awkwardly to his feet while continuing to play possum, he slipped out behind Zinaida and Pavlik toward the door. The entry was totally dark, but he was able to feel for the lock and open it. Jealous Zinaida's voice reached him from behind in the kitchen.

Filippov could hear it for nearly two floors. He didn't close the door behind him, although, naturally, that didn't make the entryway any brighter, which was why, when he ran into the potato crates he could still come up with unflattering, cobblestone-hard epithets for Zinaida for a while. When he figured out that all the crates were lined up on his left, he pressed up to the right-hand wall and the voice above finally gave out. Like Filya, evidently it too had a hard time breaking through the pitch dark.

Darting out onto the front steps, Filippov was blinded by an unbearably bright light. Aimed right at the doorway were the headlights of some car parked opposite the front door. Filya squinted, but stinging tears still managed to spurt from under his flaccid, wrinkly eyelids. At that moment Filippov's eyelids felt like paper—paper some scamp had spent a long time plucking at with his pudgy and sweaty hands— as a result of which they were now totally withered, gray, indistinct, and sore. The merciless light easily pierced through this flimsy veil and pierced Filippov's skull all the way to the occiput.

Cloaked by clouds of white exhaust fumes, the car gave a snort and crunched into reverse. Its headlights continued to blind Filya as he stood on the front steps. The cold made the air squeak and crunch, like the ice chunks under the wheels of the departing Zhiguli. In the glowing gloom, something shone and sparkled, but this celebration only made Filya feel worse. His tears instantly froze in the corners of his eyes, his eyelids stuck together as if they'd been thickly spread with glue, his breathing seized up hard, and his ears, his bald spot, and his unexpectedly defenseless legs in their thin trousers blazed, truly scorched.

Ordinarily, Filya didn't even acknowledge that these parts of his body existed, that he was made up of them in principle. Not to say that he denigrated their significance. No, they simply didn't interest him, being somewhere at the outer periphery of his notion of himself; when he said "I," that "I" did not include his ears, bald spot, knees, or ankles. Though right now he assuredly felt that he did have all these and that everything was twisted up and just about to die. Like a ruthless felt pen, the cold had marked off each and every part of him, and his idle thoughts about his special talent's otherworldly essence writhed, turning into a panicked, trembling cloud of steam at his rubber lips, which were too cold to obey him.

Nevertheless, he knew for certain he wasn't going back. He had to get to his friend. It was time. Putting off the meeting no longer made sense. Back in Inga's apartment, Filippov had realized that it was useless to hide. The longer he delayed, avoiding an unpleasant conversation—the most unpleasant and difficult conversation of his life, as it now seemed to him—the more evilly this very life served him up surprises, and it was pretty clear that its supply of shit for Filya was unlimited. He had to see his friend, tell him the truth, and get out of this hellhole.

———

But for starters, it would be nice to reach his goal alive.

The right thing, of course, would be to go back to Inga's apartment and ask for some winter clothing, but Filippov was already Odysseus and his journey had begun. The deep had been opened wide by Poseidon, and their boats had lost the way back. Racing through forty degrees below zero from the embankment where Inga apparently now lived to the center of town was theoretically possible. Even not having a cap didn't scare him that badly, because the city remained, as it had been, an artless grid of a couple of dozen streets. If he tacked from entryway to entryway, from one courtyard to the next, with Rita's scarf, which no one had bothered to take off him, wound around his head, and covering his ears completely with his hands, then, more than likely, he might not even get frostbite. Well, if he did, it wouldn't kill him. And if he was lucky and there was no security intercom in any of the entryways, then everything would be hunky-dory.

All he had to do was plan a route so that he moved only among buildings and didn't end up in a vacant lot. He had to trace a dotted line for his small ships, a line that bypassed the Cyclops, Sirens, lotus-eaters, Circe, Charybdis, and whatever else was out there. With luck, he might be able to flag down a car.

Filippov was running on disobedient legs that couldn't always bend at the knees. He took the first ten steps quickly, his soles tapping like a cheerful tap dancer, but closer to the next building he started slowing down. His legs weren't moving as confidently, the cheerful tapping there below had quieted down, and then something crunched and Filya thought he'd broken his stiffened foot, although he didn't feel any pain. Given an anesthetic that powerful, you could probably have torn off his whole leg—and he would have noticed the loss only because he'd started stepping less often.

After a while, his running stopped altogether. His legs had definitely acquired the uncompromising flexibility of crutches. But a saving entryway was near. Already within the zone of visibility. It floated out of the darkness and fog like the rocky shore the sailor's eyes seek so avidly. Not the sailor who's in the warmth and on deck but the one on the fragile board rocking over the abyss and barely paddling anymore. In that situation, the main thing is for the wave not to wash over you and pull you back into the bottomless darkness.

I hope there's . . . no intercom . . . Lord . . . please . . . no intercom, Filya thought as he stormed the front steps.

The lumpy ice on the concrete steps seriously complicated his ascent. Slipping, Filippov distinctly imagined the dull and slight smacking sound of his skull splitting against the sharp concrete edge.

I think . . . I've forgotten how to walk. Damn . . . I'm like a zombie.

"Even worse." The Demon of the Void grinned as he waited for Filippov on the front steps, scarfing down ice cream.

"Up yours," Filya muttered, grabbing onto the railing with his bare hand, his whole body shuddering helplessly. "I don't give a—"

"Up yours! Care for an ice-cream sandwich?"

Filippov hobbled past the demon and pulled on the door. It would have been easier to open a strategic bunker sealed shut in the event of a nuclear attack.

"An intercom," Filya moaned.

"Are you an idiot or something? There's no electricity in the whole city. What intercom?" The demon laughed behind his back. "Sure you don't care for some ice cream? If not, I'll eat it all."

"But why is the door locked?"

"Are you stupid? It's frozen shut. Pull harder."

When you end up in a dark foyer, the best thing is not to fidget. The best thing is to stand very still right at the door and give a good listen. You never know who's going to be there besides you. Especially if you're in the Far North, where people's customs are simple and their actions swift and cruel. Especially if there hasn't been heat for two hours and God knows what is going on in the city. And if out of the darkness something big comes toward you, and you have absolutely no idea what it might be—you can just tell it's come close and is standing a few centimeters away from you, breathing—don't be afraid. Don't jump up, and there's no point shouting. You can't change anything now, and the best thing is to reach out, feel something shaggy and warm and indeed big, and then pull *that* toward you, bury your face in its thick, stinky fur, press your entire body to it, and try to warm yourself at least a little. And while all this is happening and a shuddering chill still pushes through you from time to time, in no event should you think about how this silent mutt managed to get into the entryway, bypassing the lobby's three doors set out like a labyrinth and on such tight springs that a moment's heedlessness could snap any dog in two. Especially such a big one. Especially such a warm one. Especially such a docile one. No need to think about this, just sit there, pressing every square centimeter of yourself to it, every square millimeter, every millisecond of your body, which is now living only in time, since space has vanished. You have to absorb this mutt, swallow it, dissolve it completely. And if all of a sudden you have a flash from a silent angel that this isn't just a dog that's come to you out of the cold and dark, not just thick, rough fur that stinks of urine, loneliness, and contagion, but that very mutt, that sad creature that last year fell still in the noose four meters above the stage—if all of a sudden you realize who has come to see you, then best of all is to bury your face in this warm, suffocating stench, find the trembling ear in it, and at last whisper what you have never once said: "Forgive me. I'll never do it again."

———

The mutt heard the steps on the staircase before Filippov, who still thought they were utterly alone in this cosmos, but the dog had already tensed up, inwardly pushing him away, and started to whimper. A couple of seconds later, he heard it, too. Several people were coming down the stairs, quickly. One of them was a child. He was asking something in a high-pitched voice strange in this darkness, but getting no answer. The others were too preoccupied with walking. In their reindeer boots, their steps sounded like a soft *toom-toom*, like startled antelopes moving through thick grass. Then a patch of light flickered. The person walking in front was carrying a flashlight. Silently, they descended the stairs, silently they walked past Filippov, who pressed his hand over the mutt's snout, silently they went outside, and only the child, round as a snowman in his clothing, managed to reach out in the direction of the mutt wiggling in Filya's arms. The last second before the door shut solidly behind them, the mutt desperately jerked away, scratching Filippov in the leg as it scrambled out into the lobby.

Filya's heart started pounding madly. He felt as if he'd been betrayed again by the perfidious Nina. He gave a sniff, scrambled to his feet in fury, and rushed for the exit. He wanted to catch up to the mutt immediately and punish it for its disloyalty—kick it, beat it, rip the heartless creature to shreds.

"It's in the car," the Demon of the Void hinted, gallantly holding the heavy outside door open on the front steps. "He's leaving with those people."

Next to the garage opposite the entryway was an Uazik enveloped in exhaust fumes. Metal bolts rumbled as the man in the bulky down parka shut the garage door. The headlights were shining straight at him, which was why he didn't notice Filya, who, after slipping dangerously a couple of times on the front steps, flew down the stairs, ran toward the car, opened the back door, and dove inside.

It was incredibly crowded in the Uazik, but he managed to shut the door behind him. Landing on the child, who was wrapped up in scarves and shawls, he heard someone squawk. Then the woman sitting next to him shouted, and then someone barked at him indignantly, and the very next second the man in the huge down parka tumbled behind the wheel in clouds of steam. Sensing something wrong, he turned his head, livened up like a bear disturbed in his den, and stared darkly at a now-quiet Filya. For a second, there was an oppressive silence in the Uazik.

"Follow me!" the Demon of the Void barked, opening the door and trying to drag Filippov out of the car.

"You can't come in here!" someone hissed out of the darkness. "Have you lost your mind? What if someone sees you?"

"Don't fall behind," the demon growled, pulling Filya by the arm.

His hand was so pleasant to the touch, so reliable, and it instilled such confidence that Filippov, not doubting for a second, latched on to it the way, as a child, he used to latch on to his mama's coat sleeve on a busy street, or on to a dolphin's fin in his dreams.

"Where are you going?" There was a rustling behind Filya's back. "Go back immediately!"

"Let's go, let's go," the demon said, hurrying him along. "Pay no attention. Every flea tries to act like he's the boss. Careful here. Watch your feet. There should be a manhole here somewhere."

In the pitch dark in front of them, something began to gleam. A deadly blue light seeped under the floor.

"Don't fall in," the demon warned him in a whisper. "First feel out the step with your foot, and then there's a ladder."

Filippov, who had been stumbling time and again and getting fouled up in heavy curtains, heaved a sigh of relief. The blue light was calming, like when he'd taken up photography as a child. It had been calm, right, and safe in the endlessly cozy bathroom where he'd locked himself in with his cuvettes and enlargers all night long, only the light from the lamp was red, not blue. But that didn't matter.

"Come on," the demon whispered. "Go down that way."

"What about you?"

"I'll follow."

Climbing down the ladder, Filippov heard below him a vague, but at the same time persistent, bustling. Something was snuffling down below and whimpering reedily. The sounds were barely audible, which made Filya feel cheerful and awful at the same time.

"What's there?" he asked the demon, leaning his head back.

"A little mutt," the demon answered, stopping on the ladder.

"My little mutt?"

"Who else's?"

"Why is it whimpering?"

"I don't know. It probably misses you."

Filya let go and jumped down, counting on landing directly on the mutt. He was convulsed with a desire to feel beneath him that living muscular flesh, to have it twist in his arms, struggle, and never break away, never run away. However, the fall took a lot longer than he'd been counting on. After flying for about a minute, he tried to remember what Alice had done during her own fall to keep from being bored, but nothing came to mind, so he started patiently awaiting his landing, occasionally fluttering his legs smoothly and handsomely as if he were swimming underwater.

"In fifteen minutes our plane will be landing at the Chemukbez Airport," the demon's voice announced in the darkness next to him. "Please bring your chair backs to an upright position and open your window shades."

To Filya's right, a round window glowed in the darkness, and through it, far below, twinkled the lights of nighttime streets.

"There's no such city as Chemukbez," he said. "I don't even think there's any such word."

"Should I Google it?" An open laptop now materialized on the lap of the demon, who was now sitting to Filya's left in a huge leather armchair.

"Oops, I guess not," the demon said. "Maybe we can Google something else. You, for example."

"I'm sick of me."

"Ain't that the truth. You were so young you didn't even masturbate that often. Then let's try Nina . . . Oh, no, we aren't going to have time. Hold on."

They both got a good hard jolt, then found themselves in a long corridor with a low ceiling lit by dim lamps painted blue. But the paint on some of them had peeled, and Filya squinted from time to time at the bright beams, which were as insolent as a street thug.

"This sucks," the Demon of the Void muttered behind his back, scraping the peeling blue paint off with his nail. "I just painted it yesterday. Stop, Filya. Look."

He shook his head contritely, pointing out a peeling lamp to Filippov.

"Did you ever paint the Christmas tree lights when you were a kid?"

"No," Filippov replied. "Just light shows. I'd solder lights onto a wire and paint them. These little ones."

"Did the paint run?"

"Well, yes. It heated up."

"I have to come up with something else." The demon sighed.

"Maybe buy blue ones to start with. They have those in hospitals."
The demon's face lit up.

"Not a bad idea. There, you see, it's good you came with me. You've already been useful. Come on, move along."

They walked down the cramped corridor. The farther they went, the lower the ceiling kept dropping over their heads. At first, Filya stooped over, then he had to lean over, and thirty seconds later he was already bending his knees and walking in a demi-plié. All of a sudden, this pose struck him as funny.

"Where are we, anyway?" he snorted. "We're wandering like embryos through tubes."

"You're just about to see for yourself."

There were voices up ahead. After going another twenty or so meters, Filya could at last straighten up, but he couldn't help squinting at the bright light. His head surfaced in some kind of a box missing one side, and directly in front of him, in blinding footlights, two people were running around a stage.

"Well, what do you think?" the demon whispered triumphantly, surfacing alongside him. "Do you appreciate the surprise?"

"What's this? The prompter's booth?"

"Hush." The demon pressed a finger to his lips and then lovingly ran his hand over the wooden side. "A classic. There's nothing like this now anywhere. Vintage. I gave it a little varnish here. Touch it. You'll know how nice it is. Although, no. Come on, begin."

Filippov gave the demon a sidelong look.

"Begin what?"

The demon nodded at the actors tapping across the stage.

"Prompt."

Filya shifted his gaze to the two poor flushed devils and shrugged.

"Are you an idiot or something?" he said. "I don't know the script."

The demon grinned cunningly and nastily.

"Yes, you do. You do. At least you don't have to pretend in front of me."

Filippov did know it, actually. He'd realized that after just a couple of lines. The fat, heavily made-up lady was Nina, and running after her from one side to the other was a balding scalawag with a glued-on mustache—and that was him, Filya.

"Why the mustache?" he whispered to the demon. "I've never had one."

"Doesn't matter," the other said, brushing him off. "Directorial license. You listen carefully. If they forget the script, prompt them. Look, look! This is going to be great."

The very large lady playing Nina suddenly stopped at the center of a rotating circle, and her partner, who had rushed after her, muttering his monologue as he went, flew at her from behind and immediately bounced back like a rubber ball. He took an awkward hop, stood up to his full height on stage, and made an idiotic face. Somewhere behind Filya, the audience burst out laughing, readily and with childish delight.

"A dandy!" The Demon of the Void elbowed him. "It's a good house today. Can you sense how they're responding?"

The actors were portraying that moment in his life when Nina had left him for good, for Venechka the aviator. At the time, Filippov had taken it very hard. He'd stopped leaving the house, stopped eating, stopped getting up off the couch. Basically, he'd just stopped. For a few days, he would wake up in his empty, silent apartment, realizing that this was still him, that this sad life around him belonged to him and no one else, and then straight through until night he would watch the boring low clouds and the layer of dust that kept collecting by the day on the floor like a soft blanket. From time to time, someone would call or knock at the door, but Filippov didn't feel like disturbing the dusty canvas. He beat two neat paths in it—to the phone and to the bathroom. Other routes didn't interest him. Roaming in his head were thoughts of his own insignificance and death's inevitability. *Why doesn't it happen right now since it's coming in any event?* At the same time, he found dying scary—not breathing, not lying on the couch, ceasing to feel that you're a zero, not being.

Periodically, he would walk over to the phone and stand next to it for a long time in order to be ready to pick up the phone in case Nina suddenly decided to call. Then he would change his mind. After more thought, he'd find himself back there standing and waiting so she wouldn't have time to hang up. But she never did call.

She came. She had to pick up a few things, including the dark-blue suit Filya's mother had sewn for her after their wedding. A Chanel-style jacket and skirt. A luxury object in those days. Things like that weren't sold in the stores. Not that much of anything was. You could get oil and sugar only with the coupons they issued. The sausage line started at four in the morning. The country was in approximately the same condition as Filya—falling to pieces. The thought of this gave him pleasure. He felt he wasn't alone. With gloomy interest he watched his "I" lose, one after another, the basic features that distinguish a living person full of strength from a sorry corpse, and this process in some ways resembled the way the greatest country in the world was melting away before his very eyes—greatest in size, at least. The republics were spinning and ready to fall off like withered leaves, while Filya, in exactly the same way, had lost his confidence in himself, his curiosity and pride, his hopes and aspirations. He was quickly losing all interest in life, and it was Nina's fault. With her betrayal—not that she'd had any such intention, of course—she'd found a way to take away something so important that he ceased to be himself and saw no point in moving on.

When she came for her suit, Filya didn't open the door. He was standing guard by the telephone again. When she opened the door with the key she still had, she found him in the pose of a startled deer that senses the hunter but still hopes the hunter hasn't noticed it yet. When he heard the key turn in the lock, Filya thought it probably would have been better to be lying down, to arouse pity, but when Nina walked in and he looked in her face, he understood there would be no room for compassion.

It was this scene that his good friend the demon now showed him. However, in real life everything had been different. Nina certainly hadn't bashed around the apartment from corner to corner, or tramped like an elephant, or pulled the navy jacket over her fat body, making it strain at the seams, or hollered in a wicked voice, or goggled, or sweated huge dark patches under her arms. She'd killed Filya slowly with her new unapproachability and coldness and the overwhelming desire she stirred in him, wanting to touch her with even the tips of his hesitant, trembling fingers. And, of course, there were no fat bodies there. It was hard to imagine anyone more elegant than Nina. In her navy suit, she looked as if the local master ivory carvers had carved her out of a piece of the thinnest mammoth tusk available. With her light step, she slipped past him—Filya having frozen by the telephone in his baggy black shorts—glanced into the closet, and asked what had happened to her suit.

Her voice really had changed. That much Filya did notice. Even now, he couldn't deny that he'd been amazed at this completely new timbre. It was like talking to some other person. Or rather, the performer was the same but was being recorded by someone else, like when a famous actor's voice is dubbed in the making of the film, after which it's very hard to fight the sense of alienation. As if some stranger had taken up residence in someone you knew, and was looking at you through his eyes. Nina had the voice of someone pushing doomed men into the abyss. That is, he understood everything and was prepared to offer a modicum of sympathy, but in fact he wasn't sorry for anyone because he was a professional. Someone had to do this job, after all.

The voice of the fat lady on stage wasn't even close, though. She was squealing like the hog they slaughtered for the November holidays in his grandmother's village. Her pathetic partner tacked after her like a rabid pug, and both of them tramped so hard that each step raised noticeable puffs of dust from the wooden stage floor.

"Got anything to drink?" Filya asked the demon.

"Dry throat?" The demon grinned readily. "Me, too. Just wait, the finale's going to be a killer."

"Are you pouring or not?"

"Sure. Of course. What's the matter with you?"

The demon opened a small door in a side wall, revealing a minibar bathed in blue light.

"I want port," Filya said. "It used to be called Kavkaz. The stopper was some kind of plastic and hard to get out."

"What filth. How about slivovitz? Or French mirabelle? They make that from plums, too. There's vilyamovka from Slovenia, a good pear moonshine. Very aromatic. I recommend it."

"We were drinking Kavkaz back then. The whole town was."

"Nostalgic considerations?" The demon nodded deferentially. "I understand. Here, hold this. I've already removed the stopper. Just don't breathe out in my direction."

Filya took the homely little bulging bottle with the crookedly glued-on label and waited for the demon to give him a glass.

"From the bottle," the demon explained, shrugging. "Format is format. You have to treat traditions carefully. That'll be four rubles thirty kopeks."

"Go to hell."

"No, it's true. The price is right here on the label—for Zone 3. I have no idea what that is, but order above all."

"You're full of it, evil one."

"I don't understand."

"Hot air."

Filya applied his lips to the sticky neck and, for a couple of seconds, froze in the pose of the plaster bugler at a Pioneer camp. The poisonously sweet, warm moisture poured down his throat, and with it long-forgotten sensations; drinking this filth was practically impossible, but it was impossible to stop, too. Five or six shuddering swallows guaranteed almost instantaneous intoxication, making it worth the urge to vomit that always came with Kavkaz.

"These are morons you've got," Filya said, tearing himself away from the bottle and spitting out something at his feet. "Your director's a moron, too. Forget that by the time of this scene, the navy suit wasn't in the apartment anymore. I'd given it away to a homeless woman by our front door."

He fell silent in order to take one more swallow, then spat at his feet again.

"Listen, what's floating in there? Something keeps getting into my mouth."

"State standards permit sediment in Kavkaz port," the demon replied in an official voice.

"Fine, it doesn't matter. Just look at these jerks. You've got way too much makeup, a discrepancy in their ages, and neither one of them has the right style. Who did the casting?"

The demon chuckled unpleasantly. "This I didn't expect!" he said. "You've been drawn to realism in your old age?"

"What old age?" Filya was offended. "I'm a little over forty."

"Oh, right, sorry." The demon composed a dreary face. "Old age is when you're ninety-five. I keep forgetting your cunning ways. 'Lord, he died so soon, so young, before he'd made it to fifty.' Tell me, when you were young, did people pushing fifty seem young to you, too? Especially girls." The demon smiled innocently and winked.

"Quit trying to distract me," Filya snarled. "We're talking about something else. I realize you have your grotesque and postmodernism now. Feel free. But you could have slipped in an extra number. Something musical, for instance, or with dancing. Something with passion to grab the audience. Like the slow waltz to Tom Waits's

ANDREI GELASIMOV

'Lucinda'—slow, rough, and tender at the same time. Get it? When you love that much, you feel like strangling them."

"Like this?" The demon pointed toward the stage, where a miserable-looking "Filya" was desperately strangling "Nina," who was panting like a bulldog.

"You've got to be kidding. You know what I mean."

"I thought you meant *that*."

"No one was trying to kill anyone."

"All right then." The demon smirked. "The thought didn't even cross your mind?"

"I'm talking about dramatic counterpoint."

"And murder."

"Can't you hear me? It could have a powerful effect. It could really get under the audience's skin."

"Didn't it work? Just look."

Filya turned his gaze back to the actress, and clearly and suddenly realized she was about to die. The fat woman was suffocating in the hands of her partner, who had sunk his hands into her and was hanging from her neck like a tick, obviously not intending to let go. His wild, hate-distorted face no longer looked idiotic; all that remained of the clown in him was the stupid makeup.

"This is all the DTs," Filya muttered through his teeth. "This isn't you there. It's the shakes."

"You're offended." The demon began to laugh quietly.

"I'm not here, either. I'm in Paris . . . No, on the airplane. I fainted in the lavatory and I'm lying there, while you're all nothing but pointless raving."

"Or maybe that guy with the Uazik hit you. Then this isn't raving but your dying visions. Maybe you've died."

The fat woman kept wheezing, rolling her eyes, and not tearing her wild gaze from the prompter's booth. She obviously had not anticipated how it would all end, and Filya was unspeakably sorry for her.

He realized that she, like he, was here against her will. She'd been lured here with a promise of God knows what, and now they were killing her, and no one in the audience had any intention of helping her.

Filya heard the audience in their seats start to sob and even weep. He felt sorry not only for the actress but for himself as well. There was little that reconciled him with life, but the scene the unfortunate fat woman had just played was an exception. He treasured it, knowing that at that moment, when he'd been suffering so much, he was a human being, and now, when they'd laughed so wickedly at this, he was hurt that they were taking this scene away from him forever, and that he had no more strength, no more of the arguments that until now had helped him stay reconciled with his life. He felt he was losing it right now and forever, and because of that he wept inconsolably.

"There, you see?" The triumphant demon nudged him in the side. "And you said it wouldn't affect you."

"Go to hell," Filya squeezed out.

"Punk!" the demon exclaimed. "Fuck you!"

With a quick strike, he jabbed Filya first under the ribs and then across the face. The second blow made him lose his balance and go flying downward. This time his fall was brief. After hitting the back of his head against the iron radiator, Filya opened his eyes and saw the guy with the Uazik leaning over him. He was holding a flashlight.

"Stay right here," the guy said. "Don't go outside. Or in other people's cars, either. You might get hurt."

Filya looked around and realized he was being dragged back into the foyer. His left temple and side ached.

"Did you beat me up or something?"

"The next time I'll just kill you. Sit tight, I said."

The guy spat and walked toward the door. After opening it, he stopped for some reason, then went back to Filippov, now sitting on the floor, pulled the shaggy cap off his own head, and tossed it in Filippov's lap.

"Take it. Otherwise, you'll freeze to death."

"Thanks," Filya mumbled huskily.

His throat was totally dried out.

A joke was one thing, but he had to keep moving. Filya didn't like it when his dreams got that objective and tangible. It ruined his mood. He let reality seep through only in the mornings and put up with it until his first swallow of wine. Everything that happened after that was comfortably pushed back into a matte vagueness. Now, due to the lack of alcohol, he had no line of defense, although of the two evils he did prefer reality. His dreams annoyed him with the dismal passivity that was always his lot. In his dreams and nightmares, Filippov never played the leading roles. He was constantly being manipulated by some outside force. If for that reason alone, he now had to get up and keep moving.

"I'll just go," he mumbled, pulling the other man's hat down deeper. "I'll just go where I want."

Fumbling in his coat pockets for his lighter, he pulled it out, flicked it a few times, and blinked at the orange column of flame. The lighter lit up almost nothing near Filya, but he didn't care. The main thing was that something alive was warm in his hands. Turning the little wheel to the left, he halved the flame but didn't let go of the valve until the metal ring got so hot it burned his thumb. He flicked it again and tried to hold the valve in such a way that he wasn't touching any metal, but a few seconds later that became impossible. Also, he had to conserve gas. Even the small light and warmth the lighter gave out could come in very handy on his odyssey. His hometown—Filya could tell—had by no means put all its cards on the table. New surprises could be expected at any second.

Going out on the front steps, he saw the silhouette of the dog waiting for him. The mutt jumped to its feet, started whimpering in brief screeching bursts, and then vanished under the building. In the darkness and fog, Filya knew he might just be imagining this, of course, but in the entryway, after all, it had been much darker, so Filya was forced to admit that more than likely he did in fact see the dog.

"Mutt, I am so sick of your shit," he grumbled, cautiously descending the steps, which were bumpy from patches of ice. "What do you need?"

Looking under the building, he tried to see anything at all between the posts.

"Hey," Filya called out. "Where are you, you creature?"

In the icy, dark abyss, something started to move. Filya slapped his hand against the concrete cover overhead.

"Come here! I'm not crawling in there."

A few meters away, he once again heard barely audible whimpering. It was strange hearing sounds like that from such a large mutt, but what wasn't strange tonight?

The cold had already started squeezing Filya in its pitiless vise, so he had to decide: either go back to the entryway or onward, toward whatever was whimpering there beyond the posts. Filya swore quietly, but creatively, clutched his coat collar, and ducked into the reverberating darkness. In any case, he needed to go to the other side of the building. Circumventing this hulk and its seven or eight entryways would have taken much more time, which meant warmth.

Reaching out with his free hand, he moved for a while quite boldly between the posts. His feet had finally stopped slipping, and he could focus fully on his bat instincts. Which, actually, he turned out not to have. Clearly his echolocation skills were deficient. After he'd endured a painful bump to the shoulder a couple of times on the corner of a gigantic post, he became more cautious and decided not to rely on his hearing anymore. The whimpering mutt was constantly changing location, so ultimately Filya said to hell with the search and kept moving toward the opposite side of the building.

In any other situation, he would have compared these wanderings in the pitch dark among huge squared-off pillars to a lab mouse running through a research labyrinth, but he didn't have a shred of irony left right now. Along with everything else, the cold in his quaking body had paralyzed Filya's sarcasm, his don't-give-a-shit-ism, his wicked sense of humor, and, apparently, even his very ability to think. Viscous bursts of what previously would have been thoughts were crawling around in his head from place to place, like freezing snails, refusing to coalesce. He imagined he'd ended up under the belly of the dinosaur from the Steven Spielberg movie; he recalled the jungles and the warmth. He grinned at the fact that here, under these buildings, in summer, was the very best place to hide from the unbearable local heat, and to pee, and to drink vodka from the bottle before the school dance, or to wait for Nina to come back from rehearsal and then run after her into the foyer.

"Why the fuck did I come here?" he managed to get out, trembling. "I should have . . . there . . ."

After crashing into a few more posts, he realized that in searching for the mutt, he'd lost his sense of direction and possibly might have been going not crosswise but lengthwise to the building, like a fragment of plankton traveling in the body of a whale. Or like a Jonah swallowed not in the Mediterranean but far beyond the Arctic Circle, and he'd gotten a freshly frozen whale, not a warm and cozy one, like the primary source had suggested was his due.

With unbending fingers, Filya tried to flick the little wheel of his lighter. He might as well have tried to flick with a prosthesis or a totally paralyzed hand. Even putting the lighter back in his pocket was a problem. A familiar problem, but a problem. It was at this moment that someone gave him a slight push. He spun around in fright and flung his arm up but found no one there. Whatever had pushed him had apparently jumped back and in the next instant started to growl slightly.

"It's you, you creature," Filya muttered, lowering his hand and still not finding anything. "Come here . . . How are you doing?"

He tried to remember what they'd called the hanged mutt from the theater, but other than the idiotic name Spot, nothing came to mind. He couldn't get a whistle out, either. His stiff, frozen lips just wouldn't make the right shape, and instead of a summoning whistle, all that came out was summoning steam and a light hum. Nonetheless, that was enough. The mutt pushed him with its nose again, ran off a couple of steps, and resumed whimpering. Filya moved toward its sounds. The pushes were repeated, Filya went where the whimpering was, and soon after realized that they were in business.

"We're getting out," he mumbled, encouraging either himself or the mutt that had taken him under its patronage. "Come on. Good boy. Come on."

Once they'd gotten out from under the building, Filya realized that without the mutt he probably would have died. On that side, access to the posts was almost solidly covered over with sheet metal. There was just a small opening left, about a meter and a half wide, and it was toward this that the good mutt had led Filippov, as if toward a permanently unfrozen hole in the icy deep.

"Hey! Where are you?" Filya called out softly as he leaned, wiped out, against a tottering, crooked fence.

But the next second, he jolted alert when, two hundred meters from the building he'd miraculously just emerged from, an arrow of light slashed through the darkness and retreated infinitely to the left and right.

"Is this hell?" He exhaled. "I'm sick of your theater."

The closer he got to the flaming line, and the more solidly the icy gloom thickened around the fire blazing up ahead, the more powerfully his certainty grew that all this was once again a joke of the Demon of the Void, and nothing but no end of trouble and deception awaited him. Approaching the flames, rising a meter and a half up, Filya was already sure that the shadows cast in front of the fire were, of course, devils, and they had stoked it to give him a scare. Naturally he didn't want to make their task any easier. He had virtually no doubt that this was a taste of the next chicanery from his old friend, so he had nothing to fear.

"Come on, come on. This is all just your imagination . . . Nothing but sucky Buddhism," Filya muttered, picking up his pace. "An illusion. There's nothing here. I'm not here, either. That means I can do anything I want. Damn, it's cold."

He felt the warmth from about twenty meters away. Physically, this was probably impossible, however he not only saw the flame but literally felt it, even at this distance. Like a child's breathing that only the mother leaning over the cradle can discern, warmth touched Filya's masklike face, and he realized he was about to start crying again. He had no reason for tears this time, but the heat mounting with every step he took evoked mechanical changes in him, as if something inside were melting, disintegrating, and these changes had compelled him to pull his cold-contorted hand out of his coat pocket and convulsively wipe his cheeks, which were burning from either singeing or thawing.

"Good going, you devils," he said, teeth chattering, as he walked up to the fire.

Not one of the figures stirring the firewood under the enormous pipes turned around.

"Hey," he exclaimed quietly, stung that once again he had the smallest role. "I'm here! Have you completely lost your minds?"

Two beings wearing huge sheepskin coats, those work caps with the white strings, and bulky quilted trousers straightened up and stared at him silently. In the smoke, he could barely see their faces. Fiery flashes danced on their shoulders like diabolical epaulets, and their sheepskin coats had an oily gleam. Everything around them was hissing, crackling, droning, and gurgling. The snow underfoot had turned from a concrete-hard layer into a dark, smacking mush—dripping and coiling up in steam. Filya could feel his sneakers start taking on moisture, and the smoke stung his eyes. After standing there immobile for a couple of seconds, the two in sheepskin coats went back to what they were doing.

"Hey," Filya repeated indignantly, setting off a painful coughing jag from choking on smoke.

"Take him to the truck, Vitalik," one devil told another. "He must have run away from the nuthouse. He's about to buy it."

In the cab of the truck where the devil named Vitalik firmly seated Filya, it was light even though the lamp somewhere overhead went out as soon as the door slammed shut. The flame blazing ten meters or so from the truck filled the cabin with an even orange glow, and Filya now had an unimpeded view of the devil assigned as his escort. Vitalik was a short, sturdy fellow, about twenty-five years old by earthly measures, without any visible signs of infernality. Thickset and solid, he didn't have any horns under his cap, and despite the dirt stuck to him, he was quite tidy, neat, and well formed, like a scar after a successful operation. The first thing Filya noticed was his raptorial Tatar nose, pointed at the tip and flat as a manta ray at the bridge. Then Filya's gaze stopped at Vitalik's upper lip, which had once been torn and hadn't healed evenly. The overall picture was completed by his manner of holding his head. In this Vitalik resembled a well-trained fighting dog—slightly pressing his skull to the ground, he didn't look from side to side, just straight ahead, but very confidently and with total indifference to any possible danger.

From time to time, the flame opposite the truck picked up a merry and nasty strength, forcing Filippov to instinctively shield his eyes, which was why he didn't notice Vitalik come up holding a sandwich and plastic cup, which he silently held out to his charge. Then he reached under the quilted vest lying behind him and fished out a bottle of vodka. Filya sank his teeth into the sandwich so he could hold the dancing cup with both hands. Tasting the sharp sausage, he remembered he hadn't eaten in nearly twenty-four hours. His mouth instantly filled with saliva, though he couldn't have said with confidence that the sausage was the sole cause. The cup in his hands was still shaking hard, but this was no problem for Vitalik. Apparently, he'd encountered a similar phenomenon in his practice before, so he easily hit within the range of Filya's oscillations, calmly and steadily filling the cup as if it were resting on a granite cliff. The vodka poured serenely into the white plastic, which turned a gentle pink in the flame's reflected light, and Filya, like Pavlov's dog, salivated more. The smell of diesel hovering in the cab also contributed its mite. The jacket smelled of machine oil, but in combination with the sausage in Filya's mouth and the rosy vodka splashing quietly in the flimsy cup, smells nearer and dearer than these he could scarcely imagine at that moment. The huge world frozen through and through shrank to the size of the warm cab of a funky old GAZ-66, and in this world, peace reigned.

After waiting for Vitalik to fill the cup about halfway, Filya nodded, took the sandwich out of his mouth, and drank. The vodka was cheap and warm, but it was just the ticket. Basically, everything that was happening was exactly what needed to. Filya had landed in the right place.

He felt his strength returning and realized that everything was going as it should, in the best of all possible ways. Stylish restaurants, stylish friends, stylish scandals, showings, receptions, and trends—everything he was supposed to like because that was what other people at the top, inaccessible to others, liked—all that flew off into the black sky with the sheaf of sparks beyond the windshield, and he was left with the firm sensation that he wanted to like only this—the cab that smelled of diesel, the plastic cup in his hand, and the devil Vitalik, who'd already poured him a second round.

Filya took a bite of the sandwich, inhaled sharply, and fell still, trying not to miss the slightest detail of his happiness. He wanted to make the moment last, register it, keep it for himself forever. He didn't care that everything that was happening was just an illusion, that none of it was real. This was the best "none of this is real" ever.

"Go on, drink," Vitalik the demon said in a low but insistent voice. "Not too long ago we had a guy get thrown off the bridge."

Filya opened his eyes.

"What for?"

"He bogarted the package."

After Filya drained the cup a second time, Vitalik filled it for himself, pinched off a crumb from the sandwich, gave it a sharp doggy sniff, and downed all he'd poured in one swallow.

"Why do you just have a cap on?" he asked on the exhale. "Decide to kill yourself? Or are you on the lam? Have they got you stashed at the hospital?"

He clearly thought Filya was crazy, which was why he used a tone of voice that, in his opinion, suited a conversation with someone who'd lost his mind.

"You want me to give you my jacket? Look, it's padded." Vitalik pulled out the tattered jacket from behind. "It's warm. A filthy son of a bitch, but warm. Put it over that coat of yours or you really will buy it."

Filya was certain, in turn, that he was dealing with a devil, which was why he behaved accordingly, trying to say as little as he could. He thought it best not to draw more than necessary attention from one of these brethren. You never knew what kind of compromising material it was collecting.

"What do they feed you there?" Vitalik went on. "Do they give you vodka?"

Filya shook his head and silently started pulling the gifted jacket over his expensive cashmere coat.

"Well, drink up then. Hold on, I'll pour some more."

Filya readily took the empty plastic cup from him and waited for the refill.

"It's a good thing you showed up." Vitalik winked at him. "I'll just sit here with you a little bit. We've been lighting these bonfires all over town for five hours. I'm bushed. And I stink of smoke."

He sniffed his coat and laughed.

"A firefighter, damn it. I can't go home."

"Why?"

"My woman doesn't like me stinking of smoke. Gives her a headache."

Filya sniffed the air and shrugged. "I don't smell it. Why are you making these bonfires? Did the boss demons tell you to?"

"Who?" Vitalik gave him a slightly worried look, then scratched his forehead under his cap. "Oh yeah, right. Them. The heating mains—they say they have to be kept warm. If they burst, we'll have a city frozen solid come spring. Everyone'll have to flee to their dachas and villages. They'll have to take you fools away somewhere, too. They can't abandon you, after all. And these demons, yeah, they're really harassing us."

Vitalik grinned and wearily wiped his soot-stained face.

"My granddad's for sure as nasty as an evil spirit," he said. "Today he didn't get some money from a customer. He and his brigade sat there across the river for three months or so. They had everything nearly done, and then this accident at the power station. A rolling blackout. He never did get paid for his shoddy work. All the brigades were called into emergency headquarters. But he was building Danilov a house. He had an agreement with the bosses that he wouldn't even show up at his regular job. He wanted a lot of money. I tell him, 'You'll get it tomorrow. Your Danilov's not going anywhere,' and he chucked me out to the heating mains for that. Really angry. He loves money that much."

Filya vaguely remembered he'd already heard that name today—Danilov—and more than once even, he thought, but doubts concerning how this grubby devil could know a real person quickly evaporated.

Who knows what tricks they get up to. The thought came to him smoothly and very cozily after his third cup of vodka. *They disguise themselves, the demons. They came up with this accident. Heating mains.*

He looked at the fire, entranced, while Vitalik continued to share his resentment toward life.

"After the army I wanted to go into professional boxing, but my granddad told me I shouldn't. My mother obeys him, and she forbade me. She says, you'll be a foreman like him and get an apartment fast. But I once saw that boxer Kostya Tszyu at the airport in Tyumen. Can you imagine? Like I'm seeing you now. Just walking along, smiling. What does this have to do with an apartment?"

Vitalik sighed and poured himself another splash of vodka. Everything he was talking about sounded very much like the life of an ordinary person, but Filya had firmly decided that the devils weren't going to trick him today.

"So tell me," Filya said, "could you kill a person?"

He was sure that if Vitalik was a devil, he absolutely would try to deceive him, acting like a human being and saying you shouldn't kill, or something like that. But Vitalik was wilier.

"Probably," he said without thinking too long. "It just depends what for."

"Well, in a war, for instance."

"I could in a war. There'd be an order. I wouldn't be guilty of anything."

"What about without an order? Out of jealousy, for instance. Could you kill your wife if she cheated on you?"

Vitalik sniffed and braced his whole self, instantly resembling a huge cobblestone. "Listen, why are you asking these questions?"

"I want to check something out."

"Well, I'm about to check you out across your blockhead with a left jab. Do you know what mine's like?"

"What?"

"Slaughter."

"Then don't check me out," Filya said sensibly. "I believe you as is. You wanted to go into professional boxing. I get it."

"What do you get, you dumbass? What are you talking about, anyway?"

Vitalik started for Filya, and his left hand was already trembling suspiciously, as if taking aim itself. As a boxer, Vitalik could have given some poor slouch a thrashing in the ring, not out of hatred for the human race but just like that, unintentionally. Looking at his trembling, Filya thought there'd been no point putting the question outright. He should have taken it gradually. He could have started with something random, not necessarily actual premeditated murder. Or even better, he should have asked whether Vitalik could have, say, left a sleeping person at a dacha while knowing that someone had closed the flue by accident and the person probably wouldn't wake up because the firewood hadn't burned up completely—with the proviso, naturally, that this person had caused him the kind of pain no one ever had before.

But Filya had let go of all these diplomatic options, and so now, with a heavy heart, he gazed at the trembling left, which, according to Vitalik, was just plain slaughter.

"Wait." Filya was trying to gain a little time. "Come on, let's talk like human beings. You can talk like a human being, right?"

"Yes." Vitalik exhaled, his extremity, which had already acquired a rather formidable fist, not ceasing to tremble, though.

"Well, you see . . . ultimately we're all human beings. We like chocolate, ice cream, and dogs. We're moved at the sight of the sunset or when we hear a child's laughter, and all these other marvelous little things. Those are what make us human beings. I mean, ultimately normal, understanding, and even pleasant human beings. But . . . what if I don't want to be a human being? Don't want to like all these lovable things? What if I want to be a monster? What's wrong with that? There are so many monsters among us, and at the same time we're a great country. Are you going to argue that we're not great? You could say the same thing about America, and Europe, too. Even tiny Norway has its monsters."

Filya fell silent, staring at Vitalik and waiting for his reaction. Vitalik didn't answer right away, but his fist lost its confident outline.

"What are you talking about, anyway?" he said.

"I'll explain in just a second," Filya said, hastening to build on his success. "You see, for a long time I was sure I didn't fear my own death. I mean, even now I'm sure, but sometimes, you know, you find something that makes you uneasy. After all, even General Krakhotkin backed out. So much for being a freethinker and an atheist. He pulled his stepdaughter's hair three times before he died. Believe me, that was out of fear, not just malice. I'm not even an atheist. True, I'm not entirely sure what I am, but I don't think it's an atheist. For example, I believe in you. And not only you but all of you, in general." Filya gestured toward the firelit figures clustering in front of the truck radiator.

"In who? Us?" Once again, Vitalik started snuffling ominously, but Filya was going great guns and wasn't afraid of him anymore.

"In devils," he said firmly and even rather merrily. "You thought I wouldn't guess?"

Vitalik snickered, then pulled off his cap, scratched his head, and took a deep breath. "Damn it, what am I going to do with you? I have to get back to work. I don't know about leaving you here alone like this. You might do something odd."

"Can you put in a little word for me?"

"What little word?"

"Well, that there's this little man here, and he agrees."

"Agrees to what?"

"Everything," Filya said. "Playing for the other side. Any collaboration whatsoever. I'm ready right now. You realize I'm totally wasted. I don't understand a thing. You live and think there's some meaning to all this—it's even fun at first—but then everything gradually starts getting murky. This original sin, this senselessness, and in the end, death."

"Yeah, buddy, you really got put through the wringer. You didn't take any pills before the vodka, did you? Were they giving you anything at the hospital?"

"No, I'm serious. Talk it over with whoever fixes things there. I'd switch over. Happy to. I could even be of use. See, I understand there's an evil principle inside a man. Not only don't you have to tempt him, he'll commit evil gladly. And this has nothing at all to do with silly Eve taking the apple from the serpent but with the fact that man feels like it—evil, I mean. The more, the merrier. Because basically all the rest is meaningless. Money doesn't make you happy, success is bait for one-celled animals, and love is impossible, because each person tries to get the upper hand to be sure of being the one people like more. Life is meaningless. All motivations are just candy wrappers, the wrapping paper from cheap irises, and they sell us this bill of goods as if we were Papuans to get us to dance at their ritual bonfires. You know, I feel like I've been gulled, taken for quite a ride with this topic. As to life . . . as to living—it's great. It seems to me that thinking about death doesn't have to mean being gloomy. It has much more to do with trying to avoid deceit, which I've had more than my fair share of. I just don't have the strength to stand it. Life should be . . . not beautiful." Filya sobbed, gasping from the vague melancholy that had descended on him. "Say the word. I'm begging you."

How exactly Filya imagined this "switch," in what form, and who Vitalik should "say the word" to—all that, whether from the vodka or agitation, was a little foggy in his mind, but the main thing Filya felt at that moment was that he was utterly sincere. For the first time in a long time, he had spoken directly, seriously, and frankly about what had long lain like a monumental weight on his heart.

"Will you help?" he said.

He looked hopefully at a stunned Vitalik, who, obviously not knowing how to react and not understanding half of what he'd been told, was tapping his fingers on the steering wheel and making quiet *poom-poom* noises with his lips. That went on for thirty seconds probably, until a racket started up outside. Somewhat calmer, Filya turned toward the side window to see two more devils dragging a big dark animal by a rope toward the fire. The animal was resisting, and from time to time the devils kicked him meanly, and then he yelped piercingly, his resistance weakening as he skidded against his will closer and closer to the fire.

"What's that?" Filya said.

Vitalik leaned across him, looked closely into the blaze-torn darkness, and burst out laughing.

"Ah! That's the guys. They caught a mutt. It's been running around here all day. They sat down by the fire for dinner, and it dragged off our chicken. I told them they should have eaten in the truck, but they said they didn't all fit. They're mad now. It's going to go badly for the dog."

Filya groped at the ancient door handle, which was covered with a piece of quilt, turned it with a creak, and fell onto the snow.

"Where are you going?" Vitalik shouted after him.

But there was no stopping Filya now. Scrambling to his feet and chasing down the devils dragging the dog, he leapt from behind onto the one holding the rope, grabbed on to his coat, and toppled with him into the slush melting from the flames. The second devil froze for a second, but in the next, rushed to his comrade's aid. Filya felt a firm kick to the shoulder, but the quilted jacket Vitalik had given him softened the blow. Reaching for the hand holding the rope, he ripped it away and the devil let the dog go. Filya rose up a little, and his whole body shuddered from the second kick, this time to his gut, as he tugged on the rope.

"Run!" he exhaled along with the cloud of steam and the smoke that was already stinging his eyes.

The mutt evidently recognized Filya. Instantly evaluating the change in situation, it rushed toward the devil getting ready to kick a third time and knocked him off his feet by leaping onto his chest.

"Stop," Vitalik yelled, running up from behind.

The mutt started breathing harshly and heavily and, before Filya could straighten up, dragged him into the darkness.

"Run," Filya repeated sweetly, and not letting go of the rope, sailed after the dog, away from the heating mains flaming in the night.

———

Running through a frozen city, with the temperature a good forty below, where they have suddenly and for no known reason turned off the heat and electricity for a certain period, is best done in the company of a large dog, in which case you don't feel like an aimless grain of sand in the ocean. You're not a nonentity, a banality, a cliché in a boring conversation. On the contrary, you're cheerful and aware. You're proudly hurtling toward where destiny calls, and even if you're as tiny as a grain of sand, you're still free to dream. Those of you who don't find these kinds of comparisons grating might compare yourself to a spermatozoon. You're the manifestation of pure will. You're not just running; you're soaring above the city, like the bride in the Chagall painting, and your intended, who has taken on the guise of a big old mutt, keeps pulling you on, there, below, pawing the ground diligently. Soon you should be flying over your old school, the street that leads to the river, the monument in the shape of a T-34 tank, where in the summer everyone went to pee—you're flying toward where the most important thing happened, prepared to plunge into sweet memories—when you distinguish someone's steps behind you. You pick up speed and slip over the city a little bit faster, but the steps are obviously not lagging behind. Whoever's pursuing you isn't running anymore but truly racing, and you sadly guess your wonderful flight is about to be cut short. You don't feel like being beaten up by angry devils thwarted in their dreams of boxing, and you start going all out, so fast that your mutt can't keep up with you, gradually giving up, breathing heavily, becoming a burden. Nonetheless, you don't let go of the rope. You'll never abandon a friend again. You'd rather die, so you slow your pace, turn around, and proudly await your inevitable fate.

"You've got to be joking," Vitalik the devil, who has finally run you down, says wheezily, transforming before your eyes into your very own Demon of the Void. "Who lit a fire under you? Who do you think I am? Usain Bolt or something?"

Recognizing his tedious alter ego, Filya for the first time was happy to see him. Filya's beating had been put off, and as a result of all his recent transactions he was the proud owner of a warm cap and a thick quilted jacket, which, apparently, no one was planning to take away.

Filya, still gasping, could barely talk. "You couldn't shout?"

"You try to shout that far."

The demon bent forward and stood there, like a runner after the finish line, one hand resting on his knee, the other pressed up against his right side, as if something were jabbing him there. He was breathing even harder than Filya.

"You think it's easy running after you in all this?"

The demon was wearing his enormous sheepskin coat, a silver fox cap with earflaps, and white felt army boots.

"Where'd you get the threads?" Filya asked, catching his breath.

"You have to know where to look."

"Give me your boots?"

"You ran off."

"I could freeze my feet off. My soles are already splitting."

"Go fuck yourself."

"Punk."

"I'm no punk. I'm a demon. And you're a moron. Get out of my way. You could get run over."

Past them in the murky gloom, shining their fog lights, crawled innumerable Uaziks, Land Cruisers, and Nivas. Filya hadn't noticed them before, just as he hadn't noticed that he was running along the shoulder of the road rather than on the sidewalk.

"Where are they all going?"

"Out of town." The demon finally straightened up. "They have dachas. Stoves and stacks of firewood. They're thinking they'll sit this out."

Filya opened his mouth wide to get rid of the icy crust pinching the lower half of his face. He tried to get his finger under it but realized it was useless.

"Did Peter go, too?"

"Who's Peter?"

"My friend. I'm on my way to see him."

"I don't know about that. Maybe so. What would keep him in the city? The apartment radiators are going to start bursting soon. Does he have a wife and kids?"

Without answering, Filya climbed the snowdrift separating the thoroughfare from the pedestrian walkway. Sinking up to his knees in the deep snow, he still pulled the mutt, which readily leapt in and got stuck, too. The snow, which had gotten under Filya's trousers, didn't bother him one bit. His feet were already so numb he didn't feel anything. After floundering in the snowdrift for a couple of seconds, he climbed out onto the sidewalk, tugged on the mutt's rope, and stubbornly continued onward.

"Hey, wait up!" the demon exclaimed. "What if he's not home? Maybe it would be better if we went back."

Filya didn't stop.

"Damn!" the demon said. "I'm coming with you!"

He sailed over the snowdrift with demonic ease, caught up to Filya, fell into step with him, and was silent for a few minutes. They were walking hurriedly down the drift-heaped dark street, past a row of dead streetlamps. Time and again, the cars crawling past them on the right would catch the frozen streetlamps in their headlights and also the rare, bedraggled bushes so crushed by the frost that not everyone would guess that these poor things were bushes. The buildings looming up to the left of the road were more guessed-at in the opaque fog; only flickering matte spots at various heights spoke to the fact that these were apartment buildings and there were still people inside them.

"Listen, you were so cool with them," the demon, who was bored in the cold and silence, said, striking up a conversation at last.

"With who?" Filya pushed out, convulsively clutching the earflaps of the donated cap at his throat.

He found talking difficult. His lips no longer obeyed him, due to the thick icing of his beard, his mouth barely opened, and the words themselves—due to the chilled air's special resilience—took so much effort to push out it was like trying to speak with his face pressed up against a big piece of jellied meat. The Demon of the Void couldn't have cared less about these obstacles, though. He thirsted for company.

"Who?" the demon said. "The repairmen, that's who. The ones you took the dog from. As for switching sides, you gave them a pretty nasty shove. By the way, what side did you have in mind? In which direction?"

Filya didn't answer, furiously stamping his stiffened soles on the sidewalk.

"Are you interested for real? Or just asking for fun? Because if you're for real, you're asking the wrong people. I could make inquiries. I have some connections. But you have to decide concretely, not on impulse. You had that impulse, after all, didn't you? Yeah? A change of heart?"

Filya didn't say anything.

"I wonder why that is." The demon wouldn't let it go. "Your life seems to have worked out. Enough money, easy work, traipsing abroad back and forth. How do you put it? 'It would be wrong to complain'? That's it exactly. Wrong. You, you beast, have lost all shame."

"Get lost," Filya growled.

"Me get lost? Are you sure I'm dragging around after you because I want to? Maybe you're the one giving me no peace. You're the one who's been searching for me everywhere. You're afraid to take a step without me. You sense the void in you, and you dream of filling it. That's why you invented me."

"I didn't invent you," Filya rasped.

"Yeah, sure you didn't." The demon laughed jeeringly. "That's bullshit and you know it. You're bullshit, you jerk, and those guys by the heating main were right to say you're crazy. Time to stick you in the psycho ward if you didn't invent me. You're dangerous to those around you, especially dogs. See? You're doing in the second one right now. Look, it's done for."

Filya turned around and saw that the mutt he'd been dragging along by the rope could barely move its paws. Filya hadn't noticed, overcome by the mission of reaching his goal. He had kept striding forward stubbornly, practically dragging it behind him.

"You're going to strangle a dog again," the demon said. "Murderer."

Filya went over to the mutt, which immediately lay down on the icy sidewalk. He leaned over it and tugged its paw. The mutt raised its head, grinned, and, exhaling a cloud of steam, licked his hand.

"Let's go," Filya muttered. "You'll freeze."

The dog tried to get up, but its legs wouldn't hold it.

"Two–zero in your favor." The demon grinned behind him. "Basically, you should move on to larger animals. Given your record, dogs are on the small side. Time to be wiping out horses. That seems more respectable. Then you can move on to elephants."

Not answering him, Filya bent even lower, picked up the heavily breathing mutt, and lifted him off the sidewalk.

"Oh," the demon drawled. "Concern for one's neighbor. What a wonderful, what a marvelous deed. Are you aware that Mother Teresa's being accused of dubious political ties and money laundering? Lay off maybe? What's the point in starting? No one's going to thank you anyway."

Filya grabbed on to the dog even harder so it wouldn't slip out of his stiff, recalcitrant arms, took one step, then another, and realized he couldn't carry the mutt for long. His hands, now out of his pockets, were burning up. He hadn't felt his feet in about ten minutes. Moving them was getting harder and harder. His knees were refusing to bend, so he walked as if he were on stilts. The mutt in his arms noticeably complicated this pathetic semblance of walking.

"Ditch it," the demon said, trying to persuade him. "It's not your dog. That one gave it up for real more than a year ago. I guarantee you."

Filippov had the quickly mounting feeling that he was walking steeply uphill rather than across an even horizontal surface, and with every step the ascent got harder and harder. The dog, probably no

more than thirty-five kilos, was weighing down his numb arms more
and more, as if pig iron were being injected into it by the second and
soon it would weigh nearly a ton. Filya started being thrown from side
to side, and several times the Demon of the Void had to prop him up
so he and his burden wouldn't collapse into the snowdrift along the
shoulder.

Not quite aware of where he was or how far he had to go, Filya was
desperately attempting to make out in the fog, which was pierced by the
headlights, at least some signs of familiar places. But not only was the
city using its usual winter camouflage against him, it had also changed
maliciously and cardinally in the years Filippov had tried to forget it.
Where his instincts told him there should be a couple of wooden two-
story buildings, where the drama theater dorm used to be, a boundless
wasteland now gaped, and the site of the kindergarten built in Stalin's
day had been taken over by a multistory apartment building lit by
anxious lights. There were also new intersections that this street simply couldn't have had before. Running parallel, right at the city limits,
there was a branch of the river a couple of kilometers long—even Filya
couldn't have been mistaken about that—so the descents now leading in
that direction made no sense. They should have run into a fairly broad
channel, but they did not, and this confused him badly.

"The year before last they built a bridge there," the demon explained,
not asking why Filya had stopped at the next intersection and was looking around in terrible doubt that he'd strayed in the wrong direction.
"Now you can drive across."

Once the demon said that, everything around Filya more or less
fell into place. In any case, he recognized one building a hundred
percent. But in the windows of the second-floor corner apartment,
red and blue flames flickered, as if there were a police light flashing
inside. A little closer to the building and you started to hear bizarre
siren-like wailing.

"Did someone drive a car in there or something?" the demon conjectured slyly.

Filya couldn't have cared less about the demon's new bag of tricks. He was already climbing the steep staircase leading straight to the apartment as fast as he could. As far as he remembered, there had been no such staircase before and you could only enter the building at the front, but right now the last thing he was going to ponder was where it had come from and what that sign was looming over the front door. He had to find a perch somewhere—even if it was in this apartment, even if it meant seeing the exact spot where the sofa had once stood by the wall.

Filya had only been here once, and he'd really hoped he'd never have to come back again.

"Just look how merry it is here," the Demon of the Void shouted in his ear the moment they'd crossed the threshold. "Par-tay! Go with the flow!"

Lowering the dog to the floor, Filippov slid down the wall beside it, stuck his hands under his arms, and stared dully at what was going on. He was still shuddering from the freezing cold, which was why he now moved away from the wall, so he wouldn't hit his head.

In the apartment, which had been transformed from a residence into a fur store, a small but energetic bash was in full swing. Two people holding toy semiautomatic weapons were banging away with their guns nonstop, firing light bursts at a third person, who was pulling fur coats off hangers and quickly stuffing them into huge sacks. The multicolored flashing lights, which picked the robbers' figures out of the darkness, the crack and wail of the plastic toys, and the long-awaited warmth that brought tears to his eyes transformed this scene, as the still not entirely thawed-out Filippov experienced it, into an unexpectedly colorful and absolutely otherworldly carnival.

"Looks like they just robbed Children's World." The demon gave him a nudge. "What are you sitting there for? Don't be a lump. Over there—look. Reindeer boots."

Filya turned his head with difficulty and saw several rows of fur-lined footwear under the window. Before, there'd been an ancient bureau there. He remembered because that was exactly where he'd once noticed his own record collection, which Nina had taken when she'd left him for Venechka. All the LPs were rare, some bought from speculators for an unthinkable price, but that wasn't what ticked off Filya most when he saw his own vinyl there. What killed him wasn't even the fact that they were in some old-lady bureau—in his sense of the world, rock and roll and antique junk could coexist without offending each other much, although the very fact of old ladies' existence now made him feel nothing but disdain for those days. But, no, that wasn't what hurt most, either. What really stung, what struck and enraged him most painfully of all, was that Nina had commandeered his life. Not just commandeered it—she'd dragged it over to some punk stranger who'd had her on his granny's ancient sofa right by Filya's records and probably been crazily proud to have such a trendy squeeze. When Filya had met her, Nina liked to play songs by Ottawan on her pathetic cassette player and could hop around her room to them for hours. She didn't know Deep or Heep or Pink Floyd or Dire Straits—basically she had no idea of normal music for normal people. She was a dark horse, albeit a very attractive one, and it was he, not some jerk from the port, who'd shone some light on that horse.

"Time to get yourself some footwear," the Demon of the Void told him. "They're about to go for the boots. They'll clean this place out, and you'll get nothing."

The apartment had once belonged to Venechka the flight engineer. Or rather, to his granny, who for unclear family reasons had lived in town and not at the port. This was where Nina had run after Filya's phone rang and there was silence at the other end. The silence was a signal, a summons to copulate on the old sofa while his granny was taking a mud cure in Saky, in the Crimea. It was for this apartment that Nina had ultimately left Filippov, because the mud cure didn't do much for Granny, who six months later freed up that housing permanently. Regarding her death, Filya, still furious, decided it was he and his hatred that had buried that perfectly innocent old woman, but when he was thinking more clearly he came to the conclusion that if anyone was going to die of his black hatred then it was Venechka, and since it hadn't affected him, then there was no dark power worth regretting and repenting.

"How long are you going to mope?" the demon hissed. "They're just about to rake it all up."

But Filya was only now thawing out. He didn't have the strength to get to his feet. And even if he did, he probably wouldn't have risked it. All of him below the waist was so frozen through that it wouldn't bend; it seemed so fragile it was sure to snap at the merest wiggle of a leg. His long-frozen feelings ought to have snapped off in exactly the same way, presumably, and naturally he wanted them to, but instead of them smashing with a light ringing and melting immediately, leaving behind dirty, short-lived puddles, his aged experiences got stronger by the minute and gathered force, and Filya panicked that he was done for.

For some reason he tried to imagine what the rest of his life might have been like if Nina hadn't started running here after those hang-up calls. He thought about two sons and a daughter, about how impoverished and cheerful their life would have been, the five of them, and how little they would have needed, about how in the mornings in bed he and Nina would tell each other their dreams of war with the Chinese, and the children would bring in their potties and settle in around their bed to listen. One of them would suddenly start straining and turn bright red, and the others would start shouting that it stank. Then they'd all sit together in the kitchen and watch patiently while Nina fixed pancakes for them, because of the hundreds or even thousands of people he'd met in his whole life, she was the only creature created for him alone, and he'd known that from the very beginning.

When she cheated on him, what hit Filippov hardest was that he stopped perceiving life in its pure form. Nina was always a part of everything he did, to one degree or another. No matter what he was doing, everything was multiplied by her voice, her shoulders, her ability to lie down beside him so that their bodies were meant to be together from the very start. Nina gazed out of every film he tried—and failed—to watch. Every song was about her. She flowed from every conversation. Every passerby knew about her cheating.

"They've already gotten as far as the cash box." The demon nudged him.

Filya raised his head and saw that the attackers had indeed abandoned their sacks and were working on the cash box. They'd had no luck opening it, so they just ripped it out with a crowbar, bolts and all.

"Let's split," his demon said, trying to hurry him up. "Grab some shoes and let's go. The cops are sure to drive up any second. Or the owners."

"The alarm isn't working," Filya told him. "Split if you want. I'll stay."

He really didn't feel like going. For so many years he'd studied how to avoid any memories of Nina or what happened to her in the end, but the moment he walked into this apartment those memories ceased to frighten him. Once again, Filya was at her graduation, which he abducted her from by crawling into the school through the window in the men's second-floor restroom. Bored by the commencement speeches, the stuffiness, and her pompous classmates, she gladly agreed to run away then, and in the morning they found themselves in his best friend's apartment. After talking away about this and that, they somehow imperceptibly fell asleep in the two uncomfortable arm-chairs facing each other, and a couple of hours later they woke up simultaneously, as if they were already connected by a special disturbing thread. Nina hadn't yet stirred, had barely opened her eyes, when Filya opened his. They were sitting motionlessly, examining each other, and he couldn't find a single thing about her that was foreign to him. Before falling asleep, Nina had thrown a huge flight jacket belonging to Filya's friend's father over her graduation dress, and she looked like a ruffled sparrow that had found its way into another bird's nest. Lowering her feet to the floor, she slipped out of the jacket, huddled, and slapped her narrow bare feet toward the open balcony door. Filya turned his head to see her but immediately flinched, blinded by the sun hanging over the railings. Following Nina out onto the balcony, he looked down on the deserted streets filled with bright light, at the street-washing machine creeping solitarily behind the shimmering arc of water that made no sound at this distance, and then shifted his gaze to her white, badly rumpled graduation dress and for a couple of seconds was blinded. Nina—delicate, almost weightless—soared above the city, her arms thrown back, doing something with the shock of dark hair spilling over her shoulders and raising her sleepy, smiling face to the sun. She was so transparent that he nearly reached out to make sure she was real. Nina yawned, stretched, and shook all over, the way a senseless just-awakened kitten shakes, and Filya realized he couldn't live without her.

"Great liar you are." The demon interrupted Filya's memory. "You lived just fine without her for twenty years. And not badly, by the way. Come on, get some boots on. These jerks have finished."

The burglars had already managed to pry the cash box open and rake up the money, and now they were carrying their sacks outside, jostling in the doorway, quietly swearing at Filya, who was sitting on the floor, and sending waves of cold at him from the door that kept opening. The batteries in their toy semiautomatics had obviously run down, so they were now using their phones to light the way.

"Get up." The demon gave Filya a shove. "There are still a few pairs of reindeer boots left. Come on—shake a leg, or else you'll be like the pilot Maresyev."

The demon chuckled and sang in his awful voice:

"Gangrene, gangrene! The pilot's lost his legs!"

Filya made his way over to the window, struggled to pull off his stiff sneakers, and stuck his right foot into the narrow mouth of a boot. That foot got stuck, and Filya hopped on the other, lost his balance, and fell to the floor. One of the two burglars who'd just come back in turned around and shone his telephone in Filya's direction, but the other immediately shoved his shoulder.

"Fuck it. Let the stupid bum get himself some more clothes."

"Stupid bum," the demon repeated gloomily as soon as the robbers had slammed the door shut again.

"I can't pull them on." Filya could barely speak. "They're really narrow."

"They're women's, idiot. Feel there, it's all beaded in front."

"Which are men's?"

"Where there's no beading. Has the cold fried your brains?"

While Filya was dealing with the boots, the demon was staring out the window as if expecting someone. The mutt rose from where it'd been set down by the door and, its nails clicking across the floor, went over to Filippov, who felt the dog breathing on the open patch of skin at the back of his neck. It tickled and felt strange. His whole life, no one had ever once breathed on him so hotly. On the exhale, the mutt whimpered barely audibly, switching at times virtually to ultrasound. Shivers ran down Filya's back, but he kept trying to pull on boots that just wouldn't pull on, while the demon stood perfectly still by the window, merging in the darkness with everything else in the room. Had

Filya not known for certain that he was standing there, he simply might have thought there was no one in the burgled store but him and the badly injured dog.

"Tell me, are you happy now?" the demon asked softly. "At exactly this moment?

"Right now?" Filya said. "I think so."

"Well, you're a fool. A person doesn't have to be happy. Happy is an unproductive state. Everything most important in their lives people do when they're utterly unhappy. War, the agonies of creativity, the pain of loss—what about those comes from happiness? Only in moments like those is a person capable of the impossible. Therein lies the secret of greatness."

"So now you're the one talking about people." Filya grinned.

"Well, yes."

"Have you heard? All people aren't people. Some just seem to be."

The demon started chuckling. "Thinking about yourself? By the way, have you got those boots on there?"

"Yes."

"Good. Because time's up."

The demon shrank back from the window and dissolved completely in the darkness. The next instant, outside on the stairs, came the sounds of tramping and loud voices. The door to the store opened wide and several men tumbled in from the street. They were all wearing down parkas, reindeer boots, and shaggy caps. They were all shouting loudly, and two were waving baseball bats.

"I'll tear the snakes apart!"

"They've run away!"

"No, there's one left here!"

The blinding flashlight rested like a train's headlight on Filya sitting helplessly on the floor. He squinted and for some reason raised his hands over his head. The mutt bristled and started growling.

"Waste him!"

One of the bat-wielding men took a couple of steps forward, raising his weapon over Filya's head, but the mutt lunged at him, digging its claws into the attacker and knocking him over before rushing at the next one, who waved his bat clumsily, hitting the mutt with a glancing blow, and leapt aside. The others took a step back.

Desperately looking around in the flashlights' dancing beams, Filya saw a pile of dog furs abandoned by the robbers. Scrambling straight for them on all fours, he pulled his lighter out of his pocket, flicked it, and waved the fire over the fur pile.

"I'll set it on fire!" he shouted, breaking into a scream. "I'll burn it all! Get the hell away!"

The guys in the down parkas froze in dismay, and those seconds were enough for Filya to jump to his feet and make a dash for the door. The mutt rushed after him.

Outside they fell head over heels down the stairs, flew across a sidewalk and snowdrifts, and then jumped out into the thoroughfare. There were significantly fewer cars now. Filya ran like a swift Arctic deer through the frozen nighttime city and thought about happiness. In his mind, joyous, disconnected fragments were bouncing around about how good it was that he'd been able to run away again and how wrong his demon was in saying that a person didn't necessarily have to be happy.

"He does. He does," Filya repeated chaotically to himself. "There has to be happiness. Otherwise, you can't go on. I've got warm, comfortable shoes now, and I'm happy because it's not at all slippery running. My feet are almost warm—Lord, I can feel them. I'm running, and this sweet mutt is with me. We're all unhappy only because we have too little, and others always seem to have more. Roman Abramovich has yachts. Paris Hilton has freebie millions. But if you think about it, does Abramovich have it so easy? Probably not, really. A lot harder than everyone else. I'd definitely lose my mind. Although, more than likely, I already have. Doesn't matter. Even if I have . . . I want to be happy. I'm giving myself permission. Because none of us has the right to consider himself unhappier than Abramovich. Or Paris Hilton. Poor little rich girl. That's not even a name . . . just some address."

In that vivid moment of insight and unexpected understanding of happiness, he totally rejected his usual complaints about life and humanity. He no longer felt a void. His usual boredom suddenly receded, and everything that had seemed banal and flat acquired new meaning. Friends, celebrating the New Year, tedious children whom you had to compliment routinely to their stupid parents, the saccharine attitude toward old people—everything that usually weighed him down, that he'd always fled like the devil does incense, in the extreme case agreeing merely to pretend to be a normal person—all this had ceased to irritate him, and he felt that he was prepared to reconcile himself with this, and all this not only would not evoke in him the usual bile but quite the opposite, it would fill his void, and he would stop feeling like the half-inflated covering of a downed dirigible.

At the entrance to Peter's building, Filya again had to pick up the mutt, which could barely get up the iced-over concrete stairs. Once it had limped after Filya into the foyer, the dog immediately dropped down on the floor.

"What's with you, little buddy?" he murmured, leaning over the mutt and flicking his lighter. "Don't give up. Just a little more to go. We're nearly home."

The mutt guiltily beat its tail against the floor and dropped its head on its front paws. Filya had to carry the dog to the fourth floor in total darkness. He kept bumping into the ubiquitous potato crates and snagging his quilted jacket on the railing, but he wouldn't let go.

Next to the door to Peter's apartment, he paused for a second, because he wasn't sure whether it was the right door, and then he kicked it twice and listened.

"Please let him be home," Filya whispered to the dog. "Please let him be here . . ."

He heard firm, confident steps behind the door.

"Thank God," Filya said. "Now . . ."

The door opened, and on the threshold glowed the figure of Peter holding a huge, obviously souvenir candle.

"Petya," Filippov said. "We're freezing. Let us in."

Peter looked at Filya in silence, at his coat sticking out from under his soiled jacket, at the mutt in his arms, at his burns.

"I came to see you in person," Filya went on. "I wanted to tell you everything myself. You see, they don't need a designer for this show. They just want me."

"Go to hell, you creep," Peter said.

The next second, the apartment hallway behind his back was lit up by a flickering overhead light. Somewhere in the far rooms children were shouting ecstatically. Peter blew out the candle and closed the door in Filippov's face.

Curtain.

INTERMISSION

THE DEATH OF NINA

At the very end of August 1986, Nina and her flight engineer moved to the dacha. His granny had been sent back from Crimea for a short time to gather her thoughts before dying, so the lovers had to vacate the apartment, which smelled of old-lady medicines anyway. Venechka didn't want to bring his beloved to his parents' place in the port district, so they decided to wait out his granny's demise at the dacha.

In the North, of course, August isn't exactly dacha season, but if you've got the urge, and if you fire up the stove in the evening, you'll last until mid-September. The frosts coming on at night, the steam from your mouth when you cautiously peek out from under the blanket in the morning, the ice in the washbasin, sex very quickly and always clothed—all of that makes things tense, of course, but on the other hand, there's the added bonus of no mosquitoes. In the summer in the North, those creatures perform the same function as piranhas in the rivers and ponds of South America: they eat everything alive.

The nature of the North gives substance to its will in mosquitoes. It doesn't give birth to them; it becomes them. It takes on their image, acquires billions of stingers, and has its revenge, stealing by the liter everything a man has stolen and collected, everything he's plundered with his greedy paw. By comparison with the ordinary mosquito, which politely sucks blood from the resident of the middle latitudes, the Northern mosquito looks like a Titan of antiquity. It doesn't nibble; it bites off whole chunks, descending in droning, furious waves and capable of leaving a devastated, almost scorched wasteland in its wake.

But in August, a blissful silence ensues. Nothing is buzzing in the air, nothing is beating at the windows, and nothing is trying to drink you dry. You become trusting and gentle, like children drifting off to sleep. Nature curls up and purrs quietly, preparing for its five-month winter and total—virtually cryogenic—freeze. Everything gets slow. The river gleams unctuously and sends its dark mass along with obvious strain. A yellow birch leaf torn off by the slow wind at noon reaches the ground only toward nightfall. Everything in nature is already conserving energy; everything is moving twice, five times, slower than usual. Even the thoughts in your head move from place to place like sleepy grass snakes. Whatever you started thinking about on Tuesday won't get thought through by Saturday. The pain you felt on Monday now will never let you go.

Filippov knew that Nina and her flight engineer had moved. Basically, he knew everything about her—every movement, every new dress, every trip to the movies. He wasn't even following her or standing outside her windows and peeking in. He just knew. He sensed her like an animal, like a wistful vampire. He'd died, but he kept sensing her. Nina had left him in the early spring, and by August he was as good as dead. He walked, ate, and responded to questions, but he was dead. His life had not just lost its meaning; it had filled with antimeaning. Everything was turned inside out. Antithoughts roamed around his head, and antifeelings swarmed in his heart. He had turned into a vampire.

Loitering around town, Filippov—as you'd expect of a vampire—was aware neither of himself, nor time, nor space. Unable to stop, he moved his physical body from street to street, from sidewalk to sidewalk, but the part of him that had been him before, the part he'd once referred to as "I," remained immobilized, lost somewhere in the dusty, lifeless city, and Filippov had absolutely no intention of looking for it.

From time to time, he came across Nina's fresh trail, her imprint in the air, the invisible impression of her shoulder, her slender neck, her jawline, the echo of her laughter. When he sensed that she'd recently passed by somewhere, he froze, stamped in place, bellowed something, and tried to remember, but her trail would gradually dissipate, dissolved in the crush of endless passersby, and Filippov would calm down, forget what had upset him, and wander on.

One day, while doing a piss-poor job of pretending to be alive, he wandered all the way to the dacha. For a long time, he stood examining the stack of firewood. Then he watched a birch and counted the falling leaves. He listened to the music coming from the house and tried to figure out how many people were in there. When he saw Nina's silhouette in the window, he was vaguely reminded of something and he grew sad, snarled softly, wandered around the house, and tripped. When everyone came outside, he guessed he needed to hide. He perched by the bathhouse. In the dark, they didn't notice him. From their conversation he realized the flight engineer was flying away. Filippov waited until everyone got in their cars before he straightened up to full height. Then the cars drove off.

The windows weren't lit anymore. There was just a dim bluish nightlight on the porch. Filippov dissolved completely in the darkness. He went up the wooden stairs, a silent blob, and cautiously pulled on the door, and it yielded. Inside it was warm. And somewhere very nearby was Nina. Filippov knew she was in the house. He could smell her even on the porch. She hadn't gone anywhere. She'd stayed here to wait for her flight engineer. Alone in the empty house.

Filippov stood in the transparent light from the nightlight, listening to his instinct: Nina was sleeping in the farthest room. He quietly passed through the dacha, easily orienting himself in the darkness, as if he'd been there many times. He stopped next to Nina and for a long time listened to her breathing. Then he began breathing evenly, conscientiously copying the light sounds of her sleep, trying to coincide perfectly. He wanted to find out what she was dreaming. But he didn't.

Shifting from foot to foot in disappointment, he touched her hair on the pillow. Her hair said, *No, she's not yours.* With a heavy sigh, Filippov nodded, agreeing, and left the room. On the porch he stopped again and looked around. It was important to remember what Nina saw, which objects she was reflected in, what she touched most often. He was jealous of the old refrigerator's handle.

He took a teaspoon off the table, stuck it in his pocket, and was about to leave when his eye fell on the stove flue, which was firmly wedged in the blue wall. Filippov opened the stove door and glanced inside. The wood had obviously not burned down completely. Blue flames trembled on the glowing firebrands. One of the guests had shut the chimney a little sooner than he should have; as he left, he'd simply flipped the damper, on automatic pilot, and obviously had forgotten all about it. Or else Nina herself had done it, out of ignorance.

Filippov stood beside the stove, listening to himself. There wasn't a sound inside him. Not a single thought, not a single movement, no feelings whatsoever: total silence. His antithoughts and antifeelings were silent, too. He left the house, carefully shut the door behind him, and descended the front steps. A couple of days later he learned that Nina had died from smoke inhalation.

ACT THREE

ABSOLUTE ZERO

Noticing that the door handle had turned, Rita, who seemed to have been waiting just for this, leapt from the sofa, ran to the door that was already starting to open, and slammed it shut. Just to be sure, she threw her whole body against the door and screwed up her eyes, as if preparing to deflect a true storming, but whoever had been wanting to come in did not renew his attempts.

"Have you totally lost it?" Tyoma said. "What if it's kids there?"

"It's not kids," Rita replied, peeking behind the door. She leaned over to pick up a package that had been left on the threshold.

Tyoma got up from the sofa and walked over to her. He felt like continuing the conversation that had broken off, a conversation he found very disturbing, but Rita was already going through the package's contents.

"Just some drawings," she said thoughtfully. "Dead bodies . . . Dead bodies . . . More dead bodies . . . Look! A whole mountain of dead bodies. And designs."

"Who was it?" Tyoma asked. "Who brought them?"

"The wife of the artist who came with us. I don't remember her name. Lilya, I think. Yes, Lilya. Exactly. And she had some Chinese last name. Mama mentioned it yesterday in the car, but I forgot it. Listen, why does he draw dead people? And so many of them, too."

"Li-Mi-Yan," Tyoma said.

"Oh-ho!" Rita tore her eyes away from the drawings and looked closely at Tyoma. "How is it you remembered that?"

He shrugged. "I like unusual names."

"Or maybe you like pretty girls."

"That, too." He nodded. "Except that girl has three kids. And her husband's a famous artist. He works with your father a lot. You were wrong not to let her in. She just wanted to get the drawings to him. Must be some new project."

"She'll live. I have to talk to him first. I'll give them to him myself when he comes to. Come on, quit changing the subject. Did you get to appreciate this beauty?"

Instead of answering, Tyoma suddenly started coughing.

"Caught a cold or something?" Rita said. "I told you, don't breathe outside with your mouth open. This isn't Moscow. You have to use your scarf. Breathe through your scarf."

"Doesn't matter," he said. "You know, in my opinion, you're the one here who appreciates mature beauty. And I wasn't trying to change the subject at all. We were talking about Danilov, basically, and why he brought you here before the emergency."

Rita furrowed her brow slightly and bit her upper lip, moving her lower jaw in a silly way. She knew Tyoma liked this habit of hers, found it touching, which was why, not one bit embarrassed, she exploited it when the situation called for it.

After a second's pause, Rita sighed, shuffled the depressing drawings a little more, pretending they still interested her, and finally summoned the nerve to say something. But at exactly this moment from the next room, access to which she was guarding so jealously, there was a brief moan and then indistinct murmuring.

"Hang on."

Rita finished her shuffling and slid toward the second door. She tossed the drawings on the sofa in passing. Tyoma settled into his seat with a grim face, crossed his legs, put his hand on the file but didn't open it, and kept looking at Rita's back as she froze at the half-open door.

He could tell he wouldn't be able to hold on to her. She would slip away from him as lightly and airily as she'd just seeped into the next room, but he was angry not so much at this as at his own helplessness, his inability to counter this inevitable loss that awaited him with anything firm, clear, and masculine. He had no idea what a man should do in this kind of situation, and even though he liked to think of himself as a man, he realized he didn't quite measure up to that status yet.

Tyoma was angry at himself, his parents, Rita, and his age. He despised Danilov, and was repulsed by his house and even his couch, which was so soft to sit on. He hated this whole flea-bitten Northern burg where his parents had dragged him with servile readiness from his native and beloved Moscow, specifically because of Danilov, because he'd told them to, because he had the power to give orders, could command their fates. And the fact that Rita—the sole being who had reconciled him to the new place—had now become so slippery. Danilov had undoubtedly had a hand in that, too. He hadn't simply influenced Tyoma's life; he'd rewritten it the way he wanted, feeding him new, incomprehensible plots and destroying everything he'd come to love in his nineteen years.

"No, he's not up," Rita whispered, turning around and carefully shutting the door. "Maybe we can go down and eat something. Or no, why don't you go and I'll stay here. Then we'll switch off. Only don't let anyone in to see him, all right?"

A car gave two quick honks outside. Rita jumped on the sofa to look down at the SUV that had pulled up.

"Danilov's here," she said. "He always honks like that. Hurry up. We'll find out what's going on in town."

"You wanted to keep watch here."

"It doesn't matter now." Rita jumped off the sofa. "No one's going to come now. Everyone's wondering what's going on there."

Following Rita down the stairs, Tyoma pulled out his telephone and tried to connect to the Internet, but the network still wasn't working. Rita was right. Only Danilov could tell them anything new.

"Hi," Tyoma growled as they walked past the house's owner, who was standing in the middle of his roomy living room with seemingly no intention of removing his down parka.

"Where are your parents?" he asked Tyoma, instead of responding with a greeting of his own.

"In Karaganda."

Danilov let Tyoma's thrust go right by.

"Go get them," Danilov said. "Basically, everyone needs to gather."

Once he'd given his instruction, he stopped looking at Tyoma. The assumption was that Tyoma would immediately go carry it out.

"Well?" Danilov turned to Rita, who'd taken a seat next to the big fireplace. "Has your poor devil come around?"

"No."

"Maybe we should bring the doctor one more time. Did he get badly frozen?"

"Well, yeah, pretty much."

"Fine, I'll stop by the hospital. Although, with what's going on there . . ."

Danilov glanced at Tyoma, who was still shifting from foot to foot by the wall.

"What's the matter with you? I told you—go get everyone. I don't have much time."

Tyoma looked at Danilov sullenly.

Rita got up from her chair. "I can go. It's easy for me."

"Sit," Tyoma growled, then finally left the room.

Danilov winked at Rita.

"Hormones."

They spent the next five minutes in silence. Danilov sat down at the long table, unbuttoned his jacket, and stared at the wall with a look as if he were there alone. Not once did he glance in Rita's direction, but she knew he wasn't just looking at her but carefully examining her, studying her, waiting for her to make the first move. Absolutely not knowing what that first move should be, and not entirely sure she even wanted to make it at all, Rita squirmed in her chair from time to time, bit her upper lip, and furrowed her brow.

She knew everything her mother did about Danilov. He ran the largest construction company in town, decided certain important matters of municipal administration, was married, and was raising two daughters. Or rather, the girls were being raised by his wife, because Danilov had sent them off to somewhere in Spain long ago, having bought real estate there. One of his daughters had rashly expressed an interest in tennis, and he'd immediately taken advantage of that. A large house was instantly purchased next to some famous tennis school, and the entire female contingent of the Danilov family swiftly decamped there. Actually, they probably had no objections.

Right before his first daughter's birth, when there wasn't even a thought of a construction company, Danilov learned from utter strangers something about his wife that made him drive her out of the house after first shooting up the family couch with his hunting rifle. After these emotional experiences, Danilov's wife, who was present during the shooting, took to her bed for safety, although as a result she did give birth to a perfectly healthy little girl, whom the happy father picked up from the maternity hospital himself, having restored his disgraced wife to full rights. His daughter strikingly did not resemble Danilov, but he patiently waited for a second child from his wife. And then he packed them all off to study tennis.

Rita also knew from her mother that twenty years ago Danilov had served in the landing forces and taken part in "dispersing" the Georgians rebelling in Tbilisi. There were bloody details there about digging tools, dead women, and murdered comrades, but the story of the rifle, sofa, and birth bothered Rita much more. The revolution didn't end in the maternity hospital and paled by comparison to the couch shooting.

Danilov had met Rita at a city beauty contest, where he'd crowned her "Miss Intellect." As a bonus, he'd offered to pay for the distraught young woman's university education, and a little later he took on the then-unemployed Inga at his company. Her salary was set so high that Rita's mother naturally went on her guard; however, after a certain point, Danilov no longer displayed any interest in their family. He revived his activity only with the appearance of Tyoma, who was exactly half his age.

After what in Rita's opinion was a very awkward silence broken by nothing, the rest of the home's inhabitants started gathering around the long table. First to come was Inga—her maternal heart having hinted unerringly that she shouldn't be late. Then Peter the artist and his wife, Lilya, showed up. After them, Tyoma's parents came down. With them for some reason was the investigator Anatoly Sergeyevich, who had recently chatted with Rita about Danilov and suggested she call him Tolik. Zinaida and her husband looked extremely depressed, but they didn't trouble themselves to explain what was going on.

For an entire minute the owner of the house drilled a heavy gaze into the uninvited guest, whose response was to draw something in his notebook, unperturbed. In that minute, the general silence was broken only by Tyoma's coughing. Entering the living room behind his parents, he stood near the fireplace, closer to Rita. Everyone else was sitting at the long table.

"Fine then," Danilov began at last. "Basically, the city has been put on emergency status."

"That can't be good," an impatient Zinaida said. She reared up, but Pavlik immediately caught her by the hand.

"What exactly happened?" he asked, continuing to hold his wife's hand tight.

Danilov barely looked in his direction.

"You're interested in the technical details?"

"I'd like to understand the scale of what's happened."

"It's a bad scale, Pavlik. Very bad."

"But still?"

Danilov passed his gaze over those gathered at the table and sighed.

"The city's not going to have any heat. But have no fear. I've got generators to keep everything running here—the heating and the electricity. There's also enough food. We could sit out the whole winter here. There's plenty of snow all around, so we won't run out of water. We can bide our time."

The living room got so still that Rita could hear Tolik's pencil scratching across the paper. The investigator continued drawing something in his notebook. True, his face was no longer untroubled, but his pencil was flitting from side to side like an enraged wasp.

"And the city?" Peter put in. "Will the city freeze completely?"

"I hope not. Right now they're introducing a schedule of rolling blackouts. If they can restore operations, things will get back to normal. But right now it's better to stay put. There's room for everyone."

Danilov looked over at the investigator again, who finally responded to his glance.

"No need to worry about me," he said, leaving his notebook alone and looking Danilov coldly in the eye. "I'll finish questioning the suspects and leave."

"What other suspects?"

"That's no concern of yours."

"Listen, detective . . ." Danilov rose to his feet and loomed heavily over the table. "You haven't confused the time? Who invited you here, anyway?"

"Forgive me, but we never did learn what happened," Pavlik interjected. "What was the cause of the accident?"

Danilov lowered himself silently to his chair. The investigator answered, looking calmly at the owner of the house, as if it were Danilov and not Pavlik who had asked the question. Or as if Danilov were to blame for everything.

"A few days ago at the power station, a gas hydro turbine shut down. It was decided not to inform the public because the other seven turbines were functioning properly. Then yesterday, during a trial launch of the emergency GHT, two more turbines stopped, and, as a result, an electric power line went down. Mounting demand led to a shutdown of all operating GHTs. By three in the morning they were able to get three of them going again. As far as the rest go, we still don't know. The airport's been shut down. People are evacuating any way they can."

The investigator fell silent, casting his gaze over the grave faces.

"And what now?" A subdued Zinaida now spoke without any challenge. "What's going to happen to us?"

"To you?" The investigator grinned. "Nothing's going to happen to you. You're under Danilov's protection. But the city's not going to have such a great time of it. God only knows what's going on there now. There have been casualties."

"Excuse me?" Pavlik said, raising his eyebrows. "Are you saying people are dying?"

"What did you expect?" The investigator stared at him. "In this kind of situation, riots are inevitable."

"Is that true?" Pavlik shifted his mistrustful glance to Danilov, who wiped his brow and then hid his face in his hands and sat like that for a few seconds. Everyone else tensely awaited his answer.

"I'm very tired," Danilov said from behind his hands. "I've been on my feet all night."

Zinaida rose abruptly from her chair. "Well, I have to get to town!" she said. "I have my cousin and her children and my aunt there."

"Sit down," Danilov said in a muffled voice before taking his hands away from his face.

"Let's go!" She tugged her husband by his sweater sleeve. "Or are you going to wait for his permission again? Tyoma, take me! I have to find out how they are there."

"Sure," her son replied, and he moved toward the living room door.

"Fine, go," Danilov said calmly. "You have a powerful, expensive car. They need cars like that there right now."

"In what sense?" Zinaida was taken aback.

"The literal. People need good transportation so they can get the hell out of town. They're fanning out to their relatives in the villages. But not everyone has a car. So they'll be waiting for you there."

"Who'll be waiting?"

"Listen, you people in Moscow seem to have lost all connection to real life. People are waiting."

Zinaida became distraught. "What people? I don't understand."

"Ordinary people. With a crowbar, a hunting rifle, or a baseball bat. Something for everyone. They're killing people over cars. And you're planning to go there alone with a boy."

"Are you trying to scare me?"

"No. Yesterday they killed my secretary. In the morning her body was found next to her garage with her head bashed in. Her car was gone, naturally."

"Wait . . ." Pavlik awkwardly threw his arms up over his head. "Lyuda's dead?"

Danilov nodded wearily. Inga's eyes started to shine, and she bowed her head.

"Yesterday was the end of the world there," the owner of the house went on. "Countless people were crippled. There was a horrible crush at the bus stops, and looting and robbery. Cash boxes were torn out of stores with their bolts still attached. Anyone who tried to stop them got beaten. Badly beaten. It was kids from the countryside mainly who went at it. Freshmen from the dorms. Sturdy guys not afraid of anyone. And not a drop of pity in them, either. They grew up in nature. Meat, carp, sour cream. Everything very fatty, organic. Their blood seethes."

Danilov shifted his gaze to the investigator.

"You should be dealing with all that and not sniffing around here about me. What a moment you picked."

The investigator, looking at Danilov's back, wanted to come back with something, but he stopped himself. Danilov turned around.

A half-naked Filippov was standing at the living room threshold. His hands were bandaged up and his frostbitten cheeks were shiny from ointment. His wandering gaze slid not very intelligently over the people sitting at the table. Finally, he made a face and in an extremely hoarse voice asked, "Excuse me, please. Where am I?"

———

At the investigator's request, Filya was immediately installed in bed and barred from all contact. Rita tried to object and even faked minor hysterics, but all she achieved was getting the file of drawings handed over to Filippov.

Spreading them out on top of the blanket, he rummaged through the sketches with his bandaged hands. His fingers barely obeyed him, so pages kept sliding to the floor. Filya followed them with a brief glance under puffy eyelids and immediately picked up more. He was impatient to see them all. His vision kept betraying him. The pictures would blur, so he would blink hard, holding the drawing back in his outstretched hand, and wait for the blurry spot to come into focus. In his mind, the spots gradually formed the fairly ghastly image Peter had created for the upcoming show.

"Brilliant," he muttered. "An entire set made of dead bodies. A zombie floor lamp and a zombie armchair. It's Bosch. No, it's way cooler than Bosch."

"You're a real maniac," the investigator standing by the door said with a grin. "The minute you wake up, you're back to work."

Filya glanced in his direction with a watery eye.

"This is why I came here. But who are you?"

"You don't recognize me?" The investigator smiled. "I'm Tolik."

"Tolik who?"

"Your friend Tolik. We went to school together. You are the limit! But I recognized you right away. Even looking like this."

Filya squinted at the man. "You've changed."

"Oh, stop it," the investigator said. "It's just you've forgotten everything."

"No, I haven't. I remember you. Listen, do you know how I ended up here?"

"Yes."

"Tell me?"

"Not right now."

Filya set aside the sketch he was holding and looked carefully at the investigator.

"Why?"

"That's not why I'm here." Tolik took his ID out of his pocket. "I have to question you."

Filya looked at the name on the red cover and at the photograph, obviously taken a few years before, but he still didn't remember this Tolik.

"Don't strain yourself. We were in the same grade but not the same classes. You once gave me ten rubles. Big money in those days, by the way."

"What for?"

"Our class was on monitor duty for the school then, and I caught you in the restroom with a cigarette. You decided to buy me off."

"Bribing an official?"

Tolik burst out in fine, very broken laughter. "Something like that. If you want, though, I can pay it back. Then it won't be a bribe. Just a kind of loan."

"I don't care. What did you want to talk about?"

"So do you remember or not?"

Tolik looked searchingly at Filya. Apparently, this was important to him.

"Sure, I remember," Filya lied. "How do you forget something like that? Now, I see, you've risen to new heights. You're not catching boys in school restrooms anymore."

"No." Tolik laughed again, and in his unpleasant laughter you could definitely hear how pleased he was with himself. "Now we're just after big fish."

"Who's 'we'?"

Tolik was a little taken aback. "Well, meaning 'I.' 'We' is just a manner of speaking."

There was something fishlike in his face, and in moments of slight distress this similarity came out even stronger. Filya even thought he might remember him. There'd been someone at school who looked like a fish.

"Clearly," Filya said slowly. "For a moment, I thought there were an awful lot of you here. Listen, you don't know what happened to me yesterday, do you? I hurt for some reason. All over my body."

"You got frostbite. You came here in the wrong clothing. And on top of that, there's the accident at the power station."

"Accident? I did think there was something yesterday. Everything was kind of strange. But where's my dog?"

"I don't know. I haven't seen a dog in the house."

"I see. Is there anything here to drink?"

"Danilov doesn't drink."

"Who's that?"

"The owner of the house."

"Maybe he keeps some for his guests. Hey, go take a look. Or buy it. I should have some cash in my jacket over there. In the meantime, I'll work with the designs."

Tolik didn't budge. He looked at Filya silently, and as his gaze filled with cold, his face changed markedly. The talkative, slightly bug-eyed, but at the same time quite nice little fish turned into a spiteful, fat-lipped catfish. Filippov could almost see the prehistoric spiny fin stand up on his back, his colorless eyes get round and silvery, and his lips puff up unattractively. Up until that moment, he'd enjoyed shooting the breeze with Filya. He'd enjoyed reminiscing. He'd been pleased that his famous schoolmate had taken note of his rise in life. However, all it took was a poke, all it took was showing what to Tolik seemed like disdain, and he immediately bristled, immediately became himself. His moist eyes, which shone like cold metal, clearly said, *You'd better not mess with me. Our school days are over, and now people notice me. I'm not a nobody anymore.*

No sooner was the transformation into an evil fish complete than Tolik got down to his questioning.

"Were you in the car with the Neustroevs when they were going across the river?"

"You mean you aren't going to get me something to drink?" Filya said sadly. "Maybe some beer at least?"

"I'll repeat my question one more time. Did you go across the river with the Neustroevs immediately after you landed?"

"The Neustroevs. Is that Pavlik and Zinaida or something?"

"Yes. And they say you were with them."

"I was. I asked them to take me to my hotel, and they took me in the opposite direction."

"What for?"

"They were taking money somewhere. They said it was urgent."

Tolik pulled his notebook out of his pocket and made a note.

"And what happened on the way back?"

Filya thought briefly and then curled his lips and shrugged his shoulders. "Nothing. No, I remember. On the port road we nearly ran into Rita. She was flying like a witch to a Sabbath."

Tolik shook his head. "No, I mean before that."

"Before that? Nothing. We just drove."

"What about on the river?"

"What about what on the river?"

"Did you come across someone on the river when you were returning to this side?"

Filya sighed and shut his eyes for a second. Colorful little balls floated by under his eyelids.

"Listen, I'm pretty tired. Let's do this later. Or why don't you find all this out from them, the Neustroevs? They're funny . . . and probably remember more than I do. Lately, you know, I've been having problems with my memory."

"Pavel Neustroev admits that on the way back you drove past an automobile that had been in an accident."

"Oh, yeah. There was one crackpot who slid off the road. A cherry-red Zhiguli, I think."

"Absolutely right. License R466EV."

"Well, that I don't remember. I'm sorry. All I remember is that he ran after us with a crowbar for a long time. Pavlik freaked out because of his money and wouldn't stop. He thought they wanted to rob him."

"That 'crackpot' was trying to call for help."

"Holding a crowbar?" Filya grinned.

"He had a pregnant wife in the car," Tolik said drily. "She broke her leg in the accident. And your car was the third that drove by without stopping. Obviously, he wasn't himself."

"How do you know that?"

"A note was found with them with the licenses of the cars that drove past. Your license is third. There are four more after it. No one ever did help."

"You found a note?" Filya stared uncomprehendingly at Tolik.

"Yes. In the pocket of one of the bodies. They froze to death in their Zhiguli. And you drove on by, though you could have helped them."

Filya blinked two or three times, not taking his eyes off the investigator, who was absolutely not who he saw right now. Before him now, running through the snow, was that foolish man with the crowbar, and it was Filippov, as it turned out, who had decided whether the man should go on living or die.

The door behind Tolik opened wide, and Rita flew into the room.

"No, have a conscience, Anatoly Sergeyevich," she said impulsively. "I was waiting all morning for him to wake up. I have to talk to him, too!"

Tolik walked up to her, turned her around by the shoulders, and, without saying a word, marched her out of the room. Rita immediately started banging on the closed door.

"You've abandoned people in a hopeless situation before, after all," Tolik said, holding the door, which was shuddering from Rita pushing on it. "A familiar feeling?"

"I'll tell Danilov everything," Rita shouted behind the door. "About all your hints and insinuations!"

Tolik opened the door slightly and gave the young woman a hard shove, which she wasn't expecting. Filya heard the sound of a falling body and a brief, pathetic shriek.

"Have you lost your mind?" he said, sitting up and lowering his feet from the bed.

"Lie down immediately," Tolik commanded. "I'm not done with you."

Filippov obeyed and pulled up the blanket to his chin. Tolik finally moved away from the door.

"In the summer of '86, your first wife died under mysterious circumstances. Do you remember how that happened?" he began, advancing on the now-quiet Filya. "Naturally, you had nothing to do with it. An ordinary accident. A person poisoned at a dacha by exhaust fumes. 'So what was strange about that then?' you're probably going to ask. Are you? 'What's strange about that?' Well, go on, ask me. And I'll tell you that you were at that very dacha. That very night."

———

"Beast," Rita muttered, opening one cupboard after another in the kitchen. "Viper."

Her left sweater sleeve was rolled up above her elbow and stained with blood. Every once in a while, she would turn her arm and look at the big ugly bruise, touch it cautiously with her finger, hiss from the pain, and mutter more angry words. Finally finding a Band-Aid, she tore off the wrapper with her teeth, though she wasn't able to cover the injury. Inga walked into the kitchen.

"Rita, is there any valerian in this house?" she asked in a tone that seemed to assume her daughter should know everything about Danilov's house.

"I'm not up on that," Rita replied. "But I doubt it."

Inga stared at her bruise. "Who did that? Filya?" Fury seethed in her voice. She turned away sharply to run and immediately punish the perpetrator.

"What does he have to do with this?" Rita said, trying to stop her. "I just slipped on the stairs. Someone spilled water on the steps. Probably."

Inga froze in the doorway. Rage was still brewing in her heart, seeking an outlet, but she crossed her arms over her chest, shutting the storm inside her, and looked at her daughter. Before her was that same little girl who so very recently she had told not to cross her eyes, not to make faces on the street, not to pick her nose. In Inga's understanding, a child should remain a child—that's how she was created; that's how she had come. But her daughter had let her down badly in this regard. Inga didn't think she'd sacrificed herself to her children, naturally, but she did have a right to expect some gratitude from them. Her husband had dissolved his pathetic pinch of salt in life's waters even before Rita's birth, so Inga had raised her children alone.

Instead of showing her some gratitude, her son had chased after some beauty to Petersburg the moment beauties started interesting him. Her daughter had grown up without a conscience. All these young ladies with their slender necks, copious breasts, and elegant waists who seemed to pop up out of nowhere lately hadn't bothered Inga in the least until she sensed how much they disdained her, how much she was for them dust under their feet, ashes and decay—their terrible future, which they hated even to look at. At certain moments, she felt the arrogance emanating from them so tangibly and so directly it was as if she were a slave without rights living in ancient Egypt and all these creatures were her mistresses. And now her daughter had gone over to their side; an elegant waist and luxuriant breasts had appeared on her, too. From time to time, Inga got scared that she was losing her mind, but there was nothing she could do with herself, considering Rita in some sense a traitor.

"What's up, Mom?" Rita said, not understanding her long silence. "It's bullshit. I just knocked my elbow."

"I've gotten old," Inga said in a small voice.

Rita puffed out her cheeks and shook her head helplessly. "Here we go again, damn it. I keep telling you not to think that way. I've had enough of you turning the universe into what it's not."

"What are you talking about?"

"Tyoma has this book about Buddhism where it says that we bring on our own problems when we think about them too much. We make the universe a negative."

"You mean I'm going to stop getting old if I don't think about it?"

"Mom, what's wrong with you?" Rita frowned. "You know what I mean. Why don't you help put this Band-Aid on?"

"No, I don't understand. I don't want to understand." Inga fell silent for a second, examining her daughter. "Why did you put that sweater on again? How many times do I have to repeat that it's too tight? The investigator couldn't take his eyes off your chest."

"That's not true," Rita said, eventually patching up her wounded elbow herself. "He was drawing."

"Some drawing."

"Mama, enough already." Rita fixed her sleeve and gave Inga a stern look.

"I don't say this because of myself," Inga replied quickly. "Don't worry about that. I only say it because of Danilov. Do you think he's going to be very happy if people are going to be looking at you like that right in his own home?" As she said "like that," she bugged out her eyes, let her mouth hang open like an idiot, leaned forward, and stared at her daughter's chest. "You should wear your things looser. So you don't draw stares."

"Mama, I'm sick of you and your Danilov," Rita said irritably. "I'm being serious. You have the most incredible fantasies."

"They're not fantasies."

"Yeah? Who had her chest done as soon as she joined his company?"

Inga held her hand out in front of her helplessly. "Rita, stop it."

"Fine then," her daughter said. "I do know how you lit him up in your youth. There are legends about it in town. There's an entire mythology around you."

"Rita, don't you dare talk to me like that!"

"Fine. Then tell me where my papa is."

Inga didn't say anything, and they both stood there silently, looking into each other's eyes, until Tolik walked into the kitchen.

His professional instinct, gleaned over the years from any manifestation of fear, hatred, irritation, or other waste matter from a human soul driven into the corner, immediately told him that he had landed in his favorite situation. Shivers ran familiarly down his back, but Tolik controlled himself and showed restraint. He very much wanted to butt in, to saddle these fillies who had been badly shaken by something and exploit their conflict in his own interests, but his instinct told him that it was better to stick to the plan.

Walking past Rita and glancing at her breasts so beautifully swathed by her sweater, he opened the refrigerator proprietarily, thought for a second or two, and took out a plate of sliced ham.

"Anybody hungry? For some reason, I'm starving."

Stuffing his mouth, he bellowed to show how good it was, then winked at Rita and held out the plate to her.

"Have some? Come on, don't be shy."

Rita looked at him silently, obviously having no intention of reacting to him. The investigator dropped the plate on the counter next to the stove. It clattered loudly.

"Ooh," he said with respect. "Granite." Tolik tapped the stone surface. "Solid."

"Don't you have anything better to do?" Rita said at last.

"Sure, lots. It's just that the ham's delicious. Are you trying to get rid of me or something?"

"No, I'm not."

"Well, thank you."

He took a piece of crumpled paper out of his pocket and held it out to Rita. She didn't even stir.

"Take it. Take it," the investigator said. "You were the one who wanted to spend time with your Filippov."

Rita warily held out her hand and took the paper from him. "What's this?" she said.

"An address. Take him there right now. He wants you to."

"Now what!" Inga was immediately outraged. "Danilov said it's dangerous there!"

Tolik grinned and took one more piece of ham from the plate. "Danilov was exaggerating. He's taking on a lot, as usual."

———

On the drive into town, the road surface turned dreadful. The car ran more or less smoothly down the highway, but as soon as the first houses appeared the car started shuddering as if it were racing over a washboard. Apparently, this didn't upset Rita. She didn't even try to drive around the ruts, so Filya clutched the handle overhead. He was now wearing all local clothing. In Danilov's storerooms they'd found a nice new down parka, reindeer boots that fit, and warm snow pants.

To the right, an absolutely lifeless and flat landscape unfurled as if out of a high-budget sci-fi movie about planets frozen in ice armor. On the left, the little houses of outlying poverty ran by like a row of mice. Crooked fences, snowdrifted roofs, listing gray sheds—this definitely wasn't the city yet. Here in the sticks huddled those the city didn't want to let in. Those because of whom it had disdainfully drawn its streets, squares, and avenues—to be sure not to touch all this suburban want by accident, not to be infected by it, not to pick up something shameful.

Closer to the center of town, the streets got more decent, but Filippov was having a hard time getting his bearings in the new landscape. A few places he couldn't recognize at all. Where pathetic wooden housing—complete with private yards, sidewalks of rotten boards, and decrepit outhouses opposite every building—had previously clung together there were now faceless fortress walls surrounding labyrinths of five-story apartment buildings. In addition, from time to time, architectural installations he'd never seen before that imitated in glass and concrete the traditional Northern yurt flashed by. As far as he remembered, this kind of summer residence was called an *urasa*. But in Soviet times it wouldn't have occurred to anyone to build one in stone.

Everything around was not just covered in snow but bundled in it with the same painstakingness and unfailing care any mother would demonstrate in swaddling her own infant. The snow layer that had swallowed the city was reaching archaeological proportions. Ancient Herculaneum buried under a layer of ash, and long-suffering Pompeii— that's what one might compare the city to that Filippov was now viewing out the car window. It wasn't even normal snow but some kind of special shaggy variety. Absolutely everything was shaggy and gray—the buildings, the pillars, the streetlamps, the street signs. Only a local could identify the trees in the eccentric stalagmites running along the thoroughfare. Power lines hung heavily overhead like giant coral threads. The barbed, tousled gratings along the sidewalks were cast from liquid air, not iron.

All this colossal hoarfrost, which could be compared in intensity only with tropical vegetation, was an alternative, nonbiological lifeform. Crystals of solidified cold adhered in billions of colonies to any surface in the city the moment the thermometer dropped past forty below, colonies that led an independent and seemingly intelligent life. In their stormy growth and multiplication, one could read not simply spontaneous expansion, not only a primitive seizure of living space— no, they were obviously keeping to a precise plan. The cold here could think, and this ocean of thinking cold very obviously wanted something, expected something, was preparing for something.

Riding in a small warm car in the middle of an icy tumult capable in just a few minutes of dispatching a living creature to eternity was awful and fun at the same time. Filya glanced at Rita, who had not made a peep so far. Spying on her imperceptibly for a minute or two, he concluded that the cold bothered her only in the everyday sense. He discovered no trace of anything transcendent in her sullen gaze. He finally decided to break the silence.

"Why were you so anxious to see me? What did you want?"

Rita surfaced from some obviously not very pleasant thoughts and glanced at him.

"Take me to Moscow," she said after a second's pause.

"Moscow?" Filya repeated after her. "I'm not going to Moscow now. I'm going to Paris."

"Then take me to Paris."

"Where is this coming from?" He snickered and let go of the overhead strap. Now, in the center of town, the car barely shook.

"I'm your daughter." Rita raised her eyebrows. "You should take care of me."

Filya shook his head.

"If you're my daughter, then I'm definitely not taking you."

"Why?"

"What the hell am I going to do with a daughter there? If you were just a young woman, I probably could take you. Because young women are interesting. You can make love to them. But that's not a go with a daughter. No, I'm not that bad yet."

"Well, then I'm not your daughter. You can just take me away from here. Or else I'm going to kill someone."

Filippov didn't respond. The exaltation of youth had bored him for a long time. Outbursts like this spoke to the primitive reaction of someone who has become aware for the first time that life has turned its fat ugly butt to her. The novelty of discoveries like this upset only those not yet accustomed to those drooping outlines and offended by them because they'd, foolishly, been expecting something else. Naïveté didn't touch Filippov one bit. He sincerely found it to be the sign of an undeveloped personality.

"Tell me about yourself," he said.

"Tell you what?"

"Everything. You are my daughter, after all."

Rita squinted a little, fell silent, and looked at him. "You mean you believe I'm your daughter?"

Filya shrugged. "To be honest, I don't really care. If you don't want to talk about yourself, talk about Danilov. He's even more interesting."

Without taking her eyes off the road, Rita brought Filippov up to speed on the position Danilov occupied in the city, a position that allowed him to take a whole group of his friends out of the emergency zone and settle them in his suburban home.

"And on what planet am I his friend?" Filya said.

"None. You were just lying around unconscious by the artist's building when we drove by for him."

"Who decided to pick me up?"

"Do you care? I thought you didn't give a damn about anything."

"Well, in principle, I don't. Although . . . Give me your phone for a minute. Is there a signal in town?"

"Now there is," she said, handing over the phone.

Putting his own SIM card in Rita's phone, Filya checked incoming messages and found information about a major transfer into his bank account.

"What?" Rita asked, seeing the smile on his face. "Good news?"

"The French paid the advance. Now I'm definitely going to Paris. But most of all, I'm getting the hell out of here. Do we have far to go?"

"No, here we are," Rita replied, stopping the car beside a five-story prefab apartment building that had emerged from the fog.

"Fine. You wait right here for me," Filya said, opening the door. "I'll be exactly ten minutes. And then straight to the airport."

Slamming the door, he quickly headed for the entrance but then slowed down, stopped, and suddenly rushed back.

"Tell me, was there a dog with me when you found me?" he asked, peering into the car again. "Big, like this. Looked like a German shepherd."

Rita shook her head. "No, no dog."

"I see. All right, I'll be quick."

He came back a minute later. Sullen, he took his seat.

"Take me to the hospital," he growled. "The provincial."

"Who are you looking for?" Rita finally asked.

"I said the hospital!" he hollered. "Now she's asking questions, too."

———

Greatly offended, Rita intentionally rode through all the ruts before managing to find a parking place on the fenced-off territory of the provincial hospital—where the morgue was located, right by the gates. But then Filippov unexpectedly demanded to be taken to the nearest bank. He told Rita he suddenly knew what he needed money for, but the impulse to leave this strangely familiar place was dictated by something else. Filya wouldn't admit the real reason. So as not to rile him again, Rita didn't ask any questions.

The bank was pandemonium. Standing in line for the ATM and listening—whether he wanted to or not—to other people's agitated conversations, Filya learned that people were withdrawing cash all over town. No one could tell how long the heating outages would last or what they might lead to, so everyone rushed first thing to rescue their savings. In any difficult or confused moment, a Northerner is used to relying on himself alone, and first and foremost this meant keeping what's yours at home. The majority here well remembered the '98 default and knew exactly how much the state and its banks spat on all those tiresome little people crowding in lines like this the moment something major and frightening happened.

In the lobby where the ATMs were installed, the first swallows of mounting panic had already flitted by. Filya could almost physically feel them rushing noiselessly above the crowd, a wing touching one and then another. A short, solid guy in a black down parka with a hood trimmed in silver fox was assuring someone standing a little ahead of him, and who couldn't be seen because of his enormous hood, that some banks had stopped issuing cash. Filya couldn't see the speaker's face, but his voice, even though the guy was trying not to speak too loudly, radiated fear. Tension hovered over their heads and got denser the closer they got to the ATMs, and the front door kept opening, letting in well-wrapped, rimy people, if they'd come on foot, and unbuttoned ones if they'd come by car, but all were identically tense.

The lobby filled up quickly, so Filya was soon standing pressed between the wall and a large woman with a shaggy full-length dog-fur coat. Because the woman had come to the bank alone and had no one with whom to share the rumors that were filling her to bursting, she started telling Filya that a directive had supposedly already come from Moscow restricting flights, for the purpose of conserving fuel, and that soon it would be totally impossible to fly out of the city. She also told him about a mysterious bunker with an autonomous furnace where the city's elite would be saved when heat stopped being delivered to residential buildings. An elderly Yakut man, pressed up to Filya on the other side, objected about the bunker, citing the permafrost, in which it was even hard to dig a grave, but the woman in the dog-fur coat replied that given today's technologies, even this was possible, just not for ordinary people.

"Because no one needs you and me," she told the old man heatedly over Filya's head, which he was trying to lean away as much as possible. "They're going to let us kick the bucket here like dogs. In my apartment last night, it was five above."

"Oh, come off it," a disbelieving voice rang out from somewhere on the right. "Where's that?"

"On New Port Road, that's where," the woman responded in a ringing voice. "You mean it's warmer where you are?"

"Well, yes. It's holding at fifteen degrees."

"And where do you live?"

"Peter Alexeyev Street."

"Well! That's practically downtown!" Something akin to contempt rang in the woman's voice.

"What's the difference?"

"What do you mean what's the difference? You have nothing but bosses there!"

"Oh, come off it!"

The woman in the fur coat leaned toward Filya and demanded a report from him. "What's your temperature at home?"

He looked at her silently, twisting his singed lips, and a moment later she switched over to the rest of the line.

"Who lives where, and what's your temperature?" she shouted, throwing her head back.

"Poyarkov Street, twelve!" came an answer from somewhere to the left.

"Ordzhonikidze, fourteen!" another voice sounded.

"Khabarov, seventeen degrees!"

"Oh! Let's all go to Khabarov!" someone in the far corner hollered in a wickedly cheerful voice, and the whole line seemed to sigh and stir, and all of a sudden to smile one big, still tentative, smile.

Up until that moment, everyone stuffed into the frozen lobby had probably been connected by nothing but fear, and if there was something other than fear that brought them all closer in a strange and contradictory way, then it was the understanding that each was going to be on his own when it came to saving himself. They were here together and, at the same time, deeply divided, and this awful sensation made them feel absolutely as morbidly vulnerable and defenseless as a child left in the forest at night.

Now they listened to the nonsense two tipsy dunces in the far corner were carrying on with and laughed at their silly stories, and all this nonsense not only drove away their fear, acting like the protective spell of local shamans, it united them in a completely different way, and for a while each person in this lobby now was certain that everything would work out. Or that if it didn't, then it didn't much matter.

———

When he and Rita drove back to the hospital and parked by the morgue, Filya realized why, an hour before, this place had seemed familiar: this was where he and Nina's parents had collected her body. Since then, nothing at all had changed. The same faceless building was surrounded by the same faceless wall. As before, this gray concrete facelessness held nothing tragic, nothing beyond-the-grave, nothing terrible. The dilapidated green door certainly didn't lead to the kingdom of Hades. Filya remembered that behind it lay only an equally boring and equally dilapidated corridor. The dead here weren't people; what was dead here was life itself, which had retreated, losing all individuality, becoming a cliché, turning into this corridor, this door, and these gray bricks. Life had been wiped away, the way a school eraser rubs a line off a piece of drawing paper, leaving behind only smears and messy crumbs that could be swept or blown away. Filya always remembered that in this nondescript and utterly unfrightening place they gave you not the person but his zero. It wasn't even what was left of him. It was what he had never been. What had never been in him. They issued you a fake. As if the person had already boarded the train and left, while you for some reason were being issued a life-size copy on the deserted platform, a fairly ugly puppet. A souvenir, sort of, or something else. And the people who saw the train off left the station with these puppets and suddenly asked themselves, *And we need this awful scarecrow in order to do what?* But no one had an answer. Because the real someone they'd loved was gone.

"Come with me," Filya said, opening the door and jumping out of the car. "I don't know anything here."

"As if I did," Rita replied, opening the door on her side.

They left the car by the morgue and headed for the main building. Then they hurriedly walked past a couple of dozen cars that had jammed the lot in front of the huge building and the entry to the steep emergency-room ramp. One of the ambulances was trying to go up that ramp, but the way was blocked and none of the drivers was paying the slightest attention to its siren's wail. Coming toward Filippov and Rita in a continuous stream were people collecting their family members, carefully leading them by the arm, solicitously supporting them on the slippery steps, seating them in cars, trying to drive off, getting completely stuck, and starting to honk nervously, joining the general automotive rumpus.

Taking Rita by the hand, Filya pulled her along. Cursing, commiseration, and complaints in Russian and Yakut came flying at them from all directions. This bilingualism underscored even more the chaos and isolation that reigned here. Everyone wanted the same thing, but no one wanted to understand anyone else. Everyone thought the others had ganged up against them, that the others were their enemies, and that the best thing would be to repulse everyone else preemptively.

"Demons," Filya muttered, gasping from the cold and pushing his way inside the hospital. "Devils of Babylon."

In the corridor right by the entrance, next to the constantly slamming door, a teenager with his head shaved bare smoked, squatting. Ruffled like a sick little bird, he shielded the cigarette in his palm and exhaled the smoke at his feet. Under his unbuttoned army peacoat, which was much too big on him, all you could see was a striped T-shirt, track pants, and enormous torn scuffs. The clouds of steam that kept bursting into the hospital corridor from the street didn't bother him in the least. The people entering and exiting rushed past, ignoring him, while he was absorbed with watching the smoke from his cigarette mix with the steam. The nurse wearing a down parka over her white robe who was shouting at him didn't bother him, either. To all her complaints he responded distractedly that he was going to smoke where he wanted, that he had no one to pick him up, that he was from another town and it wasn't his fault that after he was released from reform school they'd brought him here.

"I'm real sick, lady. Don't yell. I don't know where I'm supposed to go now."

"They told me Anna Rudolfovna was supposed to be here," Filya intervened in this one-sided cross fire. "Where can I find her?"

The nurse stepped aside, letting pass to the exit an entire family that had clustered around a large, heavy woman who looked like she was from the Caucasus and who was moaning, her eyes rolling back, at every step.

"She won't be here today. Something bad happened."

"Yes, I know." Filya nodded. "But they told me she'd come in. Her neighbor said so."

"Go to the doctors' lounge, then. Maybe somebody there has some idea."

Filya and Rita moved down the corridor, while the teen behind them kept muttering, still not agreeing to put out his cigarette. "You have anarchy here, just like reform school. Nothing makes sense. Where's everyone gone? In the adult zone, there was order. Everything precise, everything according to the rules. The guys used to tell me, the ones whose fathers were doing time."

From the doctors' lounge they were sent to Neurology, but there, too, there was no Anna Rudolfovna to be found. An elderly nurse with brightly painted lips said nervously that she'd seen her in the procedures room on another floor, but outsiders were forbidden entry there. "You wait here. I'll tell them you've come to see her."

Standing in the already cool corridor, down which the patients' innumerable relatives were scurrying with plates, cans, and blankets, Rita and Filya swiveled their heads senselessly from side to side until right next to them, at the very entrance to the already half-empty and ravaged ward, a woman suddenly started shouting.

She was sitting on a bed by the door, firmly clutching her nickel-plated bed frame, as if she were afraid they would take her away by force. Standing around her were her distraught kin—her children, apparently, and even grandchildren. Not wiping the tears running down her face, she was saying she didn't want to go home, that she was a burden to everyone there, that they'd insulted her by letting her know that.

"I'll stay here. I like it here," she kept repeating, pressing up to the bed frame as if it were her sole kindred being. "I don't need anything."

Her children stamped in place mournfully, trying to object, but the woman only shook her head, refusing to relinquish her grip on the bed.

So it continued until a small Yakut grandfather whose family was also gathering in the next ward stopped by the door. Obviously, these two had had a chance to become friends. He immediately headed for the weeping woman, sat down beside her on the bed, and started talking to her quietly. The woman wiped her tears, nodded to him, and even laughed a bit, pointing to her children, as if she were suddenly embarrassed by the fuss and her part in it, as if she wanted to tell the old man that, look, she had a family, too. Filya tried to catch their conversation, but what happened after that he never found out.

The nurse with the brightly painted lips came up to him and Rita and said nervously that Anna Rudolfovna was in Psychiatry.

"The patients there are being evacuated to a suburban hospital, where they still have stove heating. Anna Rudolfovna is helping."

On the way, while they were walking down the various corridors and passageways between buildings, Rita was silent for a long time, until they entered the Psychiatric Department.

"What do we need this Anna Rudolfovna for?" she asked.

Filya wouldn't say.

In the spacious and stone-cold foyer next to the office of the department head, a dozen patients were sitting on chairs, stools, and wheelchairs, without a single relative by their side. Apparently, the rest had already been picked up, but no one needed these: a few desiccated old men and women with an identical absent gaze and identically sunken mouths and tufts of hair; two or three mentally disabled people of indeterminate age, who were surprisingly large; and a very skinny woman who sat solemnly in her wheelchair as if it were a throne.

Someone had already pulled motley outerwear onto them, obviously not their own, and now in all these padded jackets, old sheepskin coats, and ungainly overcoats they looked like a group of extras ready to go on the set of a new Jos Stelling film. One of the men had an orange construction worker's vest fastened over his shabby fur coat, for extra warmth.

"WTF," Rita said quietly.

"Life takes on many guises, daughter dear," Filya replied without any pathos whatsoever. "Get used to its multiplicity."

The sounds of heated debate flew out the office door, which was ajar. Filya glanced in, but the two women inside, who were standing in tense poses beside a large table, gave him just a cursory glance. One of them—short, with cropped red hair, a wrinkled face, and a hook nose— was talking in such a low and creaky voice she created the impression of a tree, not a human being. Her calm, intelligent eyes were riveted on an extremely agitated brunette whose entire furious outburst, all her fervor and anger, kept crashing lightly against something infinitely large and heavy that was in those eyes and the weary, smoked-out voice.

"It cannot be done without direct instruction from the ministry!" The brunette was practically shouting. "I'm going to have to answer for them. I'm in charge of the department!"

"And I'm shutting it down," the redhead rasped. "At least until the emergency is lifted."

"Anna Rudolfovna! How can you not understand? You've had something bad happen to you yourself!"

A shudder passed over the redhead's face. "What does that have to do with this? That's not important now."

"How can it not be important? They have to cross the river, too, and after that it's another two hours. Our Pazik is running on a wing and a prayer. They'll all freeze to death if anything happens to the bus. The slightest breakdown, Anna Rudolfovna! Any malfunction!"

"Larisa Ignatievna, go home."

"This is my office! I'm not going anywhere."

"Go. I'm taking responsibility for their travel."

The brunette looked at her boss as if she wanted to kill her. She just didn't know how.

"I'm removing you from management," Anna Rudolfovna said. "Another minute and I'll fire you altogether."

"That's all right," the brunette said after a second's pause. "You think the phones aren't working anymore? You think I have no one to call at the ministry?"

"I don't think anything. Go."

The dismissed supervisor wrapped her mink coat around herself in a huff and rushed toward the office door. Filya barely managed to get out of her way to let her pass.

"Did you want something?" the redhead asked him as she dropped on a chair and pulled out her cigarettes from the pocket of her worn sheepskin coat.

"I brought the money."

"The money?" She lit a cigarette and rubbed her forehead in a sudden pensiveness. "What money?" Still, judging from her intonation and her remote glance, she had asked the question mechanically. She had absolutely no interest in Filya or what he had to say. More than likely, she didn't even realize he was talking about money. At that moment, Filya would have had as much luck talking to her about elephants or submarines. Words had no meaning whatsoever for her right then. They were just sounds devoid of content, paper cups without water. And Filya knew that the reason for this was not the tumult in the hospital.

Redheaded Anna Rudolfovna only looked alive. By force of will, or the opposite—at the expense of total repression—she looked to be reacting perfectly appropriately to external signals and stimuli. But, in fact, she wasn't here, and the previous conversation had been conducted only by her trained shell. She herself was in the eye of a hurricane—not where the storm and merciless devastation were but where there was absolute calm. Literally a few meters from Filya a ferocious storm raged, shredding everything that fell in its path, but at the very center there was undisturbed silence, and the eye of whoever ended up there fixed uncomprehendingly on the wild chaos and devastation, which seemed to have absolutely nothing to do with him personally.

"Your relatives died on the river yesterday."

"I'm aware," Anna Rudolfovna said, looking at her smoking cigarette. "Can you find me an ashtray?"

"No."

"Then go."

"This money is from a philanthropic fund," he said, holding out two thick packets.

"What am I supposed to do with it?"

Filya glanced at Rita, as if she might help him in some way.

"Arrange the funeral," he said. "Here." He walked over to the desk and put the packets in front of Anna Rudolfovna. "There's two hundred thousand here."

She looked at the money for a second and then looked up at him. "Are you out of your mind?"

"Yes." Filya nodded. "Right now, yes. I'm certain."

"Who are you?"

"I'm from Moscow."

She thought about his answer and shrugged. "I think you're a fool."

"I agree. In principle, that's not even up for discussion. You know, in fact, I very much . . ."

Filya wanted to say he sympathized and that he himself had lost people close to him so he knew what it was like. But behind Rita, who was still standing in the doorway, a low, visceral wail suddenly went up that made her stagger into the office, trip over Filya's foot, and nearly fall.

"Senya," Anna Rudolfovna cried out in a hoarse voice. Her hand holding the smoking cigarette struck the desk, sending ashes flying in all directions over the glass surface.

Coming from the foyer were a melancholy lowing, soft swearing, and strange scratching noises, as if a bag of cement were being dragged over a stone floor from one wall to the other.

"Senya," Anna Rudolfovna repeated as she walked out of the office. "I just asked you to get them into the bus. What have you been doing?"

A short, scrawny Yakut man wearing an old khaki down parka was dragging the man in the construction worker's vest across the floor by the arm. The man in orange was fighting him off, moaning, rustling his vest, breaking away, and trying to crawl off, but the persistent Yakut man would immediately catch up to him and drag him toward the exit again.

To Anna Rudolfovna's angry questions the upset Senya replied that he was hurrying as much as he could, but "the damned psychos" just didn't want to get on the bus. He spoke quickly, in his indignation mixing up his Russian words and decorating them fancifully with a Yakut accent.

Meanwhile, all the mentally disabled people had gathered around their brother, who'd been thrown to the floor and who obviously had no intention of getting up; they shifted from foot to foot, mutely sympathizing with one of their own. The old people remained indifferent to it all, their mouths open, as if they were all airing out their long uninhabitable inner rooms. The thin woman sitting solemnly in her wheelchair, on the contrary, was showing lively interest in what was going on, smiling and nodding royally as if she were giving her queenly acquiescence to all this.

Filya's experienced eye read the staging, instantly determined the center of the composition, and then walked up to the woman sitting in the wheelchair and rolled her toward the exit. The mentally disabled patients immediately calmed down and trailed after him. The old people were also set in motion. Rita could almost hear their bones creaking as they started coming to life, rising, one after the other, and setting their sights on the course laid for them. It looked like the inexplicably desiccated stone giants on Easter Island had suddenly come to life and were moving toward the sea. Filya heard their unhurried shuffling behind him and slowed down.

Outside, next to the bus, Anna Rudolfovna walked up to him.

"No, you're not a fool after all," she said hoarsely, lighting up again and holding the collar of her sheepskin coat at her throat with her free hand. "You're the second person I've ever met who understands them so well."

"Thank you," Filippov replied, observing Senya seating the old people, who were swaying in the icy wind, on the bus. "Who was the first?"

"My grandson. Antoshka."

She uttered his name and fell silent, as if listening to something, took a couple of quick drags on her cigarette, and then continued.

"Once last year, I left him in my office and he ran off. Half an hour later they found him on the ward." She nodded in the direction of the man in the construction worker's vest, who was smiling broadly at her and Filya and flapping his arms as if he wanted to fly. "You know what they were doing?"

Filya shook his head.

"Memorizing poems. Antoshka was reciting what he'd learned in kindergarten so far. Pushkin, I think. And they were repeating after him. They all were having a very good time."

"Excellent story," Filya said, already starting to freeze. "Say hello to your Antoshka."

Anna Rudolfovna looked at him oddly and shook her head.

"I guess you are a fool after all."

"Why?" He stopped hopping up and down.

"Because he was in that car. He froze yesterday with his parents on the river. With my son and his bride. You brought me the money for his funeral yourself. How can I say hello to him?"

Saying this, she gasped and swayed. Her hand with the smoking cigarette still tried to reach her mouth, but her mouth wasn't opening for the cigarette anymore. Anna Rudolfovna's lips twisted convulsively, her head started leaning back, and Filya realized the hurricane's epicenter had shifted. The unfortunate woman had been caught up by the furious whirlwind that up until now had been spinning without touching her. For a rather long time she'd been able to avoid it by entering the area where everything was still fluid and not quite defined—where everything was inexact, where everything was still in the category of "maybe." Now, though, she was in its full sway. Recalling her grandson, allowing the thought of him in and speaking of his death for herself, she had precisely formulated her own grief, and because of this, it took on firm and understandable outlines. It became an unavoidable fact—and finally reached her.

Anna Rudolfovna leaned forward as if she were going to be sick and then abruptly straightened up and began arching back. Her head struck the bus with a loud boom. The mentally disabled people crowded around Senya affably turned toward the sound. Filya grabbed the unnaturally stretched-out woman, and her wide-open mouth ended up a few centimeters from his face. A scream had not yet been torn from this twisted mouth, but the body in Filya's arms was spasming in powerful convulsions, anticipating the scream, paving its way.

"Open the door," Filya managed to say in Rita's direction, but she didn't get as far as the front steps when Anna Rudolfovna screamed so terribly and so loudly that one of the patients fell down. Slipping and flapping his arms, Senya rushed to Filya's aid. The old men froze lifelessly at the foot of the bus, Rita stopped halfway to the building, and Filya continued holding Anna Rudolfovna, who was moving in his arms as if she were being torn open inside by a volcano.

To keep her from falling, breaking free of his arms, and hitting herself on the frozen asphalt, he squatted. The convulsions shaking Anna Rudolfovna's body were being conveyed to him, and he was having a hard time keeping his balance. Senya, who had run up, was pacing uselessly behind him, muttering something in Yakut. Anna Rudolfovna kept screaming and throwing her head back unnaturally. When Filya finally lowered her to the dark, bumpy ice, she darted forward abruptly, as if Filya and the whole rest of the world were preventing her from getting free for something so important that she had to do it that very moment. She flung up her arms, and the cigarette she'd been clutching pointlessly flew under the bus, hitting a wheel and scattering a small heap of extinguishing sparks right there.

The man in the construction vest readily dropped to his knees and crawled under the bus. A moment later he surfaced holding the butt. He then crab-walked toward the writhing Anna Rudolfovna and tried to put the cigarette in her mouth, but the woman's head was thrashing desperately from side to side, and all his attempts to restore harmony were in vain. Filya tried to push him away, but the good man had firmly decided to help, and time and again the hot butt ended up in dangerous proximity to the women's eyes, which were contorted in unbearable pain.

When he burned her cheek and Anna Rudolfovna screamed even louder, Filya punched him in the face. The man fell on his side and his brothers started howling, but Filya kept shaking Anna Rudolfovna by the shoulders and repeated like an incantation: "There were two people in the car. Two people. The boy wasn't with them."

—————

"Who said he was alive?" Tolik shrugged as he put the old keyboard, which he'd detached from the computer a second ago, in his backpack. "We didn't search around. Maybe he froze to death somewhere near the car. You can't search the whole river."

Filya was shifting from foot to foot. "But what if someone picked him up?"

"Who?"

"Well, the people who drove by."

"Like you and your accomplices?" Tolik glanced at Filya standing in the doorway and winked at him with a grin. "I see there's already blood on your hands. You decided to move on to active measures?"

Filya looked down at his bandaged hands. There really were blood-stains on his right hand, where the bandage was coming unwound.

"I hit an idiot," he said.

"Good going." Tolik nodded approvingly. "Why get mixed up with them? Wait for them to approach you themselves. One neat punch"—he mimicked a brief, energetic uppercut—"and that's it."

"But it's so ineffective just leaving it at that. Right, Muscovite?" Tolik said. "Tell me, did it take them long to die? You must have let them suffer, right? Don't leave them anymore. Finish 'em off right away. Again—show some mercy."

The investigator opened the safe and stared pensively inside, trying to figure out what else he should take.

"Give me the list of those license plates," Filya said.

Tolik turned around and winked at him. "Maybe I should give you my service weapon, too?"

"I want to talk to those people."

Tolik bared his teeth. "To trade impressions? You've decided to find out what other people feel when they've abandoned people to die? Laudable."

Filya lowered his head obstinately. "One of them might have taken the boy."

The investigator's tone was even more mocking. "You're taking away my bread and butter?"

"You don't want to look for the kid. You don't. I can tell."

Tolik fell silent, looking Filya in the eye, and, after a long pause, he pulled a file out of the safe. Opening it, he took out a piece of paper, put it on the table, and turned away.

Filya walked over to the table. "Is this the list?"

"Are you an idiot or something? The list is in evidence. We copied the numbers from it. The addresses are already there. Most of the owners live in outlying villages."

"They were all leaving town?"

"Not necessarily. You and your accomplices were headed this way."

"How can I find out?"

Tolik turned around and shrugged.

"However you want, go find out. Why are you pestering me, anyway? My business is to bring you in under Article 125. And I will. Rest assured. Don't think that this whole mess is going to help you wiggle out of this. They'll restore heat in the city soon, everything will shake out, and then you'll answer in full. People died because of you—just don't forget that. You got away with it once, but you won't again."

How Tolik knew about Filya's part in Nina's death remained unclear. The investigator hadn't cited any direct proof of Filya's presence at the dacha. He'd simply implied that he knew—that's it. He'd actively prodded Filya's conscience, tried to scare him. That first moment when he'd started in on the topic at Danilov's house, Filya truly had been scared. Suddenly, Tolik had risen up before him in some kind of mystical light. What he'd said about criminal responsibility, Article 125, and leaving a person in danger had dumbfounded Filya far less than the very crushing fact that this Tolik, who had appeared out of nowhere, knew everything.

Had he already been working for the police at the time of Nina's death? If so, who could he have been at the time? A rookie? A junior detective? Why had he declared Filya's involvement so confidently? Did he have witness testimony, or was this entire sortie just a conjecture, a dizzying guess? What about the statute of limitations? And, most of all, what reason did Tolik have to attack him? These questions came to Filya only later, much later, but at the time the investigator brought up the subject of dead Nina, it seemed to Filya that the fiery heavens above had gaped open.

———————

"Tell me about Tolik," he said, getting in the car next to Rita and sticking in his pocket the piece of paper with the license plate numbers. "What does he want from you?"

"I thought you were planning to go to the airport."

"You want me to leave?"

"No."

"Then tell me about Tolik."

Filya truly had changed his mind about going to the airport. He'd decided to fly out tomorrow. Or the day after. Any day after whatever day the boy was found. For some reason he was absolutely certain the boy was alive and that he'd find him. He couldn't not find him. After all, he now had the list from Tolik of the cars that had driven by. One of those people had to know something. Filya felt fresh and new.

In his eyes he was now so fresh and so new that right in the investigator's office, without even saying good-bye to him, he'd decided to go immediately to the first address on the list. He wanted, no matter what, to act on this long-forgotten freshness, to direct it into the proper channel, to be useful, worthy, and righteous. He felt a strength inside him, and this feeling, which replaced the languor he'd grown used to over the last couple of years, filled him with hope.

"I can do this," he'd said under his breath as he exited the barely heated police station and headed for the car, where Rita was waiting for him. "I can do this. It's all going to work out. I'll find you, kid. Hold on."

Muttering this "hold on" again, Filya clenched his teeth and squeezed his bandaged right hand so hard it hurt, as if he could physically strengthen his determination. However, in the warm car next to Rita, he suddenly realized he was very tired. The fog in front of the windshield was already filling with a dropsical blue. The blue numbers on the dashboard clock flickered: 16:08. It was too late to drive across the river. In town, even though it was calendar fall, the winter night had fallen, limitless, like everything in these parts. This place, this town, this piece of the planet knew absolutely nothing about moderation. Everything that happened here—night, day, people, events, cold—was excessive. All this had been so huge and perfectly resistant to the inner or outer gaze that Filya froze in dismay at the mere attempt to look at it.

The events of this strange, insane day fell heavily on him and on his pains from yesterday. He felt like a squashed worm on which the narrow underground passageway he himself had dug out at incredible effort had collapsed.

Unable to move a hand or a foot, he leaned back in the seat and repeated in a muffled voice, "Tell me about Tolik."

"Where are we going?"

"To Danilov's. The hotel's still cold, more than likely. Even the cops don't have heat. Go on, tell me."

From Rita's angry, confused, and not always well-connected statements, Filya was able to pick out a plotline. Not easily, but nonetheless. More than likely, Tolik represented a group of people interested in discrediting Danilov and pushing him out of power in the city. Obviously he'd been promised a serious promotion if he could dig up compromising material, and even better if he could lock up the local construction magnate, who was seriously hampering somebody's style.

Rita was irritated when she spoke about the investigator, so Filya kept grabbing her by the elbow.

"Easy on the gas," he said. "The fog's bad. Someone could suddenly pull out in front."

The fog lights cast a flat, wide beam in front of the car, and this was the limit of what Filya could see in the dense thickness of this already dark-blue gel. Rita let up briefly, but a minute later the detested image again aroused her anger, and the gas pedal seemed to go to the floor all by itself.

"Don't speed," Filya said. "We'll be killed."

From time to time, continuing to restrain Rita, he gradually reached the conclusion that the detective had an ulterior motive in attacking him, that it was important for him to draw Filya over to his side; he wanted to use him for something. But what? What use could Filya be in local intrigues, and to whom? Deciding that he couldn't and that Tolik's recruitment efforts in this case were more aimed at that fool Wiki-Pavlik, who'd been behind the wheel at that unfortunate moment and who, due to his closeness to Danilov, really could be of interest to the investigator, Filya was completely reassured.

"I guess it's something personal," he said out loud with a sigh.

"What is?"

"Oh, nothing. People sometimes latch on for no reason at all. They're constantly imagining things, something squeezes them somewhere, their bathing suit wedges up their ass."

"What bathing suit?"

"Doesn't matter."

They rode in silence for a couple of minutes, and then Rita spoke again.

"In one interview with you I read . . . you said each of us is a part of some text."

"Yeah? I don't remember. Probably. Sometimes I rave on like that."

"What does that mean? What text am I a part of?"

Filya snickered and held his tongue.

"You won't say?" She glanced at him searchingly.

He shrugged.

"Sure. You're part of a very nice text. You have a good text—don't worry."

"Is that true?" She looked positively joyful. "How do you know?"

"You're my daughter. Listen, can you go slower?"

Still smiling, Rita let up slightly on the gas, but the car didn't slow down so far as he could tell. The next second, the fog over the road broke up in shreds, and a few meters in front of them, Filya clearly saw a child standing right in the middle of the road.

"Stop!" he yelled, pulling on the wheel.

The car was thrown to the right and flew onto the shoulder, but in the split second before that, Filya heard a sound that made him want to scream.

"We hit him!" he shouted, jumping out of the car and into the snow. "We hit him! I heard it!"

It had been a glancing blow, so the body had been thrown to the opposite side. Filya saw him lying on the edge of the roadway. He rushed toward him, slipped on a well-worn rut, and fell—and right then an oncoming car rocketed by like a dark missile. In horror at the thought that the second car had run over the child they'd hit, Filya jumped to his feet, fell again, shouted something, and scrambling awkwardly, on all fours, wailing in terror, not noticing the burning pain in his hands, ran to the shapeless gray heap lying on the shoulder.

"Stop, don't touch it," Rita said when she caught up to Filya. "It could be contagious. Herpes, or I don't know what."

Filya turned around and looked at her from the bottom up, stunned. Nothing in Rita's face expressed great concern. It—her

215

face—held nothing but a little garden-variety sympathy. As if she ran over children every day and had long since grown used to it.

"There've been a lot of them in town lately." She sighed and shrugged. "They live in the heating mains . . . And now they've climbed out. It must be cold there, too. Maybe even colder than outside."

Filya, speechless, and still kneeling next to the dark, shapeless lump, grabbed his throat, which had suddenly been seized by the harsh icy air, and started coughing. Tears welled up. His eyelashes stuck together instantly, so he blinked hard and rubbed his bandaged right hand over his face to pull his eyelids apart.

"Let's go," Rita said. "You'll get sick. You shouldn't be out in this freezing weather for long."

Filya turned around and looked again at what they'd hit. Lying on the snow in front of him was a dog. The same dog that had wandered through the city with him half the night. And it was alive. Its left side was heaving from frequent, broken breathing. Clouds of steam were gushing from its mouth.

"Maybe we shouldn't," Rita said when Filya, carrying the mutt and panting from the strain and strange happiness, told her to open the back door. "This is Tyoma's father's car. We'll stain the whole seat. He'll draw and quarter us afterward."

"Don't sweat it," Filya said, laying the filthy, shuddering mutt on the light-colored seat. "This is just the ticket."

"For Tyoma's father?"

"Yeah, him, too."

Blood from the injured animal immediately started seeping onto the expensive leather upholstery and dripping onto the little carpet under the seat. Filya got in the front seat and slammed the door.

"Faster," he said, simultaneously exhaling a cloud of steam. "Now you can drive like mad!"

Filya kept turning around, and for a long time he rested his hand on the mutt. It was as if he were listening to it with that hand, sensitively catching the almost inaudible—practically on the edge of ultrasound—whimpering that intertwined with the dog's heavy breathing. The mutt glanced at Filya's hand and tried to wag its tail on the seat gratefully, but all he could see was a very faint shudder. The blood and melted snow caked to the fur on its obviously injured tail made it definitely too heavy to lift. The mutt kept shuddering and, with just its gaze, apologized for its helplessness.

Filya's hand rested on the cold, wet, and dirty fur, the car rattled over the ruts of the suburban road, and the dog was thrown in the air from time to time, but Filya no longer asked Rita to slow down. Like a pitiful scrap of paper in the wind, he was tossed from side to side by bursts of the most contradictory emotions. First, he rejoiced that the struck child had turned out to be a dog. Then he grieved because once again he'd nearly killed a poor mutt. Then he started rejoicing again, and frightening Rita a little by this, he even smiled—because the mutt was there, and Filya hadn't imagined everything that had happened to him yesterday, and the mutt was now lying next to him, alive and real, if slightly crippled. Then Filya started thinking that maybe it wasn't so slightly, and this thought led him to despair. But on the other hand, the mutt's existence in real life, in that part of it which Rita sitting beside him now could easily confirm, proved that he hadn't lost his mind after all and that what had happened yesterday had, after all, happened. The thought that he wasn't insane was reassuring, and for some reason Filya, holding the mutt by its dangling paw, even took pride in it.

Turmoil awaited them at Danilov's house. Tyoma was walking around with a black eye. Pavlik was trying to keep Zina in their room, but she was absolutely irrepressible and kept bursting out onto the stairs where she loudly declared that she would not step foot in this house again and she'd rather freeze in her own apartment in town than put up with this sort of thing any longer. After that, she would go back to her husband in the room, only to invariably reappear soon thereafter. To whom she was directing her philippics remained unclear. Other than Inga, who greeted Filya and Rita in the front hall, Zinaida had no other audience.

Busy with getting the mutt settled and searching for some sort of medicine, Filya at first didn't pay much attention to all this. He was just aware that there'd been an open clash between Danilov and Tyoma and that Tyoma's shiner was the result. What the cause of the conflict was, Inga didn't know or wouldn't say. Not that Filya particularly cared right now.

"Hold his paws!" he shouted at Rita. "He'll get away!"

"I am!" she replied, tensely twisting her face and grabbing the injured mutt by its front paws, which it was furiously beating in the air as if it were falling into an abyss.

The dog gave a nasty yelp and scratched Rita's jacket sleeve a few times, and if she'd had time to remove her coat when she'd come in, she'd have been left with scars on her arm.

"I'm sick of this," Rita squeezed out through firmly clenched teeth, and she let her whole body collapse on the mutt, which whimpered pathetically.

"That's easier." Filya sighed as he dealt with the broken back paw.

After pouring nearly an entire vial of iodine on the large open wound, he was now trying his hardest to bandage to the paw a slide rule he'd found in Danilov's office. Shards of glass crunched underfoot. A smashed coffee table was lying by the wall. Filya didn't remember breaking it.

The mutt, firmly pressed to the back of the couch, kept whimpering, sometimes growling quietly, and bared its nails.

"It'll bite," Inga warned, standing behind her daughter.

"Mom, lay off, please. It's scary as is."

"Didn't you think to take it to a vet? That's a special kind of doctor, by the way."

"Very funny, Mama."

"As for the couch, I doubt the owner's going to be overjoyed."

The elegant blue couch was stained with iodine and blood. Because Filya in his fit and terrible nervousness had poured enough iodine to put out a fire, and also because the spots were nearly the same color, the couch now looked like a place of pagan sacrifice. Anyone suddenly entering the living room at this minute might get the perfectly natural impression that they were trying to finish off the mutt, not heal it.

"I'll bring an oilcloth right away," Rita said, lifted herself off the dog, and rushed out of the room.

"It's a little late for that," Filya said, but Rita couldn't hear what he was saying.

Sensing the sudden deliverance from his burden, the mutt lifted its head and began whimpering reedily.

"Pretty lousy, I know," Filya said to it. "You have to forgive us, bud. We didn't mean to."

The mutt let its very long, limp tongue out of its mouth, rolled its eyes, and started breathing fast and loud. It evidently didn't care what was happening to it anymore. A minute later Filya finished fussing with the bandage. After that, as if not knowing what to do with them, he turned his iodine-stained hands in front of his eyes, took a deep breath, and, in total exhaustion, dropped to the floor next to the couch. Unbuttoning his jacket, he tried to take it off, but the awkward position and tremendous inner tension that had slackened at last had rendered Filya utterly helpless. He rustled the borrowed, uncomfortable down parka and then in a weak voice burst out laughing.

"Got a cigarette?" He raised his eyes to Inga.

"I don't smoke."

The gaze aimed up at her was the gaze of a being so tired and so defenseless that Inga, who knew from the Internet, naturally, about Filya's reputation and so had prepared for his arrival, carefully collecting all her bile, drop by drop, was taken off guard and couldn't react in line with her anti-Filya preparations. Instead of the bile, rebuff, and sarcasm she'd intended to bring crashing down on his head, Inga all of a sudden, simply and inexplicably impulsively, pitied him.

Filya was sitting on the floor at her feet, his knees bent feebly, never having undone his jacket completely, leaning back against the hopelessly ruined couch, resting his head on the dog's evenly rising and falling back, which stank of piss, heating mains, and garbage cans. He looked into her incredibly blue eyes and thought that if he hadn't known her before, then he probably would have thought she was wearing cosmetic lenses. Rita had totally different eyes.

"Is she my daughter?" he asked, skipping several stages in one leap. Inga shook her head.

"Too bad." Filya sighed. "She came out great."

"Marry her if you like her."

Inga uttered this in such an even, such an ordinary tone of voice that a foreigner who didn't understand the language might have thought it was just something polite to say—like offering a glass of water, a meaningless remark made to keep the conversation going. There weren't any foreigners here, though. And Inga had said what she'd said.

Filya stared into her face. The inner effort a retort like that took absolutely had to leave its traces—an embarrassedly raised eyebrow, a smile of excuse for its lack of tact, or at least a split-second look to the side. But Inga's face did nothing of the kind. Not even the slightest shadow ran across this still-beautiful face. Looking at him serenely with her wonderful cold blue eyes, Inga was absolutely in her element. Standing before Filya was his true teacher, a genuine extraterrestrial. The only unease he caught in her was connected definitely not with him or his possible paternity and definitely not with her unexpected suggestion. No, what was upsetting Inga was her own wounded pride.

In her regal munificence, she had once bestowed a couple of weeks of her incredible life on homely Filya, whose name now, when Googled, brought up several dozen, if not hundreds of thousands, of links. She had been convinced he wasn't good enough for a boyfriend—and yet he was good enough for those guys. Not that there was no trace left of her once-overwhelming superiority, which had allowed her to gaze down not only on him but on all other men, but that superiority had taken a significant hit. It had listed from her intended trajectory.

This listing, naturally, hadn't diminished the piercing blueness of her eyes or her still-captivating face, just as it hadn't canceled out her past confirmed wins. Inga had borrowed the term "confirmed wins" from a book about World War II military aviators left to her by a skinny, high-strung Englishman who'd come to teach his language at the local teachers college eight years ago and been put out of action by Inga. According to British aviation classifications, "likely wins" included enemy fighting machines knocked down during an air battle that managed to avoid crashing to earth and to escape the field of vision of the pilots or other observers. Inga didn't need wins like that. What she did was always confirmed with hundred-percent certainty.

Her superiority as a predator and lightning-fast ace took shape in the upper classes of high school, when, according to urban legend, grown men would climb through her bedroom window from the street, one after another. What compelled them to be so patient remained her trade secret, but virtually everyone knew that she never turned down any even mildly attractive representative of the male tribe. She was able to find something of interest for herself in each one of them. A unique men's club even formed in the city, the entry ticket to which was at least a fleeting romance with Inga. With his two weeks, Filya was far from the least in this club, and for a while he took slight pride in his membership in this unspoken organization. As did the others, naturally.

But all this was threatening to pass now. Not even threatening. It nearly had.

For Inga, Filya was like the Sulfidine powder Soviet doctors used to treat little children. And Filya's Moscow success, on whose crest he had now suddenly shown up here, did not make the pill one bit sweeter.

For various reasons, this bitter white taste wouldn't wash down, and her tongue, prone to circumlocutions, gradually started perceiving the vile taste in her mouth as something rather sweet after all.

"If you don't want Rita, marry me." Inga made her second offer of hand and heart even more calmly than the first. She knew how to dot her i's.

Filya smiled with the right corner of his mouth.

"I thought you had opened the hunt on Danilov."

"I had. But there's no certainty it's going to work out."

"Rita's getting in the way?"

Inga kept silent without averting her eyes, which were as blue as ice on a deep sea.

"You think if I take her away the hunt will go better?"

"She's the one who wants to leave." Inga shrugged.

"So I've been told."

The mutt behind him sighed noisily, started to fidget, and licked Filya's ear with its hot tongue. Filya didn't move away. Leaning his head back, he looked at Inga standing in front of him. Under her sweater, her proud breasts, free of doubt, rose and fell, and he thought that it was they who were his true teacher—not Inga but her breasts. This resolute, desperate pair had not relied on the kindness of capricious fate, had not acquiesced, had not gone with the flow. They'd resisted and struggled and, despite having minimal initial resources, like the deaf Beethoven, they had wrested a victory from a stingy life. These breasts, Filya now realized, had been his true mentor in everything—in his dissent with the world, in his inability to be surprised, in his frank and universally informed cynicism, in his abstract way of calling things by their names without worrying whether he was offending anyone. It was they that had permanently stripped him of his human ability to be embarrassed, to feel awkward or ashamed. It was they that had made him unsinkable and dead.

"The mutt probably has fleas," Inga said. "You shouldn't rest your head on it."

"I don't care." Filya smiled again. "I'll have fleas. I now take life as it comes."

"Then marry Rita."

"But what if she is my daughter after all?"

"No, Filya," Inga said, shaking her head. "The only thing here that's yours are the fleas."

At that moment, something upstairs crashed, and she looked up at the ceiling.

"Where did Rita disappear to?"

"I don't know," he replied. "She said she was going for an oilcloth."

An indignant voice, muffled by the layers of ceiling, flew down from upstairs.

"Zina, I guess," Filya said. "In search of justice again."

———

It was indeed Zinaida. She'd found Rita in her son's room, where she'd dropped by to find out the reason for the conflict, and the conflict immediately shifted to a new plane.

No sooner did Filya and Inga appear in the doorway, though, than the colorless Valkyrie's fury came crashing down on their heads with redoubled strength. Or rather, on Inga's head, because Filya's head was too busy. He was thinking about whether Inga had a soul, recalling the early Christians, who doubted the existence of a female soul in general, and thinking about himself—whether he himself had a soul, even if he wasn't a woman, and about his own paternity, the crippled mutt, and, most of all, what had happened to Anna Rudolfovna's little grandson and what needed to be done to find him in the freezing city. All this intertwined and reverberated in him simultaneously, leaving no room for colorless Zina's alarms. Therefore, Filya saw how the unattractive thin lips on her face were moving furiously, but the meaning of what she was saying reached him only in snatches. All he caught was that Zina really didn't like Inga, but she didn't like Rita even more because Rita meant there would never be peace in their home and she beat around the bush too much—much too much.

That's exactly how Zina had put it: "beat around the bush." Of this retort, which had surfaced unexpectedly from the rural impressions of his childhood, Filya was absolutely certain because he'd just stopped thinking and was hearing the penetrating voice of the colorless and distraught parent at full volume. Her son's huge black eye, according to her, was all Rita's fault.

Rita herself stood in the middle of the room looking aloof and crushing the flowery oilcloth in her hands. Filya remembered one like that from his childhood, when his parents took him to see his grandmother. The holiday table had always been covered with this oilcloth, and dishes made from a freshly slaughtered pig. The oilcloth poked up at the corners and was slippery from spilled wine and aspic. Looking at the huge rowanberry bushes generously splashed across a kind of yellow background, Filya remembered the smell—harsh, repulsive, and chemical—a smell that had always made his eyes water. He also remembered the grown-ups' voices at the table when they all started hollering together: "Rowanberry, oh, dear rowanberry, why are you so sad?" A special bravado in this "singing" was the horribly shrill note at the end of each line—and in this regard his grandmother's voice outdid them all. She would turn red from the strain, rocking heavily from side to side, emitting this inhuman sound, and proudly gazing upon little Filya covering his ears with his sticky hands.

"Give me that, please," he said to Rita as he walked past Zinaida, who was now screeching exactly the same way.

Rita handed him the oilcloth, assuming that he was planning to take it back to the couch, but Filya left the room and tossed the sticky vile thing down over the banister, into the front hall. Then he calmly walked back, stopped opposite Zina, who was still cursing a blue streak, and put his iodine-stained, bandaged hand on her shoulder.

"Shut up. I can't anymore. No one can. Believe me."

Saying this, he involuntarily glanced at her son, who'd had no reaction to what he'd said. Tyoma was basically acting as if there were no one in the room besides him and Rita. He wasn't listening to his mother, hadn't seen Inga and Filya enter in response to the noise, wasn't talking, and was only looking at Rita, not taking his eyes off her, as if he were expecting something important from her, something absolutely essential to him right then. Filya recognized that look. Years ago he'd seen in a mirror the reflection of exactly the same look on his Nina's face. This look was now reflected on Rita's face in approximately the same vein. A look of apathy.

"Don't you dare touch me," Zina choked out in hatred, flinging Filya's hand from her shoulder.

"Who's touching you? I'm just saying, calm down. Nothing terrible has happened. Some guys had an argument and duked it out. It happens. You have something else to worry about."

Zinaida stared at Filya uncomprehendingly. "I do?"

"Yes, you do. Did the investigator speak with you and Pavlik this morning?"

Zinaida's face turned to stone. "That's no concern of yours."

"Now it is. Is it ever, my dear. You and I have on our conscience not only those two bodies. There was a child in the car, and he's gone missing. Do you understand? He's nowhere to be found. If he isn't found—we might as well have sent three people to their death. The child's all of six years old. How do you like that problem? Are you sure his black eye still bothers you?" Filya extended his arm and held it there, pointing to her son's face.

Tyoma emerged from his coma finally, shifting his gaze from Filya to Zinaida. "Mom, what bodies? What's he talking about?"

Zina turned on her heel and fled the room without a word.

Tyoma strode after her. "Mama!"

"Let her go." Filya caught him by the sleeve. "Or did you enjoy listening to her?"

"I don't understand . . . I . . . ." Tyoma's face had become totally distraught.

"What's there to understand? All's well. Your mama's upset because you got it in the grill. I calmed her down. At least we solved one problem. Where's the hero of the hour, by the way?"

"Who?" Tyoma looked completely bewildered.

"Danilov. As I understand it, he's the one with the upper hand." Filya jokingly mimicked a boxer throwing a hook. "I should congratulate the champion. Where is he?"

"Filippov, wait," Inga said, intervening in their conversation. "What happened? Can't you talk like a normal person? Didn't the investigator come to see Danilov?"

"No. He didn't. But that's not important now. You tell me, where's the author of this masterpiece?" Filya again pointed to Tyoma's bleary eye. "I want to shake his hand. Now these rude young people know it's too soon to write off our generation. We can stand up for ourselves, and how." Filya assumed a boxer's stance again, and threw a few right punches.

"He left," Inga said.

"Back to town? About the emergency?"

"No. He took Peter and Lilya and the children to the country. They have a house there."

"So they left?" The joking expression slid off Filya's face. "Because of me or something?"

"The fights frightened the children. The younger ones even cried when Tyoma fell on the coffee table. After that, Lilya said she didn't want to stay here anymore."

"Ah, so that's where the glass came from." Filya heaved a sigh of relief and grinned again. "I guess it was lively here. Too bad I missed the fun."

He wanted to get in another jab on this topic, but the next second, his thoughts skipped to something else and he literally ran out of the room. Hurriedly entering his room, he rushed at the unmade bed and started rummaging through the covers. There was nothing there.

Filya felt himself break into a sweat. He tore at the annoying jacket and finally just pulled it off over his head.

The file of drawings lay on the windowsill. When he saw it, he actually started laughing. All the drawings were there. Peter hadn't taken anything.

———

Half an hour later, Danilov returned and told them that after the country, he'd stopped by the city, where things had become more complicated over the last day. The emergency situation had notched up another level. Neither municipal services nor the Emergency Ministry big shots who'd come from Moscow had been able to do anything about it. The security agencies weren't handling it well, either. Looting and theft had crept through the whole city. People were smashing shops, stocking up on food and warm things—basically, anything that came to hand. In one of the outlying districts, they'd cleaned out a whole warehouse of industrial heat insulation in just a few minutes. They'd trucked out fiberglass baffles.

"People got organized fast," Danilov said, standing in the middle of the glass-strewn living room and sipping burning hot tea from a huge mug. "Tomorrow they'll probably start selling all that somewhere."

He said nothing about the ruined couch or the mutt sleeping on it. He held his gaze on it for a second but brought up something else. "No one is going outside if they don't have to. We're staying in the house. We aren't reacting to signals from outside. Don't open the door to anyone. Tomorrow I'll leave someone here who will make all decisions."

"What kind of decisions?" Zinaida asked.

"Who to let in and who not to. And who can be trusted with a gun." Danilov looked at the gloomy, sulking Tyoma but said nothing.

———

Late that evening, Rita slipped into Filya's room. She may have just wanted to talk, to discuss what had happened to them in town, or to confer about her obviously tangled relations with Danilov and Tyoma, but Filya never learned any of this. Before a single thought occurred, glancing at her sweet pajamas, which were poking out from her long knitted cardigan, his body jumped off the bed, turned the taken-aback Rita around one-hundred eighty degrees, and pushed her out of the room. Standing by the closed door and listening to what was happening on the other side, Filya was amazed at the reaction of his carcass, which had suddenly become quite active. But he wasn't about to bring Rita back. He waited for her furious puffing to quiet down, and only after that did he peek out into the hall.

Evidently, everyone in the house was already asleep. The only light was on the second floor. Actually, it wasn't even light but its dim remnants. Filya pulled on his pants and, half-naked, left the room. He stood on the staircase a moment and listened hard: absolute silence reigned in the house. From time to time, something clicked in the radiators and heating pipes, but Filya caught no living, organic sounds. Everything that might think, rage, amuse, hate, frighten, delight, and, most of all, disappoint—all that had quieted down and slunk off to hide in some corner.

Filya, stepping carefully, went down the stairs and into the living room, which was lit only by an orange spiral heater. The rug by the couch was still strewn with glass. The shards blazed and flared orange, which made the carpet seem to bloom with bizarre, living flowers. Above this sudden magnificence, in the half dark of the couch, lay the mutt he and Rita had crippled. Sensing a human's presence, it opened a shining orange eye but didn't lift its head. Like an independent being, this eye lived its own life and moved, following Filya's displacements across the rug. Filya hadn't taken the time to put on shoes, so he was trying not to step barefoot on the shimmering shards. The living room was noticeably cooler than upstairs, and shivers were already running down Filippov's bare back.

It turned out to be not so easy to ascend the stairs in the dark carrying the heavy mutt. A couple of times Filya tripped and nearly lost his balance, stubbing first his right toe and then his left on a high step. The mutt took these shocks rather hard and both times clasped Filya's naked shoulder in its teeth, not really clamping down, but still making it clear that Filya shouldn't do that anymore.

It was warmest by the closet next to which Filya lay the mutt in his room. To clarify this, he had spent a minute walking from corner to corner with the mutt in his arms, and in the end his bare feet told him where would be best. Back on the floor at last, the mutt yawned loudly, sneezed, and shut its eyes. The move to the warm room had worn it out.

Filya squatted next to the dog and put his still-bandaged hand on its evenly rising and falling side. The mutt opened one eye slightly, inquiringly.

"You and I are playing for the same team again," Filya softly said, explaining his attack of tenderness. "Downed pilots. All I need, bro, is this thing."

He touched the slide rule poking out of the dressing on the dog's leg.

"A classy item, by the way. Look what you can do with it."

Filya tugged at the slide rule, which pulled out of the bandage like an antenna.

"Listen, what if I use this in my new show? Mummies and zombies could wander around the stage in bandages, and then these things come out of their arms."

He fiddled with the slide rule a few more times and looked into the mutt's half-open eye.

"That would be some show. Come with me? Want to see it? This time will be different. I promise you. Will you come?"

The mutt breathed a sigh.

"Only first, help me find this kid. Help me. Okay?" Filya started getting busy. "You don't have to do anything. Lie here and recuperate. You just have to want me to find him. That's enough—I know it is. All I need is for you to want it."

Filya didn't know whether he had the right to ask the dog such things after what he had done to it at that performance, nonetheless he did ask, and now the mutt had to decide whether he deserved its help or not.

"No rush." Filya, happy that he had shared the responsibility at least a little, straightened up and rubbed his feet, which had fallen asleep. "You go think. We've got plenty of time 'til morning."

Waking up a couple of hours later from strange scurrying sounds, he saw in the dark someone's silhouette squatting in front of the mutt. Other than the Demon of the Void, who'd gone missing all day yesterday, no one else should have been sitting in his room in the middle of the night, squatting like that.

"Get away from the dog," Filya demanded in a voice caught half-asleep. "I need it."

The silhouette turned and spoke in Tyoma's voice. "You should have hit me, not it."

"Tyoma?" Filya half rose in bed. "What's the matter? Why are you acting like a lunatic?"

"Danilov said Rita slept with him."

Filya took a deep breath and sat up on the bed.

"Listen, let's do this tomorrow," he said after a long pause. "I have one very important thing to do. I need some sleep. Want to go with me in the morning?"

"Yes."

"So we have a deal."

They both were silent a little longer.

"Can I take the dog to my room?"

"No."

Filya was awakened a second time, by shots outside. Surfacing convulsively from sleep, gasping and grabbing for something in front of him, he had time to be scared but immediately decided he'd dreamed the shots. But in the next instant, there was another bang right outside his window.

Filya hid under the blanket and held his breath. No more sounds came in from outside. He waited about ten minutes, thinking he probably should get up and look out the window, but then, imperceptibly, he fell asleep. Nothing else disturbed him until morning.

"Who was shooting last night?" he asked when he went down to the living room, where at seven thirty all the house's residents had already gathered.

"Those were my men," Danilov replied, turning his head away from the TV for a second. "Scaring off looters."

Filya surveyed those gathered in the large room. Everyone was listening tensely to the news about the situation in the city.

"We've got television," Filya said. "That means it's not the end of the world."

No one responded to what he'd said. Only Tyoma looked his way.

The newscaster started reading out the weather reports. "Over the entire republic, temperatures are significantly below normal. The villages of Anabarsk, Bulunsk, and Verkhoyansk are down to minus fifty. In the republic's capital, it's minus forty-four . . ."

"Lord, it's like we're in an Agatha Christie novel," Zina sobbed.

"Stop it," Pavlik responded immediately. "Agatha Christie wrote exclusively in the detective genre, whereas our situation is more of a disaster novel. To be absolutely precise, she has six nondetective novels, but they were written under a pen name, Mary Westmacott. Therefore, technically speaking—"

"Pavlik, quit it, I beg of you," his wife's voice flew up. "You know what I mean. We're cut off from the world, the killings have started around us, and we aren't getting out of here."

So he wouldn't have to hear any more of this raving, Filya nodded barely noticeably to Tyoma and turned an invisible steering wheel. Tyoma rose immediately. However, before exiting the room, he turned and looked at Rita. She didn't respond to his look.

———

"Why is living so hard?" Tyoma asked when they were well away from the house. Ten minutes had passed in silence as they looked into the dense, dark predawn fog.

"I don't know," Filya replied. "I wasn't the one who thought it up."

"But after that . . . does it get easier?"

"Not necessarily."

Of the list of car owners Filya had taken from the investigator, only two were registered in the city. The first was Pavlik. Filya was well acquainted with the second address. The building was next to the theater where he'd once worked as fire warden. Jumping out of the car and looking at the columns of the front entrance, blurry in the fog, he thought he'd come full circle. Or was just about to. His course was coming to an end.

People were crowded on the square in front of the theater. Despite the early hour, there were forty or fifty people jumping up and down around the huge bonfires they had going next to the theater's tall staircase. Clustered around two Kamaz trucks piled to the top with firewood, they were wreathed in steam, busy doing something important. A welding iron sparked and hissed, and the strikes against the metal rumbled. The fog had transformed the scene into a spectral and seriously infernal act in a play, but Filya wasn't thinking about devils anymore. Now he had a genuine and all-encompassing mission.

"Let's go. What're you standing there for?" He gave Tyoma, who had fallen still next to the car, having forgotten to fasten his down parka, a shove in the shoulder.

"What are they doing?"

"I don't know. Do up your jacket or you'll get sick."

"I don't care."

Filya recognized this indifference. Not even indifference but the desire to shift emotional pain into the physical sphere, to make his suffering perceptible bodily. A naive desire. Anger, dismay, and the feeling you've been betrayed have no physical analog. If they did, there'd be nothing but invalids crawling through the streets.

One of the blurry shadows by the Kamazes leaned over, picked up something, and flung it in their direction. A substantial piece of ice went flying into the Land Cruiser's side with a dull thud. The shards flew off in different directions, and Filya could feel them cutting the back of his neck, where his cap didn't cover it.

Tyoma picked up a similar piece and drew his arm back to throw it.

"Don't even think about it," Filya said.

The men crowding by the trucks were now nearly all looking their way. And although he couldn't see their faces in the fog, Filya knew what was written on them.

"Don't," he said softly. "You'll be one against all of them. Or do what you want, but they'll rip both our heads off right here. Tyoma, I have something very important to do."

Tyoma lowered his arm and dropped the ice.

"Well done. To entertain you, I'll tell you about other means of suicide. There are less painful ones, believe me."

Barely had they gone through the creaking front door overgrown with a gigantic frost beard when it slammed behind them and Tyoma's phone came to life in his pocket.

"Oh, that means there's service now," Filya said. "Life is getting back to normal."

Tyoma took out his cell phone, looked at the screen, and then put the phone back. "Rita."

"Aha. You mean it's already reached that point?"

"I just don't want to talk to her."

They went up one flight, and the phone in Tyoma's pocket cawed.

"You can read it." Filya nudged him with his elbow. "The woman did try. She did text, after all."

Tyoma stopped on the landing between floors and drilled his inflamed gaze into Filya's face. You could tell he hadn't slept at all.

"What are you standing there for? Check it, I'm telling you. Maybe it explains everything. Maybe Danilov lied to you."

Tyoma took out his phone, clicked some buttons, and froze for a few seconds, his head leaning toward the screen's ghastly glow. The steam that had been tearing from his lips even before this and was hotly and nervously forming clouds before dissolving in the perfectly still, cold air now stopped right there, not rising to the frost-shaggy ceiling. For a while, everything stopped in that rimy space. Everything in general.

"It's a message for you," Tyoma said at last. "Some Anna Rudolfovna called. She asked that someone tell you to come by this address."

He held out his hand and showed him the text on the screen.

"Yaroslavsky Street," Filya read. "Is that anywhere nearby?"

"In the neighborhood, I think. It runs parallel to the avenue."

Filya looked into Tyoma's eyes to figure out just how disheartened he was. Tyoma looked back with morose indifference. His look reflected nothing Filya had expected to see in it—no anger, no pain, no dismay, no self-pity. Gazing at Filya was an oppressive void, and for a second he even wondered whether instead of Tyoma standing in front of him it was his old friend who'd enjoyed sulking over him.

"What's with you?" Tyoma asked, watching as Filya started shaking his head.

"It's all good. Let's keep going."

But it was all far from good. Filya had lied to the young man in a desperate attempt to protect himself, although the void revealed to him in Tyoma's gaze had already surged, already penetrated Filya, and he didn't have a chance in hell of withstanding it. The heavy indifference of someone who'd suddenly had taken away from him what he'd lived for was sucking at him like a greedy, champing bog, pressing on his rib cage, cracking open everything there was to break in it, and Filya was helplessly falling into it, into this indifference, looking at the surrounding world now with the eyes of the crushed Tyoma. It was as if Filya were once again in his hated past and could feel the familiar, icy deafness, which not only sounds but generally everything in his life had such a hard time passing through. This deafness was as viscous as the local fog, as the cold. As limitless as winter.

Now Filya knew the boy hadn't been lying to him the previous night. Tyoma really did regret that Filya and Rita had hit the dog and not him. He truly did not want to live. Why the boy's misery had gone off the charts and reached this incredibly high pitch in a single night was beyond mysterious. The fact was, though, that Tyoma had taken a leap and was flying off into an abyss, even though just two days ago he'd seemed absolutely fine. At his first meeting with him, Filya never would have guessed at this forgotten but nonetheless kindred hatred for the world. A lot changes in boys' worldviews when they find out their girlfriends sleep with other guys.

———

The door was opened by an unpleasant, fussy little man who obviously took them for who he'd been expecting and so let them in without question. He was a little man not because of his physical size but because he was fussy on the inside. Although significantly taller than average and fairly solidly built, inside he obsessed, endlessly and minutely, and unable to make a choice, he grabbed everything at once. While he was leading his early visitors to the kitchen, hopping like a grasshopper over the boxes that blocked the entire entryway and hall between rooms, he managed to inform them that this wasn't all the goods, that he had his own Azerbaijanis at the market, that fruits would be a little more, and that he'd nearly solved the problem of a second heated truck.

Listening to his murmuring with half an ear, Filya realized why the apartment smelled of tangerines. The little man had bought up everything that might freeze in city traders' now-unheated warehouses for cheap and was quickly sending these perishable goods to the villages, where prices were not about to fall. By all accounts, the take promised to be considerable, so the little man was sincerely pleased by the municipal accident.

"Did you see the master craftsmen on the square in front of the theater?" he said quickly. "Those guys figured it out. That's class for you. Riveting sheet-metal stoves together and selling them with firewood on the spot. People've come flocking. They've been open for business for more than a day. They take rubles and hard currency both. Even gold jewelry—whatever deal you make. Beauties. What can you say?"

His voice held so much sincere admiration and envy simultaneously that Filya couldn't stop himself from kicking one of the boxes of tangerines, which before this he had politely stepped over.

In the kitchen, Tyoma immediately hunkered down on a stool in the corner and fell quiet, though Filya could sense him the whole time. An invisible but very strong umbilical cord stretched between them, pulsing with disaster.

"It's warm here," Filya said to the trader bug, who'd hastily cleared the table of his unappetizing dinner remains.

"Uh-huh," the man said, nodding readily. "Yesterday the cold was nasty, but last night I took a bottle to someone from a local furnace that's autonomous from the main line, and he patched me in. They promised not to turn off our building anymore. They put us on emergency status."

"Emergency?"

"Well, yes. Emergency resources, like for hospitals. I have to go from apartment to apartment and collect a kopek from everyone."

"You grovel?"

"Why do you say that?" The bug smiled easily. "I was looking out for people. I paid for the whole building myself. You should give back something."

"You were worried about the tangerines," Tyoma said quietly, staring at the floor in front of him.

At that moment, Tyoma's face changed, as if he'd arrived at a difficult but very important decision for himself, and now a strange half-smile roamed across it. Without tearing his frozen gaze from the invisible spot on the dirty floor, and obviously not aware of that fact, he kept slipping the wide silver ring that adorned his left thumb off and on. Filya hadn't noticed the ring before, but now, together with his strange smile, this repetitive gesture made a sinister impression.

"Did you drive across the day before yesterday?" Filya finally asked the trader bug. "Or lend your car to someone?"

"I did," he answered, taking a big fish frozen like a log from the cupboard under the window. "Care for some stroganina?"

"No. Frozen fish slices were never my thing."

"Wait. How do you know I went across the river?"

The bug had already slapped the huge fish on the table by its tail, getting ready to slice it, but froze with the knife in his hand and looked searchingly at Filya. His knife was a good one, a hunter's knife, with an ivory grip.

"Doesn't matter. Did you see a dead car on the road? Next to the island?"

"Yeah, I saw it. But what does that have to do with—?"

"Quiet. Just answer my questions."

"You mean you're not here for the fruit? Who are you guys? You didn't send a text?"

"Not us."

He reacted to the news about the dead people as if it had nothing to do with him. He stopped slicing his fish for a second, frowned slightly, and then renewed his smooth and confident movements, which absolutely did not match his previous inner fussiness. The alarming news seemed to have stymied him momentarily, but he pulled himself together, stopped fussing, and prepared to defend himself. Filya watched the thin pink slices with amber veins curl off the sharp Yakut knife and listened to the cold, absolutely calm explanation of the apartment's owner, who assured him that neither he himself, nor Filya, nor anyone else was going to answer for that incident.

"Maximum—a fine or community service. But probably not even that. For them to charge us, they have to prove that we're required by law to concern ourselves with the safety of the victims. That is, that we're their guardians, or that we were the cause of a dangerous situation."

"How do you know all that?" Filya asked.

"I studied law. They kicked me out third year. So don't get your panties in a twist over this, buddy. Tell that cop of yours to get lost. Sure you won't have some stroganina? I've got some vodka. We can raise a glass to the dead at the same time."

He winked at Filya, who nearly nodded. Nodding would have been so easy, so natural and pleasant, that Filya almost did it, but then he remembered Anna Rudolfovna falling down next to the bus, her mouth open in a soundless shriek, and the man in the orange vest trying to stick a cigarette in her face.

"So why didn't you stop?" Filya asked. "Why did you drive on by?"

"Me?" The owner of the apartment and the tangerines shrugged. "I was loaded up. My Uazik was topped off—Snickers, different soda pops, gum. I didn't have anywhere to put them. On my head or something? Even the cab was crammed full. And I was in a crazy hurry. I had to drop off the goods at the village. The insanity had already started in town, and I've got a buddy in Nizhny Bestyakh who had a whole shipment of heaters from last summer in a warehouse. I had to get them here fast. They sold like hotcakes the same night."

"And the kid?"

"What kid?"

"What happened to the kid?"

"How should I know? I didn't see any kid. Maybe he wasn't in the car with them."

"He was. The three of them had left town."

"You're sure?"

"Yes." Filya sighed heavily. "I'm sure."

"Well, I don't know. Maybe somebody picked him up. Only, you know what I'd say? Your piece of paper with license plate numbers won't cut it. You won't find the kid that way."

"Why?"

"Because they only wrote down the ones that didn't stop—like you and me. And since we drove past, how could we know whether there was a kid there or not? No one's going to tell you anything useful. Watch out—they'll crack your skull for good measure."

Filya realized this unsinkable little man was right and said nothing in reply. He'd been so inspired yesterday and this morning, too, at his great and important deed, so much had he believed in this chance and the new meaning that had suddenly appeared in his life that now he was unbearably bitter. Filya listened to the apartment owner continue with his jokes, shook his head at his offers to drink, and was angry that all this was like water off a duck's back for him. At the same time, he couldn't shake the persistent and unpleasant feeling that he could see himself in this little man. His frivolous attitude toward life, his little sayings, his easy and even enchanting cynicism, and, most of all, the temptation right now to forget it all—all this was more than familiar to Filya, who'd consciously cultivated these qualities in himself, spent years cultivating them, but right now, in this tangerine-fragrant kitchen, he could barely hold back waves of revulsion.

"Never you mind," the trader bug, fussy once again, said, keeping up the press on him. "Mind you never! Ha! Let's have a drink, why don't we? Dunk the nice stroganina in here. Here's some dip I've got left over from yesterday. Sure makes your mouth water. Well, it takes all kinds. Hey! It's good for what ails you. No? Well, I will. Here's to it, boys. God willing, this isn't the last."

All this armor he'd managed to provide for himself notwithstanding, he needed Filya. This man was trying as hard as he could to pull him into his orbit, trying to get him to share what had happened, as if he'd forgotten or was still afraid to admit that they'd shared it for all time. Not eliciting the desired reaction from Filya, he shifted to the taciturn Tyoma sitting in his corner. Tyoma frowned at his familiarity, but still wouldn't talk.

"Why the sour puss?" the apartment's owner asked. "Head hurt or something? We'll fix that in a jiffy."

Tyoma pushed away the glass yet again, but the owner slipped around to his side of the table and grabbed the youth by the head.

"Hey, let go of him," Filya said.

"No, no, I know how! I cure everyone's headache this way."

The next second, the fussy little man who sold heaters and fruit squeezed Tyoma's head the way strong-armed buyers at the market squeeze watermelons to test, waiting for them to crack. Tyoma cried out in surprise and intense pain, and gave the merchant a good shove, sending him flying back. Tripping over a half-open box of tangerines, he crashed to the floor and you could hear his fussy head hit the floorboards.

"What if he dies there now?" Tyoma asked as Filya dragged him out of the entryway.

"Nothing's going to happen," Filya said. "He was asking for it."

The right side of their car had a new long, deeply drawn furrow. Lying in the snow by the door was a piece of metal. Filya automatically turned toward the men crowding on the square by the trucks but then opened the door and pushed Tyoma inside.

"It doesn't matter. Sit."

Driving up to the address from Rita's text and making out the number through the fog, which had thinned a little by then, Filya turned to Tyoma, who was glumly looking straight ahead into space.

"You know, why don't you sit here for now. Or else you'll shove someone else by accident."

"Tell me," Tyoma said heavily, "what does a person feel when he's killed someone?"

Filya snickered. "You didn't kill him, so calm down. I barely saw any blood even. Just the least little bit."

"I'm not talking about myself."

"Then who?"

"You."

Tyoma finally turned his head and looked Filya in the eye. Filya was silent for a second, then opened the door and, before jumping out of the car, breathed out clouds of steam that boiled up on his lips.

"Why don't you ask your parents? I wasn't the one behind the wheel."

———

He climbed to the fifth floor very quickly. On the way here, Filya had managed to convince himself that Anna Rudolfovna had some news about her missing grandson, and this news absolutely had to be good because otherwise she wouldn't have tried to find him through Danilov and Rita. Who needs to share bad news? More than likely she wanted to tell him something good.

A little girl in a mouton coat opened the door, and he entered the apartment breathing hard and loud. Yesterday's hangover had exacted its due. There was steam coming noticeably from Filya's mouth. The temperature in the apartment was obviously within ten degrees of freezing.

"Hello," a vaguely familiar woman in a mink coat said as she rose to meet him from behind a table. "My name is Larisa Ignatievna. Anna Rudolfovna suggested how we might find you. We've been waiting for you."

There were three other people in the room—a man and two women. All wearing outerwear and fur caps. Filya shifted his gaze from them to Larisa Ignatievna, who was talking to him, and recognized in her that same head of psychiatry Anna Rudolfovna had been arguing with over sending patients across the river to a rural clinic.

"Where is Anna Rudolfovna?" he asked, not understanding what was going on.

"She . . . I guess she's at home."

"At home? In what sense? Isn't this her apartment?"

"Oh, no," Larisa Ignatievna said. "I used her name because you're the fund."

"Fund?" Filya was understanding less and less. "What fund?"

He stared at the woman in the mink coat. Some doctors he knew had once told him that psychiatrists sometimes lose their minds, and for a second he considered that possibility. The newly arisen circumstances in the city might well have activated strange and unpredictable processes dormant in that brunette head.

"The philanthropic fund," the woman in the coat said, holding his long gaze. "You brought Anna Rudolfovna the money. Two hundred thousand rubles for the funerals."

"Ah . . . That."

Filya exhaled, dropped to a chair, and started slapping his pockets. It was as if he suddenly needed to find something in them, but what exactly he hadn't figured out yet.

No, she wasn't crazy. This woman knew what she wanted.

"All famous people are philanthropic," she went on in an understanding and even, for some reason, justificatory tone. "Chulpan Khamatova, for instance . . . the marvelous actress . . . Ingeborga Dapkunaite. Tatyana Drubich does fund-raising for hospices. And now you've decided to, too. Especially since you're no stranger to our city. And we have such misfortune. You got up and running so quickly, as soon as you knew this misfortune was impending."

"I didn't know," Filya said.

"Of course, of course. Nonetheless, it was quite wonderful. A good deed."

She suddenly held out her hand to him, the way bureaucrats and officials do, and he automatically held out his to her in response. Larisa Ignatievna grasped his palm, shook it energetically, as if congratulating him, and then started to laugh very artificially.

Filya smiled stupidly in response, not knowing how to cut this awkward scene short, but from somewhere behind him, behind his back, the dark eyes of the man who'd been sitting on the couch, eyes filled with hope and fear, surfaced. Mumbling something, he handed Filya medical documents from a stack on the floor, and ultrasound pictures and EKGs started falling out. Not letting go of Filya's hand, Larisa Ignatievna started bending down to pick them up, which meant Filya, too, had to bend his knees.

Filya gathered—not right away but eventually—from the man's mumbling and Larisa Ignatievna's disjointed explanations while all three were collecting the scattered papers—that the man was married to her cousin, who was still sitting silently on the couch. His mother had been operated on the day before yesterday, and during the operation, because of the general emergency, there'd been a blackout. The woman didn't die, but something in her was badly damaged, and now she had to be taken to the mainland to be treated and cut open again, and all this was very expensive.

The man repeated the word "mainland"—which sounded slightly odd to Filya's ear, as if they were all on an island here—and tugged his sleeve but unconsciously shifted his attention to the third woman. Evidently worried she might miss her chance, the woman got to her feet, clasped her hands to her chest, and hurriedly explained her difficulty from the far corner of the room. The man kept interrupting her, and she raised her voice, and Larisa Ignatievna tried to outshout both, explaining that this was her friend, that looters had burned down her dacha, and she needed some compensation. Then, as if she'd come unhinged, Larisa Ignatievna shouted at the girl in the mouton coat standing by the door to go run to the neighbor and tell her he'd come.

These people were obviously frightened by everything that was happening, desperate in the extreme but, at the same time, full of such strength and zeal that they had overcome their shyness and embarrassment at having been carried off to this unfamiliar country and were prepared to behave worse than the boldest lout. These helpless people's requests for money were no sweat to Filya. He was really disappointed in just one thing, that from this sudden bedlam with all its icy obviousness, only one thing had emerged: the child had not been found. It had been a complete waste of time rushing here.

"Yes, yes, I'm a fund," he said, taking money out of his pockets. "A fund. The genuine article. Reliable. Here you go."

He put everything he had with him on the table, everything left since his visit to the bank yesterday. So he wouldn't be like the little man selling tangerines, wouldn't feel any kinship to him, Filya was prepared to give away much more. But that was all he had.

"Seven thousand five hundred?" Larisa Ignatievna turned to him after counting the money. "One ticket to Moscow costs more than thirty thousand."

When Filya jumped in the car, Tyoma wasn't inside. He turned around, deciding the youth had fallen asleep on the backseat, but there was nobody there, either.

"What the fuck!"

Naturally, he couldn't leave without Tyoma, although now he was in no great hurry. He realized this disappearance probably boded no good.

In the fog, Tyoma was not immediately to be found. He was sitting on a playground, at the top of the slide, hunched over and pressing his hands to his ears. His down parka and shaggy cap were lying in the snow by the ladder.

"I'm so sick of you," Filya snapped, dragging him down.

Tyoma clung to the railing, as if he were being dragged into a bottomless maelstrom. He started bellowing and jerking, and the whole rickety construction swayed, threatening to come crashing down on Filya, who was standing under it.

"What are you? A cosmonaut?" Filya said, apropos of nothing. "You decided you wanted to go into outer space, damn it? I'll show you outer space! Come here. Do you hear me? Let go!"

While he was pulling the resisting Tyoma toward the car with all his might, Tyoma managed to bite him twice. The first bite was to the thick shoulder of his down parka, and all Filya noticed was the light rustle of Tyoma's teeth over the thick rubberized fabric. But the second time, the youth twisted desperately in Filya's arms, and the bite landed on Filya's right cheek.

Filya screamed from the unexpected pain and banged Tyoma's head against the hood. For a moment, Tyoma stopped twisting. Throwing him onto the backseat, Filya ran for the things he'd left in the snow, and when he returned, Tyoma was sitting vertically, whining, his whole body shaking, as if he'd been plugged into a high-voltage power line.

"Here," Filya yelled, flinging his jacket and cap at him, and then slammed the door with a crash.

In the car, he turned the rearview mirror toward himself. He could see the bite mark distinctly on his frozen right cheek.

"Moron!"

Filya looked at Tyoma in the rearview mirror. He was sitting still as a statue, with his jacket on his head.

"I'll fix you . . ."

Jumping out of the car, Filya again opened the back door wide and in one jerk pulled Tyoma outside. Tyoma wasn't resisting anymore. His jacket fell on the snow, but Filya paid it no attention.

"You drive!" he hollered, pushing Tyoma behind the wheel. "You drive!"

"I can't," Tyoma bleated.

"You can, you freak! Drive us! People need help!"

Filya slammed the door, stopped for a second by the bumper, caught Tyoma's crazed look through the windshield, shook his fist, walked around the SUV, and collapsed in the passenger seat.

"Move it, moron!"

The car, its wheels having frozen flat to the snow, crunched heavily and pulled away from the building. The jacket was left lying in the middle of the road.

———

Filya couldn't get money at the first or the second bank they stopped at. The ATMs weren't working in either establishment, and the tellers were besieged by such awful crowds that he had a very hard time even squeezing into the room. The third bank was just plain closed, but the people gathered near it told him they were promising to open up at any moment. The crowd, shifting uneasily from foot to foot and hopping in place, was covered by a gigantic cloud of the combined steam being exhaled by all these people put together, and for some reason Filya decided he couldn't wait in the car; it would be warmer in that cloud.

Looking back at the SUV to make sure Tyoma was sitting calmly at the wheel, Filya dove into the cloud, which hummed from all the conversations, and where he immediately ran into a piercing voice taut as a crystal string.

"Don't talk to me like that!" a young woman in a dirty gray down parka and a polar fox cap exhorted. "Don't you even dare talk to me at all. You don't understand anything. My mama died. She's gone. But I'm Alena Frolova! I exist! I exist! Is that clear?"

She continued insisting that she existed, stubbornly repeating her name, while Filya pushed on until he was stopped by someone's shout.

"Hey, people, you're nuts! The kid's got no clothes on! Send him to the car!"

Filya craned his neck and spun around, but he couldn't see anything over the backs and shaggy caps, so he turned around and moved in the opposite direction.

"You can't get back in line if you leave!"

Someone shoved him in the shoulder, but he didn't stop.

"I wasn't in line," he muttered under his breath in a voice gripped by the cold. "I wasn't."

———

Tyoma was sitting immobile at the wheel, gazing sullenly at the steam-making crowd. "What do they need money for now?" he asked.

Filya put his shaking hands in front of the car's life-giving heat vents and shrugged. "They probably want to fly away. Tickets are very expensive."

"Sheep."

When Filya told him they were going back to Danilov's, Tyoma suddenly dug his heels in. He wanted to stay in his city apartment. This was evidently what he'd come up with while he was sitting in the warm car gazing at the crowd. He said he couldn't stand to see Rita, or his parents, to say nothing of Danilov. "I'd rather freeze to death alone. I don't care anymore."

Listening to his voice trembling on the verge of hysterics, Filya made one more effort to find a shred of sympathy or interest for the young creature's bad nerves, but then he had to admit it was boring, and without saying anything he just punched Tyoma in the face. The punch caught him right in his motormouth, but since Filya was sitting to his side and couldn't take a good swing due to the close quarters, it came out fairly crookedly and surprised Tyoma more than causing him any pain.

"Are you bonkers?" he said after a moment's delay during which he realized what had happened.

"I could do it again," Filya replied. "Want me to?"

He'd decided not to go to any more banks. It was much simpler to borrow cash from Danilov. In addition, Danilov had access to the city administration and so could render substantive support in the search for the missing child. In any case, it would be more effective than stupidly running around town or across the river, wasting precious time on the other car owners. The trader was right. Filya now knew that none of them could help.

No sooner had the car turned onto the suburban road than Tyoma began to flex his muscle. Driving around uneven surfaces, he kept throwing the car onto the shoulder, where it would rattle over the deep ruts in the frozen earth like the centrifuge in an ancient washing machine. The Japanese had built their car for off-road use, of course, but they hadn't bothered to learn about the shoulders of Yakutsk roads. Filya grabbed on to the handle over his head, bounced patiently on the seat, feeling like a badly folded, decrepit blanket cover, and restrained himself for the time being, allowing the kid to express his attitude toward the unjust and cruel world.

Actually, his patience didn't last long. When the SUV started swerving harder and sharper to the right, Filya pressed his temple firmly to the glass. Hitting his head on the window, he hissed, swore, and gave Tyoma a good clip on the back of his head.

Tyoma first tucked his head into his shoulders, like a tortoise into its shell. And then suddenly he let go of the wheel, shouted something, and, turning his whole body toward the passenger seat, started slapping Filya with both hands—as if putting out a fire that had broken out in the car—while shouting something unintelligible. He did this in such a heated and chaotic way, and Filya was so taken aback, that neither one saw the Kamaz leap out of the fog and come hurtling toward them.

The deafening honking paralyzed them both, but in the next instant Filya pulled on the wheel, and the SUV skipped completely off the road. The car flew across a field, and Tyoma grabbed on to the wheel at last, but he obviously had no intention of returning to the highway. Drifting farther and farther across the open ground, he steered into the fog, as if he were taking a frail little vessel into open waters. As the car was tossed around, Filya grabbed the handle. He no longer understood where the shore was, or rather, what might have played the part of a shore: dry land, reliable and solid ground.

Tyoma, his face distorted with rage, was muttering something under his breath, driving the gas pedal deeper and deeper into the floor. The car was speeding off into nowhere, and Filya, transfixed, with a desperately beating heart, looked into the fog in front of him in anticipation of a concrete barrier, a solid wall, or a tree.

Ultimately, it was a hole.

The car dove into it hood-first, like a small boat into a swelling abyss that had opened up before it. Filya's heart lit out for parts unknown. His seat belt jerked his tension-twisted body back, breaking his collarbone. His head, like a soccer ball kicked through a goal, flew forward completely independently until it was stopped by his neck, which was prepared to stretch infinitely but not to be torn off. Filya heard the windshield shatter just a few centimeters in front of his face. After that, everything went black.

———

Consciousness returned a few seconds later—possibly even the next instant. Filya thought he could still hear the last strokes of the engine running. In the bowels of the car, something was still turning, making a muffled sound, but then there was a clunk, and total silence ascended, flooding the teetering SUV like dark water rushing into the breached hold of a sunken ship.

Filya had decided the blow had deafened him, so he was amazed to hear his own moan. And in that amazing, weightless silence, the moan sounded vulgar. An offensive, grating sound on the backdrop of the purest silence. Filya frowned and at the same moment was overtaken by excruciating pain.

He started moaning again and turned his head. His broken collarbone didn't let him see all of Tyoma—only his oddly bent knee and the right hand lying on it motionless. All the rest was hidden from Filya where the pain was.

Falling still for a second and then nonetheless moving toward the fiery burst, he reached out to the youth, screamed from the ferocious pain that pierced his right shoulder, and grabbed Tyoma's hand. He didn't stir. His hand remained lifeless.

Grinding his teeth, moaning, and breathing brokenly, Filya fiddled with his seat belt for a whole minute until he finally unfastened it. Now he could reach the key to the ignition. He realized he had to get the engine going immediately. Otherwise, the temperature inside would soon be the same as outside. He had to maintain the heat in the car.

Tyoma still hadn't come around, but he was alive. Filya could see him breathing. Barely noticeable steam was coming from the youth's lips. Judging from that steam, Filya had spent more time unconscious than he'd thought. The car was cooling off. He had to hurry.

Turning the key and getting nothing, he remembered Tyoma's phone. A couple of hours ago it had been working, which meant he could call someone for help. But the telephone wasn't in Tyoma's pockets. Filya tensed and looked behind the seat, figuring that Tyoma might have dropped the cell while he was in back, but there was nothing there, either.

He sat perfectly still for a moment, trying to concentrate and figure out where the phone could have gone, and then, in the light of a vivid flash, he saw Tyoma's jacket falling off his head onto the sidewalk when he'd dragged the boy out of the car in Larisa Ignatievna's courtyard. The telephone was probably in the jacket—in that stupid, useless jacket. By not picking it up, Filya had doomed them both to the saddest lot possible.

Now you'll find out what it was like for them, stirred in his heart. *What they felt.*

For some reason he couldn't even say the names of the people who'd frozen in the car and so got stuck on the faceless "them," as if he were still hiding, trying to hide behind the fact that he didn't know them, and since that was so, then they were people only in the most general, abstract sense.

More or less like you right now, flashed through his head. *An abstract dude no one needs who's about to freeze to death in this abstract car.*

The thought of imminent death restored his strength. Filya roused himself and with his left hand tried to start zipping his jacket. He had to get to the road. People were driving there. Someone would stop, and he'd lead them here.

Now you'll find out, sounded once again in his head, but he drove *that* out.

He still couldn't do the jacket zipper, which required the use of his right hand, so in the end he jumped onto the snow without ever zipping up. The cold clutched at his rib cage with steel claws. Filya closed the jacket as best he could, holding the flapping edges with his left hand, and moved toward the road.

By now the fog had turned from the thick and dark gelatin it had been that morning into a translucent rice water, and Filya could make out certain surrounding areas through it. Behind him was a long line of low hills covered with scanty vegetation. Right in his way were light poles, which Tyoma had been lucky not to hit when they'd run off the road. Actually, if the SUV had hit one of those poles Filya would be a lot closer to the road now. The extra hundred meters played a large part.

Awkwardly turning his whole body around and looking at the abandoned vehicle in order to remember its location, he tried to pick up the pace, but the pain from that exhausted him even more. After ten meters or so he gave up and meandered the rest of the way like a sleepwalker, trying not to jiggle his right arm. Added to the incredible cold in this vast field was the light ground wind that singed his already frozen face. To hide it at least some from this icy napalm, Filya walked with his head well down and squinting and so didn't realize right away that he was now on the highway.

On his left, the sound of an approaching vehicle mounted swiftly. He looked up, and the next moment a big army truck moving fast rumbled past him from behind. The honking crashed down on Filya and the wave of air burned him with such force that he could barely keep his feet. If it hadn't been for that truck, he probably would have kept going.

Stopping in the middle of the road, he raised his left hand and waved it weakly in the hope that the truck driver was still looking at him in his mirror. But evidently he wasn't. Filya's jacket flew open, and the cold, like an experienced fighter who patiently waits for his foe's mistake, pierced him straight through in a single blow of its sharpened silver claws.

For fifteen minutes or so, Filya was dying on the deserted highway. At a certain point he had the vague feeling that he was no longer on earth. With each second, this feeling got stronger, and in the end he was fully convinced of it. Truly nothing human remained around him. Even the road under his feet and the power masts blurry in the fog were nothing but relics of an alien ancient civilization. Strangely enough, this didn't discourage him one bit. On the contrary, having clarified this for himself, he suddenly regained his strength, and the distressing despair that had not quit him since the moment he'd woken up in the silenced car finally receded.

Now he didn't care. And this sensation gave him tremendous freedom. He agreed that he was freezing, falling into anabiosis, shutting down like a switched-off device.

The only thing that still tied Filya to the earth he'd abandoned was in the SUV that had died somewhere in the middle of the field and was swiftly losing heat. He vaguely remembered that Tyoma wasn't wearing a jacket, and he wandered back, tripping as he went. The light poles served as guides, although fairly quickly he thought he might be going the wrong way. Returning to the highway, he made one last effort to stand for another five minutes in hopes that someone would drive by, and then he moved back to the field virtually at random. Everything alive in him at that moment had frozen so badly, had ceased to be alive to such a degree, that he was deeply indifferent to whether or not he was headed the right way.

Nonetheless, about twenty-five paces later he came across the distinct tire tracks left by the SUV. Following these still-fresh ruts, he limped as far as the car. Opening the door took some doing. Even his healthy left arm responded with such a delay it was as if the signal to it was coming from a neighboring galaxy. Filya climbed onto the passenger seat. Then, whining convulsively, he pulled off his jacket and threw it on Tyoma, who was still unconscious but also still breathing.

———

Filya would have been hard put to say how much time passed between when he climbed into the car and the moment he heard steps outside. The snow's persistent creaking forced him to open his eyes halfway. Someone wearing a bright-yellow down parka was standing by the door on the driver's side, leaning toward the window, looking into the car.

Filya straightened up in his seat. The yellow jacket noticed he'd moved. Making the snow creak, the bright spot walked around the car, stopped at the passenger door, and rapped something metal on the glass. Filya turned his head toward the window. The man standing outside gestured to him to open up.

"Hello," the Demon of the Void drawled, smiling. "Been waiting long?"

"I'm not waiting," Filya replied, frowning.

"All right, let's go, my friend."

The demon held out his arm for Filya to lean on.

"I can't." He shook his head and nodded in Tyoma's direction. "He'll die."

"Let's go, let's go. They'll save him in ten minutes."

"And me?"

"I'm saving you."

As they walked even farther from the highway, toward the low, endlessly stretching ridge of hills, the demon jabbered incessantly, as if making up for the time he'd been absent. Laughing at Filya's adventures, he assured him that in the last two days he'd dealt with at least three different mutts, and not one of them had had the slightest connection to the poor thing that had croaked during his show.

"You're so sweet." Filya's tried and true old friend laughed at him.

As it turned out, there'd been nothing between Danilov and Rita, either. The Demon of the Void wittily mocked the suspicious Tyoma, and then Filya himself for running around town in vain and as a result nearly putting the unfortunate boy in his grave.

"I was looking for the child."

"What child? He wasn't in that car. They left the kid in town."

"Who with?"

"Do you care? They're taking him to his grandmother right now. Actually, they already have."

The demon continued to scoff, sharing far from the most chaste details from the lives of the people our protagonist had had occasion to encounter in these past few days in his hometown.

Filya shook his head and covered his ears, but his troublesome friend's voice penetrated through his pressed hands, and he did learn a thing or two anyway. About Pavlik and Inga and about Zina—something he had no desire to know about her. About Danilov, and even about his old friend Peter. Actually, none of this surprised him. He'd supposed more or less these things in general terms and didn't judge anyone in the slightest. Only the mention of the investigator Tolik wounded him. It turned out that Tolik had never spoken with him about Nina or his possible guilt in her death. Tolik didn't even know about that tragic incident.

Filya flew into a rage.

"You think I invented that conversation myself? He was constantly dropping hints to me."

"I don't know." The demon shrugged and nodded behind Filya, who had stopped in front of him. "Look. Recognize it?"

Filya turned around and saw a small dacha. The light wasn't on in the windows anymore. There was just a dim bluish nightlight on the porch.

"Go," the demon whispered to him. "It's okay."

Filya hesitantly climbed the wooden steps, pulled on the door, and it yielded. Inside it was warm. Somewhere very nearby was Nina. Filya knew she was in the house. He could smell her even on the porch. She was sleeping in the far room. He walked softly that way, easily orienting himself in the dark. He stopped next to Nina and for a long time listened to her breathing. Then he left the room. On the porch he stopped again and looked around. It was important to remember what she saw, which objects she was reflected in, what she touched most often.

His eye fell on the stove flue. The metal was firmly wedged into the blue wall. Filippov opened the stove door and glanced inside. The wood had obviously not burned down completely. Blue flames trembled on the glowing firebrands. One of the guests had shut the chimney a little sooner than he should have.

Filippov stood next to the stove, then pulled the flue, and left the house, gently shutting the door behind him.

Curtain

ABOUT THE AUTHOR

Photo © Lutz Dursthoff

Born in Irkutsk in 1965, Andrei Gelasimov studied foreign languages at Yakutsk State University and directing at State University of Theatre Arts in Moscow. In 2001, he became an overnight literary sensation in Russia when his story "A Tender Age," which he published on the Internet, was awarded a prize for the year's best debut. It went on to garner the Apollon Grigorev and Belkin Prizes, and his novels have regularly enjoyed critical and popular success in Russia and throughout Europe. This is his fifth novel to be published in English, following *Thirst*, *The Lying Year*, *Rachel*, and *Gods of the Steppe*, winner of Russia's National Bestseller Prize in 2009 and praised by *Bookslut* as "a very rich, good book." Gelasimov adapted *Thirst* for the screen, and the film, directed by Dmitriy Tyurin, won first prize in the Moscow Premiere Screenings at the Moscow International Film Festival and the Jury Prize at the Sochi Open Russian Film Festival.

ABOUT THE TRANSLATOR

Marian Schwartz is an award-winning translator of Russian literature. She is the recipient of two translation fellowships from the National Endowment for the Arts and a past president of the American Literary Translators Association. Her translations include the *New York Times* bestseller *The Last Tsar*, by Edvard Radzinsky, Leo Tolstoy's *Anna Karenina*, Andrei Gelasimov's *Thirst*, *The Lying Year*, *Gods of the Steppe*, and *Rachel*, Olga Slavnikova's *2017*, and Mikhail Shishkin's *Maidenhair*.

29285214R00155

Printed in Great Britain
by Amazon